MW01173709

Letters in the Attic

BY

MEREDITH LINDSEY

Second edition
ISBN: 9798375942261
Editing by Sasha Boyce
Typeset by Meredith Lindsey
Cover design created by Meredith Lindsey

Contents

For Kendahl Clevy and Anna Pougas,

because sometimes the fulfillment of childhood promises is all that keeps us going.

Chapter One

I had never experienced motion sickness before. In all my seventeen years, I'd never asked my mother to pull the car over so that I could empty my stomach contents along the side of the road.

I'd never dreaded the act of driving until very recently. My whole life had been changed by a single car ride, and I wasn't even present when it happened.

"Pull over!" I gasped, already clutching my stomach in one hand and covering my mouth with the other.

"Really, Camille, again?" My mother sighed and directed the car to the shoulder just in time.

There wasn't anything left in my stomach by that point. I'd already purged myself three times during the four-hour drive from Colorado. Even so, dry heaves wracked my frame painfully as I tried to regain control of my body. My skin was covered in a sheen of sweat that seemed to sparkle in the midday sun, and I wondered how much longer I would have to endure this.

I looked up from my position on the ground and received my answer. Fifty yards ahead of me stood the city sign, casting a long shadow that almost reached my hands in the overgrown grass. The green paint peeled in several places, and the battered wood revealed years of wear and tear. The fancy cursive writing had faded over time, but I could still make out the greeting.

Welcome to Green Peaks, Wyoming! We hope you have a pleasant stay!

I sat back on my heels and allowed my stomach to settle. The sign might have been old and worn, but it was the most welcoming thing I'd seen in weeks. It could've read "Welcome to Hell! Have a wretched stay!" and I still would have preferred this place over the one I was leaving behind. As if to prove my point, my cell phone buzzed in my back pocket, alerting me to another text message.

I ignored it.

As I reclaimed my place in the passenger seat, I observed the green patches on my jeans from repeatedly propping myself up on my hands and knees. I hoped the grass marks wouldn't stain.

"Do you think it was something you ate?" my mom asked, using her concerned-mother voice. I refrained from rolling my eyes.

"No Mom, it wasn't something I ate."

The silence stretched between us. We both knew the real reason the never-ending car ride was upsetting my stomach. It was the same reason that I was sitting in the front seat instead of the back.

I couldn't pretend we were heading toward a family vacation, not without my dad acting as the DJ in the shotgun spot. The trunk full of luggage might depict the illusion that we were simply off on a weekend getaway, but the trailer bouncing and squeaking behind my mom's SUV told the truth.

This was a one-way trip, and we were never going back.

As we neared our final destination, I got my first look at what Green Peaks had to offer. The town founders hadn't had to stretch very far to come up with a suitable name. Both sides of the highway were furnished with long stretches of forest, a sea of rolling hills that were capped by green leaves and ferns. I didn't know how far the lines of trees expanded, but it was evident that they encompassed the entire town.

We turned onto a smaller road that lacked a middle line, and it carried us into the center of town where there were exactly three four-way stops. I thought my hometown of Plainfield had been small, but at least we had stoplights. I didn't think the blinking red lights perched on these stop signs like angry, guarding vultures really counted.

The town consisted of a volunteer fire station, a park bordered by a couple of elementary schools, a sleepy-looking gas station with two measly pumps, a post office, and a small home-owned pharmacy. There was a police station, a tiny hospital that looked more like a clinic, and a school that housed both the junior high and high school students two roads over.

And that was it.

"Where's the Walmart?" I gaped out the window as we passed the tiny businesses. My mom turned the wheel and followed the twisting road the GPS directed us to.

"Green Peaks is too small for Walmart," my mom said with a shrug, as if I should already know this. "There's a Walmart in Rawlins a little over thirty minutes away. Pete said the gas station, G.G.'s Oil, has most of the groceries we'll need, so we shouldn't have to make the trip too often anyway."

This new piece of information pulled me up short. I wouldn't call myself a city girl by any means, but *no Walmart?* Were we living in the stone age? The homey feeling I'd first received when entering the small town suddenly turned into suffocation.

"Breathe, Cami." My mom chuckled at my reddening face. I gasped in response and laughed as air filled my lungs.

"Amazon still delivers here, so you can order your art supplies online."

I relaxed a little. I guessed it wasn't the complete stone age if we still had Amazon. The meager art supplies I had left were packed up neatly in the trunk, but they wouldn't last long if this place was inspiring enough for me to get back to my canvases. I hadn't touched a paintbrush in weeks, and my fingers itched at the thought of capturing the sunlight breaking through the trees.

The road we followed eventually narrowed onto a gravel drive, and within a couple of minutes, we arrived at the new house. My mom had told me we were getting an upgrade in the quantity of our space and a downgrade in its quality, but I still couldn't believe how big the house was until I saw it with my own eyes.

It was Victorian-styled, with a tower that cast a pointing shadow over half the yard and a spacious front porch that I could see continued to wrap around the back. The crown molding was falling off in places, and the white paint was peeling even worse than that of the sign at the town's border. The windows were dusty and probably no longer opened, but they were at least intact.

I loved all of it.

A red pickup truck waited at the end of the driveway, and the driver laid on the horn as we approached. The engine died and a man and woman stepped out just as we parked beside them.

"Lacey!" My mom cried as she bolted from our still-running car. I sighed and hit the button to stop the engine before opening my own door. I was lucky she'd managed to put it in park at all, but I didn't hold her carelessness against her. She was as fragile as I was at that point, maybe even more so.

"Oh Terri, it's so good to see you! I'm sorry we couldn't make it to the funeral."

My mom hugged her sister fiercely, and I could tell as the tears began to flow and the sobs racked her body that Aunt Lacey was doing a good job of holding her up.

Uncle Peter walked around the car with his arms wide, and I allowed him to crush me in an embrace.

"Good to see you, kiddo."

He hadn't called me kiddo in five years. But then again, I hadn't seen him in five years either. Ever since my grandmother passed away, our families had stopped getting together for the holidays. Since I didn't have any cousins to be friends with, it didn't bother me too much. They still called each other and touched base a few times a year, but other than that we had all been content to just live our lives with the Wyoming and Colorado border between us.

It looked like it took a family crisis to bring my mom and aunt together again.

My uncle's strong cologne filled my nose, and I tried not to scrunch my face up against it. After what felt like an eternity, or maybe that was because I was holding my breath again, he pulled back and held me at my elbows.

"You're a senior now, huh? Almost a real adult? I can't believe you got so tall!"

I thought about informing him that five feet and three inches was on the lower end of average for an adult woman, but considering how short I'd been the last time I saw him, I understood where he was coming from. I had been the shortest girl in my grade, and probably the grade below me too, up until I turned fourteen and hit a growth spurt. Now I was the same height as my mom, the spitting image of her with our long, dark hair and grayish eyes. The only things I inherited from my father were the waviness of his hair and the presence of a single dimple in my right cheek, assuming I smiled enough to show it.

"Yeah, I turn eighteen in two months," I agreed, and gently backed away from his hands to turn towards the house looming in front of us.

"It's a beauty, isn't it?" Uncle Peter asked in my ear.

I nodded. I couldn't agree with him more.

I gave Aunt Lacey time to put the pieces of my mother back together while her husband and I started unpacking the car. As we carried the boxes into the house, I was struck again with the sheer size of it all. There was absolutely no reason my mom and I needed this much space, and I wondered how we could afford it.

"How did you pick this house out for us, Uncle Pete?" I dropped a box of kitchen utensils on the counter.

Uncle Peter lowered his own box of miscellaneous items and leaned against the bar that was larger than our old kitchen table.

"The school board is kind of like the city counsel of this town. We pretty much run things around here," he began. "This house has been sitting for a hundred years without an owner and belongs to the township. It's not in the best shape, but all things considered, it could be much worse. I was able to get a very good price for your mom."

I nodded my head and looked around. Sure, the wood was dusty and the floor creaked with every step, but there were no signs of mice or any other creature trying to make this place its home. The house was like a black and white picture, a snapshot of what it had been a hundred years ago, almost perfectly preserved over time. The more I saw of the house, the more amazed I became.

I was suddenly very grateful for my uncle and his ties in this tiny, overlooked town.

Uncle Peter was the principal at Green Peaks High School, and apparently held a high seat on the school board as well. Only in a town this size would he be allowed to do both, but there probably wasn't a lot of competition or people who even wanted to fill the positions.

Not only did he score this house for us, but he was able to find my mother a job as well. While fifth grade had always been my mom's favorite class to teach, she was happy to accept the second-grade teaching position that had just opened up that summer. With only one adult to provide income for the family now, it was essential that she found a reasonable job to pay the bills.

My mom and Aunt Lacey walked through the door and praised all the hard work we had accomplished so far. We didn't have a ton of belongings to bring with us from Colorado, but I'd carried enough heavy boxes to work up a sweat.

"This place is amazing, Pete! I can't believe you found this for us!" My mom kissed Uncle Peter on the cheek, and he batted her away playfully.

"You girls are my family; I'd do anything for you!" He smiled at me widely before turning to grab more boxes.

Upstairs, I picked out the room that seemed the biggest to call my own. My mom preferred a room on the lower level, so I basically had the whole second floor to myself. Surprisingly, the house was furnished for the most part, lacking only appliances and a good cleaning, and the queen-sized mattress I plopped down on exhaled a much smaller plume of dust than I'd been expecting.

My room faced the back of the house, and out the smudgy window I could see the lines of trees that began on both sides of the backyard. Our property had to be on the very edge of town because the forest surrounded us on three sides and left the only opening to face the road that brought us here.

I was gazing out the window when my phone buzzed again, like a little incessant creature that demanded I know it was there. I'd considered asking my mom to get me a new phone with a new number, but I didn't want to bother her with everything else she had going on. Figuring I might as well get the beating over with, I extracted it from my pocket and lit up the screen. Three new text messages stared up at me.

You and your family are total trash.

There's not enough booze in the state of Wyoming to satisfy your alcoholic family.

Your father got what he deserved that night.

Three messages from three different numbers I didn't have in my contact list. I might not have known their names, but I knew they had to be my fellow Plainfield High School classmates.

I'd always known my father liked to drink, but it had never been an issue in my household. He would have a few beers, many times more than just a few, but he never grew mean or hostile or ever treated my mom or me harshly. If anything, the alcohol made him rather silly and sometimes more fun to be around.

He had not, to my knowledge, ever driven drunk before.

The night we received the phone call, everything changed. It was a Friday night, and Dad had been at the bar with a few of his friends having a good time. Witnesses say he didn't seem incoherent, but the bartender encouraged him to call a cab, supposedly. I had a feeling he added that detail to protect his bar's reputation.

Dad didn't call a cab, though. He tried to drive home after too many drinks. If he had simply driven off the road and met his end against an electric pole or tree, I wouldn't have been receiving nonstop text messages for the past two weeks. If he'd simply taken a cab, the entire town wouldn't hate us.

Roger Stone met his end when his Chevy Malibu made contact with the little Mazda Miata that was heading home after a date at the movies. They said it was a head-on collision, and both drivers and one passenger were pronounced dead at the scene.

That night, my mother and I lost an essential unit in our family and Plainfield High lost its star quarterback and cheerleading captain. Amelia Piper and Nathan Miles, winners of the cutest couple award three years straight. They were in my class, both about to begin their senior year, and both holding scholarship offers to colleges across the state.

It was funny how one day no one in the school knew my name, and the next everyone had my number and was sending me death threats. Overnight, I'd become a sort of celebrity. I had exactly one friend left, a flamboyant boy named Michael Varner, and he was the only one sad to see me leave.

My mom and I needed a fresh start, and here in Green Peaks, Wyoming, we were hoping to get just that.

I shoved my phone into the bedside table and slammed the drawer a little too hard. Even if I blocked those numbers, more would take their place. Their words were already branded on the inside of my eyelids, reminding me not only of my father's death but also that he had died a murderer.

I closed my eyes and leaned my forehead against the window, not caring about the layer of grime anymore. I tried to relax and let my emotions take over, but the tears still wouldn't come.

As I stood there staring out the dirt-streaked glass, I couldn't help feeling drawn to the forest spread before me. Something inside me was being tugged forward, like it needed to be lost in the sea of green and leave this life and all my sorrows behind.

Within the shadows of the trees, I thought I saw a figure move. But then I blinked, and there was nothing but green leaves and darkness.

Chapter Two

We spent the rest of the weekend settling into the new house that I was starting to think of as our mansion. I hated sweeping and dusting, but the necessary chores helped turn my mind away from the depressing thoughts that tried to crush me every time I found myself alone.

The living room was too big, with tall ceilings and a fireplace I could almost stand up in. The family room became the place my mom and I congregated, where we could sit and talk and watch TV or sprawl out on the couch with a book. I was surprised by how quickly the place began to feel like home.

We only had a few days to unpack before Monday arrived, marking the first day of the school year for both of us. I was glad to be starting a new school on the first day, rather than jumping into a class of students that were already in the middle of all their subjects. It was smoother this way, and all I wanted was for my senior year to go smoothly and not create any more waves.

The part I was dreading the most about my first day was my method of getting there.

"Are you ready to go, Sweetie?"

My mom was dressed in a glittery purple top and long, polka-dotted skirt for her first day on the job. I knew she was hoping to impress the second graders with her bright clothes and convey the message that she was a fun teacher, one that they could expect to have a great time with. Next to her sparkles and polka dots, my jeans and black T-shirt seemed very drab.

"Yeah, I just need to grab my backpack."

I sincerely hoped the students at Green Peaks High School were unobservant, or, at the very least, kinder than those in Colorado. I didn't want everyone to see me carted to school in my mother's SUV like one of the second graders she was on her way to teach. It was embarrassing to have to arrive this way instead of driving up in a cute sports car and parking with the rest of the student body. I could emerge from my car in a gust of wind that swirled my dark hair around me, and the other students would stop and stare and wonder who the cool new girl was.

Who was I kidding, though? I had never been the cool girl.

Back home, before all of this happened, my family had owned two cars: my mom's SUV and my dad's Malibu. When I turned sixteen, I sort of inherited my dad's car, except his name remained on all the paperwork. It was mine to drive to school and take to the movies with the few friends I had, and my parents shared the SUV since they had always carpooled to work anyway. But sometimes my dad still drove his car, like on the night of the accident.

After the initial blow of learning about my father's death, the hits kept coming. Our car insurance wouldn't pay to replace my father's car because he was intoxicated when he wrecked. The life insurance wouldn't pay out either. So, there we were, one family unit down in an already struggling household, with one less car and salary to pay the bills.

I wished for the hundredth time that he'd called a cab.

The drive to school passed in a matter of minutes, and then I was looking up at a two-story building lined with white stones and dark windows that reflected the early morning sun and prevented me from seeing what horrors might lay dormant inside.

The parking lot was half filled with students hanging around their cars and chatting about their summer vacations before being forced to return to the penitentiary of a school. As my mom drove around to the office entrance, I was happy to note there were no heads turned our way. I might get out of this unscathed after all.

"Are you sure you don't want me to go in with you?"

I tried to hide my horror at the thought of my mother escorting me into the office with her glittering shirt and carrying voice, shouting for the world to hear that Camille Stone had arrived for the first day of her senior year. She might as well hang a "kick me" sign on my back.

"That's okay, Mom. I'll tell you how it goes later." I grabbed my bag and turned to the door.

"Have a great day, Sweetie! I'll meet you back here as soon as I can get out of work."

I didn't want to think about how long I might be stuck waiting around for her to pick me up. There were some benches I could sit on, but they were in clear view of the parking lot and all the students that would be leaving and staring at the new girl who didn't even have her own car. I needed to focus on one thing at a time, or I might start hyperventilating.

A gust of frigid air washed over me as I opened the heavy door, making me feel like I was stepping into an oversized freezer rather than a place for learning. I hadn't brought a jacket because it was eighty degrees outside, but apparently Green Peaks liked it cold.

Everything inside the office was white. The walls, the tiled floor, the countertop separating me from the secretary, and even the secretary's hair. I wondered briefly where they kept the padded room in this asylum.

"Can I help you, dear?" The woman's voice was stronger than I was expecting from someone who looked like they should have retired ten years ago. I noticed the silver name tag pinned to her shirt that read "Martha."

"Yes, my name is Cami Stone." I tried to match the strength in Martha's voice, but I knew I was failing miserably. I sounded like a terrified child, and probably looked like one too.

At the mention of my name, the secretary's face lit up. "Oh yes! Miss Stone. We've been expecting you! Principal Morse told me to notify him as soon as you got here."

I started to tell her that that wouldn't be necessary, that I just needed a class schedule and a locker number and I could figure the rest out on my own, but she had already pressed a button on the wall and I could hear an answering buzz inside a room deeper in the office.

Half a second later, Uncle Peter emerged from one of the rooms within the office with a huge smile on his face.

"Cami! So great to see you! Are you ready to start your first day?"

I shrugged my shoulders. "I'm here, aren't I?" He frowned, and I made a mental note to try and tone it down on the sarcasm. I didn't want people to see me as a loser, but I didn't want them to think I was stuck up either.

Uncle Peter exited through a door on the side of the office and re-emerged through the door I had just entered. He held a sheet of paper, my class schedule, I presumed, and an index card that revealed my locker number and combination.

"We've got twenty minutes before your first period starts. I'll show you around so that you don't get lost."

I had a little more trouble hiding the emotions on my face this time. What was it with the over-helpful adults today? Was there a sign hovering over my head, flashing "Incompetent Teenager"?

"Oh no, Uncle Pete, I really don't want to trouble you with that! I can ask around if I can't find a classroom."

Having the principal hold my hand while he showed me around the school? That was definitely out of the question. I had a feeling this wasn't the normal routine for new students, and if it was clear on my first day that I was going to receive special treatment from the guy running the school, it could only mean bad things for me in the eyes of the other students. My mind was flashing back to the text messages that reminded me I was already hated at one school.

"Nonsense!" Uncle Peter cried, walking me back towards the door with a hand on my bookbag. "It isn't any trouble at all, and I want to make sure you're comfortable here."

It looked like I wasn't going to get through this unscathed after all.

The school was small, much smaller than the one in Plainfield, and that one had been strictly for high school students. Apparently the whole second floor of this building was reserved for the junior high kids.

"You shouldn't have any reason to go up there," Peter said as we passed the staircase. "There are strict rules in place to keep the high schoolers and junior high students separated. Parents were afraid the youngsters might be bullied if they had to share the halls." He smiled and shrugged, almost like the thought amused him.

The logic made sense to me, but so did simply having two separate buildings to keep us apart. Money didn't grow on trees, I supposed, but if there was that much concern from the parents then I figured it would be worth it to work a new building into the budget. Then again, the chance of something happening to a young kid in a town this size was pretty small.

"Your first class is American History, which is in room 110."

Peter walked me around the school, pointing out each of my classes and their teachers. White seemed to be the recurring theme, and the intensity of the color bleaching the hallways and classrooms left me with a headache in no time.

The tour took less than ten minutes because of the school's small size, but by the time we made it back to my locker the other students were filing in through the front doors, making their way to their first classes.

I froze behind my locker door and began to search frantically for an escape route before someone saw me with the principal. I could feel my face turning hot and red as the students drew nearer, and I noticed Uncle Peter's smirk at my obvious discomfort. I had just slammed my locker and turned to leave when a voice spoke directly behind us.

"Hey Mo!"

Crap. I had almost made it.

I turned reluctantly to find a tall, blond haired boy with dark blue eyes leaning up against the wall of lockers. He spoke to Uncle Peter, but his eyes were on me.

"Mr. Mitchell! Did we behave ourselves this summer?"

The boy looked back at Peter and grinned mischievously. He swept the wavy, long hair out of his face and managed a one-arm shrug, his other shoulder still pressed against the locker.

"If you didn't hear anything bad about me, then I guess there wasn't anything to hear."

I glanced between the two males, a little taken aback. Did everyone talk to the principal so cordially here? Where I was from, the principal was the man everyone avoided and only spoke to when absolutely necessary. He was the one that handed out the punishments and had no concerns about making friends with the students. But even as I thought this, several more kids greeted him as they passed us to their lockers. No one was glaring at me or coughing "teacher's pet" behind my back. Everyone seemed to genuinely like my uncle.

Peter rolled his eyes at the boy and shooed us along.

"You better get to class, Cami. I'd hate to make you late on your first day, although I'm sure I could get Mr. Angle to let this one slide."

Uncle Peter waved good-bye and turned towards the hallway that would take him back to the office. I was left with the blonde "Mr. Mitchell" who was staring at me as if I were an algebra equation he needed to solve. The devilish smile never left his face.

"So, your name's *Cami?*" he finally said, ungluing himself from the lockers. Other kids were moving around us now, shoving notebooks and binders into their allotted homes. The hall was quickly filled with the buzz of teens talking and laughing and the slamming of locker doors. "Like a shirt?"

I rolled my eyes at him as I deposited a few items into my own locker. Like I had never heard that one before.

"No, it's short for Camille, but no one under the age of sixty should have to go by that name."

The boy laughed, and I couldn't help admiring the way his blue eyes crinkled with the motion. He extended his hand. "My name's Jason. It's nice to meet you, Cami."

I shook his hand, and that's when I noticed the dried purple and yellow splotches that had hardened into his skin.

"You paint?" I asked, gesturing towards his hand.

Jason's eyes widened and an embarrassed look crossed his face, possibly because a girl just pointed out that his hands were dirty. I softened my face into a playful smile, trying to show him that I really didn't care. My hands had been stained the same way countless times, and I knew what it was like to be absorbed by a canvas.

"Yeah, some." His voice was a little more shy than it had been when he talked to Peter.

"Same here." I said.

The first bell sounded, making us both jump, and I took the opportunity to rip my eyes away from the boy in front of me. Seriously, I couldn't let myself fall for the first guy I met in this town. I was just in Green Peaks for one year, and then I'd leave the mess of my adolescence behind and hopefully start a new and better life at whatever college I chose.

Still, it was nice to know there was at least one friendly face here.

I walked towards my history class and found Jason following along beside me. I guessed it wasn't that much of a coincidence that we shared the same first class in a school this small. Probably a fourth of the student body was in my history class. Suddenly something occurred to me, and I had to ask.

"Why did you call Principal Morse 'Mo'?"

Jason laughed again and shook his head. "I'm not even sure when we started that. It's just short for Morse, but all the cool kids call him Mo."

Cool kids gave their principal a nickname here? It baffled me how the peer system from one school could be so drastically different from another.

I also couldn't believe how easily I seemed to fit into this one. The day flew by, and within the first couple of periods I already had more friends than I could handle with my brain's limited capacity for new names. No one seemed to mind when I had to ask two or three times for them to repeat them. Everyone was friendly and inviting, and no one accused me of being a raging alcoholic like my father.

I soon learned that I shared almost the exact same schedule with a girl named Natalie Morgan, another tall blonde who looked like she could be Jason's sister. They weren't related, I discovered, but they did happen to be in the same group of friends. I walked with her from class to class and sat with her posse, which included Jason, a short boy named Taylor Garner, and a dreamy girl named Carly Thacker who could be found doodling in her notebook in the back of every class. As it turned out, they were all just as big of art freaks as I was.

"You should join the Art Club!" Natalie shouted as we dug into our lunch of chicken nuggets and mac and cheese. No one turned their head at her sudden outburst, though. Another thing I quickly learned was that Natalie had only one volume: loud. These kids had probably grown up with her loud voice and high energy over the last eighteen years and could tune her out by now.

"Yeah, we meet every Friday after school and work on projects for the shows we put on throughout the year. You should definitely join," Taylor said quietly. I had to strain to hear all his words after the ringing that was left in my ears from Natalie's voice.

It sounded like fun, and I really wanted to get back into my art after neglecting it for the last several weeks, but I hesitated.

Did I really want to get attached to these people when I was going to leave them all behind in a year? Not to mention, being a part of a group like theirs probably meant drama down the road, as all high school cliques seemed to carry some degree of drama. I didn't want to make waves, I reminded myself. I just wanted to get through my senior year in one piece.

"I don't know," I started. All their eyes were fixated on me, even Carly's, who had given her notebook a short reprieve so that she could join in on the conversation. I could tell they weren't going to let me off easy. "I don't have a car to drive home from any after-school clubs, and I don't want to make my mom come back and get me."

There. Let them see how truly lame I was and decide if they wanted a loser in their group. I cringed as I waited for them to disperse, halfway expecting them to get up and eat at another table without me. It wouldn't be the first time something like that had happened.

"If that's all you got, I'd be happy to drive you home. From what it sounds like, we only live a few minutes away from each other anyway."

Natalie's eyebrows were raised as she stared me down and took a long swig of her chocolate milk. The others were nodding too, waiting for me to accept her offer. They didn't think I was lame for not having my own car, and they seemed like they actually wanted me in the club. I felt like my brain was firing neurons in every direction as I tried to catch up with what was happening here, now, at this new school.

Somehow, I was being accepted.

"Yeah, okay. I think that'd be fun." I heard myself say the words before I could swallow them back. There was no turning back now, and the part of my mind that had been keeping her mouth shut for so long asked me why I should want to turn back anyway. Here was a group of kids that wanted me in their circle, a group of *cool kids* in their own right, and I'd be stupid to turn them down.

Maybe Green Peaks was the new beginning I so desperately needed. Maybe I wouldn't have to wait until college to start my new life. As I finished my lunch and continued the school day with my newfound friends, I let the tight ball that had been clenched in my chest ever since my father's death loosen fractionally. I let myself breathe a little easier, and for the first time, I let myself hope.

Chapter Three

Natalie Morgan, the loud girl everyone rolled their eyes at and was constantly telling to "shut up," quickly became my saving grace in this new town.

Instead of ditching me after school, she hung around with me on the uncomfortable stone benches for the full thirty minutes until my mom arrived to pick me up. She talked about art and the different projects she had been working on during her summer break and even showed me pictures of the completed paintings, sculptures, and carvings on her phone. She talked about the kids in our class, which girls were friendly and which I should avoid, the couples that had been dating since junior high, and the ones who had broken up over the summer. She talked about the teachers, the ones that were most likely to give pop quizzes and the ones that could easily go off track when asked a well-targeted question.

I barely had a chance to get a word into any of the conversations, and that was just fine with me. I was happy to listen to her ramble on about inconsequential topics and take it all in quietly. Her personality reminded me of my friend Michael Varner from back home, who I knew from experience could talk for an hour straight, never pausing to take a breath. My neck would sometimes get sore from all the nodding during his one-way conversations.

While I knew I could never replace Michael as a friend, and I planned on staying in touch with him as much as possible through texting and social media, it was still nice to meet someone that could fill the role of my loud and obnoxious best friend almost perfectly.

Natalie eventually exhausted her list of conversation topics and turned the questioning onto me. I knew it was only a matter of time until someone asked the obvious question, but my whole body still tensed when the explanation was finally requested.

"So why did your family move to Green Peaks?"

Her green eyes were soft and curious, holding none of the accusations I'd feared would accompany the subject. It did look strange, a mother and her almost eighteen-year-old daughter moving to an insignificant town with little to offer. My aunt was here, so we did have one tie, I supposed, but it wasn't like she and my mom were close enough to warrant the move by themselves.

I didn't want to reveal the gory details behind our flight from Colorado. I didn't want to see judgment in the eyes of all my peers or hear the words "useless drunk" and "alcoholic family" thrown behind my back. I didn't want anyone to know the truth behind my father's death. My phone buzzed in my pocket, and I could only imagine what line of text could be waiting to break me down all over again.

I had been expecting the question to reveal itself at some point, so I'd practiced a simple line to use in response.

"My father passed away recently, and my mom and I just needed a change of scenery. Since my aunt and uncle live here, Green Peaks seemed like the best option."

My answer contained no lies, but I hoped she couldn't detect the ugly layer of secrecy hiding beneath my words. I was spared from learning what she thought on the matter because my mom chose the perfect time to pull up and roll the window down.

"Cami! I see you made a friend!" My mother's voice was high and excited, and I had to stop myself from slapping my hand against my forehead. Really, it wasn't like I was five years old.

Natalie played it off well, though, and I thanked God again for sending me this high-spirited soul. It seemed like no situation could be too awkward for her, and I wondered if she had ever been embarrassed in her whole life.

"Hi, Mrs. Stone!" Natalie sang after jumping up from the bench. Her long hair had become tangled from the half hour of sitting in the wind, and she brushed it back from her face. "It's nice to meet you! I'm Natalie."

Natalie extended her hand through the open window and my mom shook it graciously. Judging by the look on her face, my mother hadn't expected me to talk to a single person today, let alone make friends with an exuberant girl like Natalie. But I could hardly be angry at her lack of expectation when I had planned on staying quiet and laying low. My new friends just hadn't given me a choice in the matter.

My mom chatted with Natalie for a few minutes about school and work, and before I could get into the car, she informed my mom that she would drive me home from school from now on. I tried to tell her she didn't need to do that, I absolutely hated to be a burden on people, but she wouldn't budge. Another wave of gratitude washed over me that I had met and made friends with a girl like Natalie Morgan.

In the car, I watched as my new friend walked to her own vehicle, a baby blue and white striped truck sitting by itself in the now near-vacant parking lot. I smiled to myself as she got in and revved the deafening engine. Leave it to Natalie to buy the only vehicle that held a chance of being louder than she was.

As we drove away, I could feel the excitement rolling off my mom in waves. I knew that she had hoped beyond reason that I would end up liking it here, and apparently the evidence of a single friend was enough to confirm that I would. I tried not to roll my eyes and allowed her to have her moment.

"So, you made a friend on your very first day? That's wonderful, honey!" Her eyes were sparkling as much as her purple shirt. Was she actually getting teary at the thought of me making friends? I didn't think I had been that unsocial before the move, but maybe I was. I didn't realize how important it was for her that I found a way to fit in here. Maybe she was just happy that I was capable of fitting in *somewhere.*

"Yeah, I made a few friends, actually, and they invited me to join the school art club. I think I'm going to do it."

I decided I would put all my mom's worries to rest. While I wasn't completely sold on Green Peaks yet, it wouldn't kill me to let on like I was for her sake. I remembered how fragile she still was in the aftermath of my father's death and resolved to be a little more generous with my attitude.

"That's fantastic, Sweetheart!" She was definitely crying now. I chose to pretend like I didn't notice and instead focused on the road in front of us, prepared to grab the wheel if it looked like her tears would land us in a ditch.

To change the subject, I asked how she liked her new students and if they appreciated her outfit. One girl had been brave enough to compliment her shirt, she said, but most of the children were shy and reserved. There was one boy named Tommy Higgins that had the potential to be a troublemaker after he "accidentally" tripped his neighbor on his way to his seat, so she was going to have to keep an eye on him. She thought it would take a week or two before they all became comfortable enough with her as their teacher before they returned to their goofy selves.

It sounded like we both had a good first day of acclimating to the town. I just hoped our good fortune here would last.

When we arrived home, I dropped my bookbag on one of the kitchen stools and made my way to the family room to relax. None of my new teachers were rude enough to hand out homework on the first day, so I planned on sinking into the cushy couch and napping before dinner. I had just wrapped myself in a soft, pink blanket and closed my eyes when my phone began to buzz again, demanding this time.

I squeezed my eyes shut tighter. *Just ignore it,* I thought. They'd get bored texting me eventually, wouldn't they? Three more buzzes revealed that they wouldn't.

Fine, I fumed. I disentangled myself from the blanket and half fell off the couch in my annoyance. Grabbing my phone from where it landed on the floor, I pressed the button on the side to turn it off. When I saw who all the messages were from, though, I stopped and smiled. I unlocked my phone and opened the texts.

So? How'd your first day go?

Still waiting...

Hello?? I'm still your best friend aren't I?!

Camille. Jean. Stone. Answer me right now!!

I should have known that Michael would want to hear how my first day went.

Relax, Varner, I typed. *It went surprisingly well. I met a few art freaks who are pretty cool.*

Three bubbles appeared at the bottom of the conversation, his response quickly being written out. I could just see his fingers flying over the screen as he typed out a snarky reply.

I sighed and got up, knowing this would take up most of my afternoon. I made my way into the spacious kitchen and extracted a water boiler from the cabinet next to the stove where I'd watched my uncle unload it a few days before. I got the water boiling and spooned some black tea and rose petals into the infuser before setting it into my favorite mug, a large black cup with my initials engraved in gold. It had a chip in the handle where my father had dropped it last year.

My phone vibrated noisily on the granite countertop. It was Michael yelling at me from a hundred miles away.

About time! Here I was thinking you had been kidnapped and murdered, skinned alive and buried in a shallow grave. They do that over there, ya know.

I rolled my eyes and replied. *How do you know that I'm not? This could be the murderer using my phone...*

I smiled and watched the bubbles blink as he typed. It was nice to get back into our bantering routine. We had been texting each other this way for four years, from our bedrooms late at night to mere seats away in Algebra class. It was easy for me to pretend we were only a block away from each other now, back in our little suburb of Plainfield. We could be breaking down our first day of senior year together, gossiping about the cheerleaders that gained weight over the summer and the teacher who tried out a hideous new haircut with the attempt to look younger.

The teapot began to whistle, reminding me I wasn't in my tiny kitchen in Plainfield anymore. I poured the water over the infuser and stared out the window, watching the trees of Green Peaks Forest sway in the wind. At least it was beautiful here...if one loved the color green.

I talked with Michael for over an hour, breaking down every person I met and which classes I thought would be terrible. He didn't share many details on how his own first day of school went, and I knew it was my fault. Michael was guilty by association in the eyes of our student body, and while he didn't have many friends before my father's accident, he certainly didn't have any now. I felt terrible for leaving him behind to deal with the hostility alone, but I didn't have a lot of say in my mother's decision to move. Besides, if anything could help him return to the social standing he held before, it would be my absence.

I was still sipping my tea, which had cooled immensely since the start of our conversation, when I read a line of text that made me splutter back into my mug.

Does Green Peaks have any hot guys I need to know about?

I laughed and rolled my eyes. Of course he would want to know if I'd met any hot guys. I thought of Jason and his long blond hair and surprisingly warm, blue eyes. Blondes had never really been my type, but I couldn't deny that he was cute. And he was into art, which pulled more weight in attractiveness in my book. Despite the qualities in his favor, though, I knew I wouldn't pursue anything beyond friendship with him. It just didn't seem like the right time to get into a relationship, and honestly, I barely knew him. I had always been the type of girl to become close friends with a boy before thinking about turning it into something more.

I'm not hooking you up with any more of my friends. Remember how Danny Rochester turned out?

We reminisced about the last boyfriend I tried to set him up with and the disaster that ensued. Danny believed in open relationships, and neither of us were aware of the three other boyfriends he kept from different schools. We texted and teased each other until supper time, when I was forced to leave my phone on the counter and join my mom at the bar in the kitchen. It was an unspoken agreement that the dining room was too grand for the two of us to dine in alone.

It was only seven in the evening by the time we finished eating, and I didn't feel like watching TV or reading a book. It was too early to go to bed, and I didn't want to join my mom's lesson planning at the table. I was about to accept that it would be a boring night, one of many to come, I was afraid, when a sudden inspiration hit me. Here I was in this enormous house, and I hadn't even taken the time to explore its depths yet.

I had seen most of the first floor, which consisted of the living room, family room, dining room, kitchen, two bathrooms, and my mother's bedroom. A door set into the wall beside the staircase revealed another set of stairs that descended into the cellar.

I took the stairs downward one step at a time, feeling the cold leach into my bones. The room was small, and it seemed the previous family hadn't needed the storage space because no boxes or rogue furniture made its home there. The lighting was nonexistent, but by the flashlight on my phone I could make out the grime and possible mold caked on the walls. I made a mental note to steer clear of the basement from then on.

I dusted myself off after emerging from the cellar and continued up the next flight of stairs to the second-floor landing. The dark hardwood floors extended through every room of the house thus far, but the peeling wallpaper changed patterns from one room to the next. Yellow poppies in the kitchen, burgundy stripes in the living room, and now subtle blue flowers in the upstairs hallway. I could feel the bubbles in the paper as I ran my hand along the wall, the product of a hundred years of aging.

Three more bedrooms lined the hallway along with two bathrooms. I had chosen the larger bedroom next to the bathroom with a huge vanity sink and clawfoot tub. The water had run orange for the first minute of use when I tried to take a bath that first night, but the rust had all washed away by now and I was content that the water was clean enough.

At the end of the hallway, to the right of the window on the far wall, I found another door that I hadn't investigated yet. The brass doorknob felt cold and small in my hand, and the door squeaked loudly as I pulled it open. The stairs that had been hiding behind the door were dusty, showing no footprints or evidence of a person setting foot on them in a very long time. They looked creaky and worn, scaling upwards into darkness like a horror novel. I considered turning around and calling it a night, but it couldn't have been worse than the cellar and I was determined to see the whole house through.

I took three steps up and was surprised when none of them creaked. Even the main staircase in this house groaned on every other step, and yet this one remained silent as I continued upward, disturbing the hibernating dust.

The door at the top of the stairs opened just as soundlessly as the steps that had carried me to it. I felt the room sigh as I entered, as if it had been waiting the last hundred years for someone to explore it. The air was cooler than I had anticipated, not at all what I predicted a musty attic should feel like. I flipped the light switch up with little hope of success and was surprised again when a single bulb flashed to life overhead.

This space was much larger than the one in the basement and was clearly where the family stored their extra belongings. A wooden rocking chair sat in the corner with a white cushion strapped across the seat, now yellowed with age. A grandfather clock stood beside it, the glass face coated in enough dust to prevent me from reading whatever time it was frozen on. Scattered throughout the room was an abundance of miscellaneous items, ranging from piles of leather-bound books to a crate of wooden children's toys. I stepped past a box containing glass bottles and flasks that looked like they belonged in my chemistry classroom, then a basket of unidentifiable herbs. A funny scent tickled my nose upon further inspection, and I dropped the basket to move on.

It was there in the center of the room, against the far wall and directly in front of the attic window, that I found it. A small wooden table, perfectly circular with soft, smooth edges. It was the only piece of furniture in the entire attic that wasn't covered in layers of dust. Situated on top of it was a thick, white candle with wax hardened down its sides next to an old, dull pencil. A matching wooden chair sat in front, inviting someone to sit down and write with the Green Peaks Forest spread out below.

I was pondering the absence of the dust, wondering how the table could possibly be so clean amidst the state of the rest of the room, when I noticed the piece of paper.

It was folded into the shape of a bird. A perfect bird, a beautiful representation of the art of origami that I had never been able to master. I picked the bird up and felt the weight of it in my hands. It was definitely a very old piece of paper, that much I could tell, but like the table it lay on, it was free of dust. As I peered at it closer, I realized there were words written within the folds.

The bird was a beautiful piece of art, one that I usually wouldn't dream of disrupting, but curiosity got the better of me. I unfolded the note one wing at a time, being careful not to rip the old material. When it was finally spread flat on the table, I gasped.

It was a love letter, a poem perhaps, written a century in the past by a man who was certainly dead by now.

Are there words that can describe your beauty?
Vowels and consonants capable of capturing the essence of your perfection?
I think not, my dear.
A fool I might be, but words are all I have.
Your eyes, though often sad, bring warmth to an eternally damned heart.
Your smile, so coveted, could bring a man back from the brink of death.
And your heart, my God.
That you simply cannot hide.
Your love may not be directed at me, but I feel it, my sweet girl, and I ache with the knowledge that it exists.
That you exist.

Love,
Z

My eyes swept across the page, reading it twice, then three times. I didn't know who the poet was, or the girl he so obviously admired, but I could feel the love and care that were taken in writing these words. I couldn't remember ever reading something that made me feel so deeply, like I was exposed to a love that in no right was mine, but I desperately wanted it to be. I knew it was crazy, but I felt like the letter writer knew I was reading his words, wherever he might be.

A drop fell onto the paper, alerting me to the fact that I'd begun to cry. Maybe I was being hit with whatever wave of emotion had crossed my mom earlier in the car, because I'd never been much of a crier, nor was I known to reveal any emotion, really. I typically bottled my feelings up and only allowed them to escape into my art. Perhaps they were coming out now because I'd neglected my emotions the past three weeks. I knew I needed to change that.

I tried to match up the fold lines and reassemble the paper bird, but it was no use. My fingers simply weren't built for origami. I folded the letter into a simple square instead and placed it carefully into my pocket. I knew I would be reading it again.

My life right then might have seemed dark and ugly, but I decided to focus on the beauty when I was able to find it. An old friend, a group of new friends, a loving mother, and a letter that was so beautifully written it caused me to shed my first tear since my father's death.

For a school with only two hundred students, Green Peaks had a decent turn out for the first art club meeting of the year.

I counted roughly twenty other kids scattered around Ms. Carson's classroom, some chatting in groups and others sitting by themselves, already diving into another project before the meeting had even started.

I sat with Natalie, Jason, Taylor, and Carly, and was told that we were the only seniors in the club this year. That explained why I didn't recognize any of the other students from previous classes. My friends didn't bother introducing me to anyone else, and I didn't ask to be. I was secretly grateful when Ms. Carson began the meeting by talking about the upcoming Art Show the school would be putting on and didn't force us to go around the classroom introducing ourselves. My palms had been sweating at the mere thought of the group's eyes on me. I hated being the center of attention, even for a second.

I was already getting used to having more than a single close friend. It'd been years since I had a group of friends to sit with at lunch and hang out with after school. I'd spent plenty of one-on-one time with Michael throughout my high school career, but the group dynamic was different. I realized I liked being able to remain quiet and listen while the others talked and add my own input and stories as I desired.

I had only been a student at Green Peaks High for a week, but people were already treating me like I'd been there my whole life.

I pulled my attention back to the classroom and Ms. Carson, who was continuing to relay information about how the art club worked and what we could expect out of every meeting.

"The Art Club will put on three shows for the town throughout the year. Our Fall Show will be held the first week of October, the Winter Show shortly after you return from Winter Break, and the Spring Show in the middle of April."

Ms. Carson's eyes swept around the classroom as she continued. "We have two months to prepare for the Fall Show, where you all will be expected to submit two or three pieces to be displayed for the school and entire town to admire. Fall themes are appreciated, but not necessarily required. You'll need my approval before displaying them at the show, so don't even think about trying anything inappropriate." She turned her head and found Jason at our table, who was staring at the ceiling innocently. After a moment of trying to hide his amusement, Jason's face erupted in a huge grin.

"What?" He laughed, as the whole class followed the direction of Ms. Carson's glare. I squirmed in my seat and reminded myself they were looking at the boy next to me, and not me. I supposed I should get used to attention being drawn to us, with Jason and Natalie as my friends.

"I won't do it again!" Jason promised, and the way he batted his eyelashes at the teacher made everyone laugh. Ms. Carson failed to hide her own smile, and she turned away from our table and continued giving directions.

Natalie and Taylor were still giggling at the memory of what Jason had done, and I could only guess what it was.

"What did you do?" I whispered to Jason. His eyes were bright and animated, his smile returning to the mischievous smirk I'd witnessed in the hallway on my first day. He leaned toward me, and my breath caught at how close we were sitting.

His hair tickled my face as he whispered in my ear. "Let's just say Ms. Carson isn't a fan of nude paintings."

I leaned back and averted my eyes, feeling my face redden under his gaze. Natalie and Taylor tried to cover the next laughing fit that ensued, but luckily Ms. Carson was on the other side of the room and didn't hear them. Jason went on to tell the story of how he tried to enter a painting of Marilyn Monroe wearing only a Santa hat into the Winter Show his freshman year. He had almost gotten away with it, he claimed, until the teacher went through the displays to straighten everything up and found his precious gem. From then on, all pieces of art had to be cleared by Ms. Carson days ahead of the show.

By the time she made her way back to our side of the room, we had let our laughter die down and were smirking at each other silently. Ms. Carson gave Jason another steely glance before turning away, and Jason winked at me behind her back.

"I would like for you all to work on a collaborative project to submit to the Fall Show as well," Ms. Carson went on. "I suggest you break into groups of four to six people and start coming up with ideas over the next week. At our meeting next Friday you'll be able to get started on them."

All around the room, students began to break into groups to discuss ideas for their projects. None of us moved from our secluded area of the table, and no one approached us asking to join our posse. Maybe it was because we were seniors and somehow came off as intimidating, but I had a strong feeling it had something to do with Jason's record of trouble making. As we brought our heads together, I could tell they were just as happy as I was to keep our project between the five of us.

"So, what do you guys want to do?" Natalie asked, getting straight to the point.

I looked around at the others' faces, remaining silent. I had never been a part of a group art project before and didn't really know how it would work. I knew a little about Natalie's style of art from the pictures she had shown me, but I had no idea what the others liked. I was spared having to speak when Taylor made a suggestion.

"We could paint Marilyn Monroe in different positions covered in Autumn leaves?" Taylor asked, his face composed.

Everyone laughed, including Carly, who was still doodling in her notebook.

By the time the club concluded, we still hadn't thought of a good project to make for the upcoming show. We glanced around the room as the other groups huddled together, sketching ideas and dividing tasks. It was the disappointment clouding Natalie's face and the slump of Jason's shoulders that led me to open my mouth.

"We could go back to my house if you guys want," I suggested quietly. "I'm sure my mom won't mind if we hung out for a bit."

Actually, I could already see her bursting into tears again at the sight of four friends coming to spend time with me at our own house. I decided not to mention that detail and planned on texting my mom to give her a heads up. Hopefully that would allow her enough time to get the tears out of the way before we arrived.

"That would be great!" Natalie shouted. She shoved her notebook into her backpack with a lot more exuberance than she had been moving with before, and then zipped her bag shut with a fierceness I was afraid might cause it to break.

"I've always wanted to see the inside of that house," Carly mused quietly. Her eyes were dreamy as she followed us out of the classroom, her mind a million miles away until she tripped over a freshman's bookbag. Taylor helped her easily to her feet without cracking a joke. They were as used to Carly's daydreaming as they were to Natalie's volume and energy.

We all headed towards Natalie's pickup truck, threw our bags into the bed in the back, and then climbed in. I offered the shotgun spot to Carly and found myself sandwiched between Jason and Taylor in the backseat.

I'd grown used to Natalie's truck over the past few days, but it still cracked me up how much the interior differed from the exterior. From the outside, the truck looked like any old rusting pickup that might be on its way to carry a load of hay or offer aid to any of numerous farming tasks. On the inside, the truck was transformed into a preteen girl's bedroom.

The front seats were draped in hot pink slips that matched the polka-dotted floorboards, somehow kept clean despite the rainy weather we'd had. The steering wheel was lined with a fuzzy purple cover, and the equally purple rearview mirror sported an air freshener that caused the entire cab to smell like cherry blossoms. The boys on either side of me had ridden in there before, I presumed, because neither made a comment about the girliness of the vehicle.

"I've always wondered what your house was like on the inside too," Jason said as we pulled away from the school.

"My older brother and his friends almost broke into it one Halloween on a dare. But they chickened out, said the place gave them the creeps. A lot of the town thinks it's haunted."

Natalie gave Jason a sharp glance in the rearview mirror, and I could feel her eyes turn to me, gauging my reaction. No one had told me they thought our house was haunted. Jason's eyes widened as he realized what he said, and he tried to back-pedal.

"I doubt it's actually haunted though," he said quickly, nudging my knee with his. "My brother's a big sissy. He wouldn't know a ghost if it slapped him in the face."

I laughed and shrugged my shoulders. The house didn't feel haunted to me so far. It was quiet, peaceful even—until I walked around, that is. There wasn't much to be done about the creaking floorboards, but that was to be expected in any old house, wasn't it?

"Why do people think it's haunted?" I asked.

Everyone turned to look at me, then shared eye contact with each other, trying to determine whether they should tell me something. No one said a word for several minutes, and my skin began to crawl at their prolonged silence. I hadn't been worried about the house being haunted before, but their refusal to answer my question was putting me on edge. What weren't they telling me?

"What, did someone die there?" I asked, my voice hitching up in my sudden urgency for an answer.

Natalie laughed shakily, and stared at the boys through the rearview mirror until they joined in. Carly was staring out the passenger window, oblivious to the conversation as far as I could tell.

"No, of course no one died there," Natalie said unconvincingly. She cleared her throat and threw daggers at Jason for bringing it up.

"Look," Jason said, finally turning to me and looking me squarely in the eyes. "As far as we know, no one died there. But there's just a funny history around that house that no one seems to know the truth of. No one has lived there in a hundred years, and no one knows why. People have gone and looked at it, outsiders like you, but no one could ever close on it. You're the first family to show a serious interest in the house, and we were all shocked when you actually moved in."

Taylor nodded in agreement. "The fact that you guys moved in just shows that there's nothing wrong with it though," he added. "It's a really pretty house, and it's a shame no one has occupied it for this long."

I took in everything they said and thought it over. At least no one had died in my house, to my friends' knowledge anyway. It made sense that the locals would be superstitious about a house that had been abandoned for so long. It was something to tell stories about and scare each other over the crackling of a bonfire. The best ghost stories were those that resided in the story teller's own town, and my new house made for the perfect centerpiece.

"Maybe people are afraid of the house because it's surrounded by the Cursed Woods." Carly said, her voice low. We all looked at her, startled that she even knew what we had been talking about. Her dreamy eyes flashed back and forth, following each towering tree we passed out the window. The forest was getting thicker here as we drew closer to my house.

"The Cursed Woods?" I prompted. Apparently it was a day for all sorts of scary stories. At the back of my mind, I was glad they had waited until Friday evening to share these creepy tales with me. At least if I couldn't sleep tonight, I wouldn't have to worry about getting up early for school the next day.

Natalie chuckled for real this time, and I was glad to see her eyes held none of the hesitation that had been present a moment before.

"I forget you don't know things, Cami!" She laughed. "I should have told you about the Cursed Woods days ago. It's just what the locals call the Green Peaks Forest. Man, I'm really slacking on my friend-of-a-newbie duties."

I laughed and shook my head. She still hadn't explained why it was considered cursed.

"They call it the Cursed Woods because of the strange things that happen in it," Jason said, reading my mind. "Sometimes there are weird colors in the sky over the forest, and animals have been seen coming out of it that have no business in Green Peaks. There have been sightings of tropical birds, wild horses, and even a kangaroo, supposedly."

"These are all legends, of course," Taylor added, giving me a small smile. "None of us have ever seen anything odd in the woods. I think it's our parents' generation that are all super weird about it."

I didn't have time to consider the Cursed Woods, or my own possibly haunted house, because at that time we reached the end of the lane and both of them stood before us. The house seemed to stand even taller before me, more menacing, and the woods stretched behind it, dark and foreboding. I felt like the trees that were now swaying in the wind were laughing at me, wondering how I could turn into such a coward over the course of a single car ride. Neither had scared me before, but now?

Now they were simply more interesting.

My mom was waiting for us in the entry hall, and the smudged eyeliner on her face told me she had already cried over the text I sent from the truck. I hoped she could at least keep her eyes dry for the next hour while my friends were here.

"It's great to see you again, Mrs. Stone!" Natalie said as we entered the house. She bounded forward and gave my mother a hug, resulting in a startled choke my mom quickly turned into a greeting. She appeared to be too surprised by Natalie's animation to break out in more tears, and for that I was grateful.

I introduced my other friends, who all shook hands with my mom before letting their eyes travel the length of the room, taking in the faded wallpaper and recently glossed floorboards. My mother announced she had made us a snack, and we all followed her through the living room and into the kitchen where a cheeseball and plate of crackers waited for us.

We helped ourselves to the crackers and cheese, and then before my mom could start interrogating them, I led my friends on a tour of the house.

They were just as impressed with its grandeur and homeliness as I had been. I avoided the basement and explained the probable mold that coated its walls but showed them every other room on the first and second stories, relieved when we reached my room that I hadn't left it in a complete mess. They all agreed the house certainly wasn't haunted after witnessing it for themselves, and I breathed a little easier when they laughed the notion off.

As we exited my bedroom, I turned toward the attic door before stopping myself. I could show them the little room with its intriguing objects and mysterious table that somehow repelled dust, but something stopped me. I realized I didn't want to share the attic with anyone yet. As I considered the implausible theories Jason would come up with after inspecting the dustless table, I knew I'd tell them the whole story about the paper bird I'd found up there.

I felt the weight of the note in my pocket, which I had begun carrying around with me to read whenever I felt compelled to. I certainly wasn't ready to share my love letter with anyone, especially a couple of boys who would probably make fun of it and belittle the words that, for whatever reason, seemed so important to me right now.

I stared through the window at the end of the hall, at the trees that were growing darker in the setting sun. Suddenly, I knew what our art project should be about.

"Guys, let's do something on the Cursed Woods for the project," I said excitedly, turning back towards the others. I was happy to see surprised and elated faces as they considered the thought.

"That's actually a really good idea, Cam," Natalie said, punching me in the shoulder. "We could do something with the animals in the woods and show the trees changing colors so Ms. Carson gets her beloved fall theme."

Jason and Taylor agreed, and even Carly voiced her consent.

A warm glow spread through my body at having come up with an idea they all liked. It would be fun to share this experience with them, and I had the bonus of living right on the edge of the woods. I could gaze at it and work on my part of the project any time I wanted.

"You know what would give us some really good inspiration?" Jason asked, his eyes mischievous once again.

I shook my head, but Taylor rolled his eyes as if he already knew.

"Let's go out in the woods right now! It's not like we have anything better to do!"

The trees waved at me eagerly through the window, beckoning me in. I was reminded of the pull I felt on my first day, but hesitated before agreeing to Jason's proposal. Why did I feel drawn towards a forest of trees that had been nicknamed the Cursed Woods? The feeling frightened me, but even as I considered declining the idea, I heard the others agree and start making their way down the stairs for the front door.

I didn't want Jason to think I was a sissy like his brother. So, despite my reservations, I followed.

We didn't plan on going in very deep, but the sun was falling quickly below the horizon and the shadows were growing into darkness. I grabbed Natalie's arm as we entered the trees, then covered my fear by pretending the vines sprawled across the forest floor had tripped me. She smiled and slid her arm through mine, matching her pace to my hesitant crawl.

Maybe the stories of the weird lights and animals were getting to me, but every snap of a branch and hoot of an owl had me whipping in the direction of the sounds. Taylor and Jason trekked a few yards ahead of us while Carly dragged behind. Natalie was making a habit of glancing back at her periodically to make sure she followed us and didn't get lost.

I had the itching sensation that someone was watching me. I knew it was paranoia getting the best of me, but I couldn't stop myself from glancing over my shoulder almost as often as Natalie, not to check on our friend, but to watch for a figure that didn't belong.

The sun was almost completely down, and I considered getting my phone out to light our way when Jason suddenly stopped ahead of us.

"Do you hear something?" he asked quietly. His eyes were wide as he looked around us slowly.

None of us made a sound as we quietly glanced around the darkened trees, straining our ears for anything out of the ordinary. The crickets chirped, another owl hooted, the wind whispered as it lifted the leaves in the breeze. Then I heard the crunching. Footsteps, approaching us from behind.

Before any of us could whip around and see who the invader was, a loud voice boomed from directly behind us, silencing all the woodland creatures and momentarily stopping my heart.

"What do you think you're doing here?"

Chapter Five

A chorus of shrieks filled the night. They echoed and bounced off the trees, making it sound like there were dozens of us rather than the handful of a group we truly were.

Despite the terror and shock my mind was thrown into, I found that I was aware of everything around me in clear detail. I was surprised to discover the loudest scream erupted from Carly, her tiny frame emitting what had to be the most ear-piercing cry I had ever heard. Who knew a tiny person like herself could create such a large sound? The noise coming from Jason was just as high pitched and shrill, and a part of me knew I would laugh at the situation later. If I was alive to laugh at all, that was.

My own scream was lodged in my throat, and I held my hands over my mouth as I stared at the dark form of our assailant in wide eyed silence.

The sudden blaze of a flashlight forced me to squint as the figure closed the remaining distance between us. Natalie squeezed my arm in anticipation, and I squeezed hers back, calculating whether we should run or try to swarm the stranger all at once. There was only one flashlight, which meant we had them outnumbered five to one. A voice in my head whispered there could be more of them waiting in the dark trees, though, and who knew what kind of weapons they might hold? I hushed the voice and tried to concentrate.

As the echoes of my friends' screams died away, a laugh erupted in front of us. It was a tone I immediately recognized, and the scent of the man's cologne washed over me as he drew nearer, allowing me to release a sigh of relief. I didn't need to see his face to know who had snuck up on us.

"Uncle Peter!" I shouted hoarsely, finally locating my voice. I dropped my arms from Natalie's hold and crossed them squarely over my chest. My uncle was close enough now to make out the dark green jacket he had worn to help us unpack, and the short strands of his brown hair caught the glow from the flashlight as he tipped his head back to laugh even harder.

My friends' eyes adjusted to the beam of light as mine had, and it took them only a moment longer to recognize him.

"Wait, Mo?" Jason yelped, his voice still high and alarmed. I suppressed a giggle as he coughed and forced his vocal cords to go deeper. "What are you doing out here?"

Peter stopped laughing and brought the flashlight up to his chin, illuminating his suddenly serious face. The light turned his skin a ghastly shade of orange and transformed him into something sinister.

"I was following the children," he breathed, his voice scratchy and ominous in the now quiet clearing. His words hung in the darkness for a moment, undisturbed, before I broke apart from the group and shoved him lightly. The flashlight caught his emerging grin of straight, white teeth before being redirected to the trees that led the way back towards the house.

"Really kids, it's too dark for you to be out here," Peter said finally, all joking aside. "And where is your jacket, young lady?" He looked at my bare arms sternly. I was about to pop off and accuse him of being as overbearing as my mother, but then a cold breeze blew through, causing me to shiver. I admitted I probably should have worn a jacket this late in the evening.

Uncle Peter led us away from the trees and onto the path that would carry us back to my house. He explained that he had stopped by to drop some papers off for my mom, and when he heard we were troping around in the forest he just couldn't resist scaring us. I felt the tension in the group dissipate as everyone accepted we were no longer in danger. Jason and Taylor joked with my uncle and Natalie and Carly replayed the scene, Carly's face red as she thought about how loudly she had screamed.

Everything was as it should be. Our mysterious stalker was revealed to be my harmless uncle, and my friends were back to their joking selves as we prepared to exit the Cursed Woods. Why, then, did I still feel like I was being watched?

We reached the end of the trees and the rest of them continued on ahead toward the welcoming lights shining from the house. I strayed behind and turned my gaze back into the depths of the forest. It was too dark now to make out anything but the first few rows of trees. The moon shone brightly overhead, illuminating the clearing of my backyard, but the canopy of the woods was too thick for it to penetrate. Still, I felt like something was waiting in the darkness, just beyond the moonlight's reach.

"Coming, Cami?" Uncle Peter called. They were almost to the house now and had just realized I wasn't in their midst. I nodded my head but wasn't sure if they could see the motion in the night.

"Coming!" I called back. I shook off the paranoia, accrediting it to the stories of haunted houses, cursed forests, and the most recent scare from my uncle.

I gave the trees one last glance before turning to join my friends and family.

The next school week passed uneventfully. I'd survived my first two weeks in Green Peaks and had even retained the friends I made on my first day of school, despite them learning that their high school principal was my uncle. He was a *cool* principal, they insisted, so he must be an even cooler uncle. I had rolled my eyes and laughed with them as we all recalled the freakish face he made with the flashlight. Maybe Dad jokes were cool here too.

I celebrated my successful assimilation by sleeping in on Saturday morning. I didn't have any plans for the day, and it was nice to finally relax and stop worrying about everything. My friends didn't appear to be going anywhere, and I hadn't received a nasty text in over three days. Things were finally starting to lighten up for me.

I emerged from my bedroom around ten o'clock and stumbled down the stairs, yawning twice on my way to the kitchen. I could hear my mom moving things around in the dining room, and after brewing a cup of tea, I walked to the doorway to investigate.

"What are you doing?" I observed the various cardboard boxes covering the dining room table. I leaned against the doorway and sipped my steaming mug as my mom dropped another full box onto the polished mahogany.

"That's the last of it," she stated. Sweat shone on her neck and forehead, sticking to her long, dark bangs. She was already dressed for the day, and based on the array of boxes before me, she had been up for quite a while.

"The last of what?" I stepped forward and peered into the closest box, which was full of button-down shirts. The next box had blue jeans in it, and I noticed a smaller one heaped with men's ties.

"Your dad's stuff," she said simply and walked around the table, passing me on her way into the kitchen. She was quiet as she helped herself to a drink of water, the ice clinking in the glass making the only sound.

I took in the sight of my father's things, objects that seemed greatly reduced in his absence that could be stored away in six or seven boxes. Was this all that was left of my father's being? Lifeless scraps that were meant to be hidden away? My mom must have spent the entire morning going through all their things, sorting the living from the dead's.

"I need to run some errands before lunch. Do you mind taking it all up to the attic for me?" she asked. Her gaze was on the floor as she went on. "I might donate them eventually, but I don't want to think about that right now." When her eyes met mine, they were red and glistening. I nodded at her mutely.

"Unless you wanted to come with me on my errands?" she added as an afterthought. Her eyes had strayed away from mine again, and I could tell that she wanted nothing more than to be alone. To get out of the house and away from the only things left of her husband. By the time she got home and had pulled herself together again, she was hoping they would be gone from her sight.

"I think I'll stay in my pajamas for a while," I said lightly. I had a feeling Green Peaks wouldn't judge a teenager walking around in sweatpants and a T-shirt, but I didn't mention it. "Don't worry about the boxes. I'll take care of them." It seemed easier to refer to them as simply boxes and not mention the treasures that hid inside.

My mom voiced her thanks and then disappeared into the next room to find her purse and car keys. I listened to the engine start up, followed by the crunch of gravel as she departed. I sank into one of the dining chairs and regarded the boxes before me.

They were more like tombs than boxes, cradling my father's belongings like the coffin that held his remains before we lowered it into the ground. I knew these boxes would sit and collect dust, forgotten, just as my father's coffin would slowly degrade into the dirt of its surroundings.

My light mood from having discovered I might fit into this new environment came crashing down around me. I wondered, not for the first time, what my father would think of this new place and its people. He had never cared much for my uncle, saying he was too stuck up to respect our family, but he tolerated my aunt for my mother's sake. He had a fun time joking with Michael when I invited him over to hang out, and I knew he would get along just as well with my new friends. If only fate had moved us here before my father's accident, maybe I could have had a future where our time wasn't cut so short.

I took my time rinsing out the empty mug and set it carefully in the rack to dry. I knew I couldn't put off moving my father's things for too long. I at least needed them to be gone before my mom returned, and I didn't know how long she would take.

Sighing, I grabbed a box full of shirts and carried it up the stairs.

My feet kicked up more dust as I ascended the steps to the attic, and I made a mental note to clean them off later. We might not go up there often, but I didn't want the residue to irritate my mother's allergies.

Inside the attic, I flipped the light switch up even though the rays streaming in through the grimy window offered plenty of sunlight to see. The yellow glow from the bulb added an eerie coloring to the already strange collection of objects. I scooted the box of glassware with my foot, making room to set my father's shirts down. I then moved a few other objects to create a space large enough to hold all my father's other belongings. Somehow, it seemed like they should all stay together.

It took me five trips of walking up and down the stairs to transfer all the boxes into their new home. Ten flights of stairs later, I could feel my muscles screaming at me in displeasure. I wasn't used to all this cardio.

The last box was duct taped shut and was surprisingly heavy for its small size. By the time I made it up the stairs, my back was screaming in protest. I finally dropped it on the floor in relief and heard what sounded like metal clanging together on the inside. I was sweating and out of breath, but I had always been a curious person. I spied a rusty looking knife in the box with the mysterious glassware and used it to make quick work of the tape.

Free from its bindings, I opened the box and felt my breath catch. No wonder it had been so heavy. Inside, three handguns were nestled together, like three siblings huddling for warmth. They shone in the lightbulb's eerie glow, the silver of the revolver glinting like molten steel and the black of the pistols glistening like midnight oil. The rest of the box was occupied by boxes and sleeves of ammunition, golden bullets that seemed innocent without my father's hands to load them.

It seemed like a lifetime ago that my father drove me out into the country and set up a target to teach me how to shoot. It was our little secret, he said, because I very well knew how my mother felt about guns. But one day I might need to defend myself, and he said it was his duty as my father to make sure I knew how.

At the sight of the weapons, I sat in the rocking chair to catch my breath, not caring if my clothes got dirty from the layers of dust. They were already going to need to be washed after the sweat I just worked up.

I was leaning back in the chair, testing the limits of the old wood slowly, and taking in the peacefulness of the attic when something caught my eye. The light spilling in from the window lit up an object laying white and still on the table. *My table,* I found myself calling it.

I stood up and crossed the room, the guns temporarily forgotten, and weaved my way through the now very cluttered area. When I drew near enough to clearly see what the object was, I halted. It simply wasn't possible. I blinked my eyes closed tightly, thinking the image might disappear, but when I opened them the white shape remained.

There on my round, dustless table sat another paper bird.

How did you get here? I thought wildly. The letter I had found over a week ago was right where I left it in my bedroom. I remembered seeing it on the nightstand this morning before getting out of bed. Even if it was somehow the same letter, nothing could explain how it had become folded again and then returned to the attic while I had my back turned. Was it possible there had been two letters that first day I found the attic? Maybe I had just missed this one. Even as I considered the thought, though, I knew it was a lie. I could remember the details of my table, with its candle, pencil, and lone paper bird very clearly. There had certainly only been one.

I gingerly picked up the new bird, testing the weight of it in my hands. It was warm from the sunlight streaming in through the window. I glanced back at the attic door, standing half open. The knowledge that I was home alone in this big, new house gave me a chill for the first time since moving here.

Maybe I should have left it. Just dropped the bird and exited the attic, never to return unless absolutely necessary. But what could be the harm in opening it? I could see the ink that bled through the paper, adorning the bird in place of its typical feathers. I ran my thumbs over it, knowing that it wanted to be read.

I took a deep breath and slowly unraveled the letter.

Hello again, my darling.

It truly has been too long.

I thought I could stay away from you, but the challenge was just too great.

I know that you cherished my words, and I wonder if you'll cherish a few more.

Please believe me when I say, you are no ordinary girl.

I can feel your spirit like a lost kindred soul.

It calls to me, despite our distance, and I cannot ignore its summons.

These words, though not enough, are all I can give you in answer.

I will continue to write, as long as you are there to read.

Every night, sweet girl, you can expect another bird.

May their wings give flight to the feelings I can no longer contain.

Love,
Z

I dropped the letter on the table with a gasp, as if it had burned me. Swinging around toward the door, I half expected someone to be standing there waiting for me, but it was empty and dark, the doorway revealing nothing but dusty stairs.

I could hear myself wheezing as I tried to force air into my lungs, knowing in a small part of my brain that I was hyperventilating and needed to calm down. I couldn't calm down, though, not in light of the mystery that had presented itself before me.

Was someone breaking into the house and leaving these letters? It was the only explanation that made sense. They could have dusted the table off and left the bird in the only clean area. That would explain why everything was coated in dust except for them. But my mind jumped back to the image of the dust covered staircase the first time I opened the door. There were no footprints in the dirt until I climbed the stairs and disturbed it. Unless the intruder had literally flown up the stairs, they couldn't possibly have left the steps so clean and untouched.

Maybe the house actually was haunted. I tried to remember everything I knew about ghosts, but even if I did believe in their existence, I'd never heard of one having the ability to write a letter before, let alone fold that letter into a perfect piece of origami.

None of it made sense. I glanced down at the letter again, finally gaining control of my breathing. Maybe I should have been less concerned with *how* the letters were arriving in the attic, and more interested in *why*.

They were left for me. Someone knew that I had read the first one, loved it enough to carry it around with me, and decided to write me a second. There was a stranger that had feelings for me, and I didn't even know if they were alive or dead.

Maybe the "Z" stands for "Zombie," I thought absently. A smile broke across my face, and I quickly covered it with my hand. I was obviously growing delirious. No part of this was funny. But as I tried to convince myself of the seriousness of my situation, a few giggles escaped from behind my hand. Within moments I had collapsed into a full-on laughing fit. I was a teenage girl, laughing by myself in a hundred-year-old attic, with two love letters in my possession written by a possible stalker or ghost. Or possibly a stalking ghost. What a mess.

"Cami?" My mom's voice called from downstairs. In the midst of my hysteria, I had failed to hear the front door slam.

Making a split-second decision, I folded the letter up and shoved it into the pocket of my sweatpants. If my mother decided to go through my father's things again, I didn't want to risk her stumbling upon it.

If I was smart, maybe I would share the letters with my mom and voice the concern I was feeling over what they might mean. Then again, if I was smart, I wouldn't be planning on staying up that night and trying to catch the letter writer in the act.

I may not have been in my right mind, but the reckless part of me that was beginning to take charge didn't care. I was going to get to the bottom of this, even if I had to take some risks to get there.

I left my table and attic behind and closed the door softly behind me. As I descended the noiseless stairs, I mentally thanked the old house for making my next step easier. I would need to be quiet if I was going to sneak up there again that night.

Chapter Six

In the dark of the thickening night, my eyes strained to make out the words of my most recent letter. There was just enough moonlight filtering in through the dirty attic window for me to read the last lines.

Every night, sweet girl, you can expect another bird. May their wings give flight to the feelings I can no longer contain.

If I took the letter writer at his word, then my next letter would arrive tonight. My chest was already filled with bubbles of anticipation. Butterflies were setting in from excitement, or maybe downright terror. My mind was in too much of a whirlwind to try and figure out which.

I didn't know how early or late the letter would be delivered, so I told my mother I was going to bed early, feigning a headache that warranted immediate rest. My mom had been quiet since her return from town, barely speaking two words at lunch and dinner, and she didn't question my motives. In her dejected state, she would probably be going to bed soon after me.

Despite my mother's preoccupation, I went ahead and made a show of getting ready in the bathroom before not quite stomping back to my bedroom. I knew she could follow the sound of my footsteps overhead, and I hoped my tiptoes that succeeded them to the attic were inconspicuous in comparison.

So, there I sat, wedged behind an old dresser and a stack of boxes that concealed me from most of the room. A gap between some boxes gave me just enough space to watch my table, the unspoken beacon that called the letters home. I was confident that I could remain hidden from whatever person or being was leaving the precious birds, but I still hadn't fully worked out what I would do once I discovered their identity.

I had one of the pistols loaded and ready at my side, but I didn't trust myself to hold it in case I got too jumpy. I clutched a heavy flashlight in my hand, knowing it could do just as well as a weapon if need be. The gun would stay in its place on the floor all night if things went my way.

In all honesty, I didn't have a clue what to expect from my night's excursion. I wanted to know who was leaving the letters and how they were managing to do it in a house like ours. If the previous two notes had been delivered at night, I didn't see any possible way they could have walked through our entire house without either my mom or myself hearing them. Our house was *loud*, especially on the main staircase, and both of us were very light sleepers. Not to mention that we lived out in the middle of nowhere, our closest neighbor stationed at least a mile away. We should have heard a car engine outside the window, or some means of transport to carry them all the way here.

The more I thought about the mystery, the more I itched to uncover it.

The soft glow from my watch told me it was ten o'clock. I'd only been hiding in my corner for an hour, but my limbs were already turning stiff, my bottom sore from sitting on the hard attic floor. I wrapped my arms around my knees and gritted my teeth. I was determined to see this through.

Around eleven my eyelids turned into cement, gaining hundreds of pounds of weight and becoming nearly impossible to keep them up. I fought to hold them open, even using my fingers to try and prevent them from closing, but it was a losing battle. My sleepless, worry-filled nights were catching up with me.

A distinct *creak* broke the silence, and my eyes flew open, alerting me to the fact that I had nodded off. I noticed absently that my watch read midnight.

The moon had risen high in the sky and seemed to be perched right outside the window with all the light it offered the room. With the help of the clear night sky and my eyes, which had adjusted to the darkness hours ago, I could make out all the shapes in the attic clearly. The grandfather clock stood across the room, as silent as ever, the rocking chair sitting immobile beside it. Everything seemed to be in the order I had left it in, and the door I had come through remained closed. What, then, had woken me?

My eyes were drawn to the smooth, undisturbed table and the window right above it, which had apparently opened of its own accord. It gaped half open, like the room had opened its mouth to grin, taunting me.

I stared at the smirking window and felt a warm September breeze swirl around me. I was still frozen in place when I saw a white object fly through the window, hover in place by its two fluttering wings, and then land gently in the middle of the table.

My next bird, my letter, delivered right on time.

I silently screamed at myself to move, to see who was outside the window, but my body was anchored in place. I sat motionless as the glass slid slowly shut, barely making a sound as it clicked back into place. When I could finally move, I raced to the spot as quickly as I could without disturbing any of the items that would inevitably make a crash loud enough to wake up my mother.

As discreetly as possible, I peered out the window at the ground below. The grass in the backyard was clear, revealing no trespassers or mysterious letter writers. The edge of the forest stood a hundred yards away, creating a barrier between the moonlit grass and the shadows within the trees. Separating the known from the unknown. Any manner of person or creature could have escaped into its depths. And I had missed them.

I shook my head in dismay. *No,* I thought. *There's no way someone could've been outside this window.*

I considered the evidence before me, trying to coax my thoughts back toward reason. I was on the third floor of a very old house that creaked and groaned simply from walking around the inside, let alone if someone tried to scale the roof on the outside. I definitely would have heard it if someone had been above me.

Not to mention, there's no perch for someone to stand on to open the window, my subconscious reminded me. Even if there had been something to stand on, how did that explain the way the bird flew through the opening, *hovered in place,* and then settled on its spot on the table, almost alive? A person couldn't do that.

Cautiously, I poked at the paper bird a few times, holding my flashlight up in case I needed to smash it. *Like a bug,* my subconscious smirked. But the bird stayed dormant on the table, showing no signs of taking flight again. The idea that the house might be haunted was gaining authority in my head.

Was I losing my mind? None of this was possible, and I refused to believe that a ghost was at work here. Besides, why would a ghost send the letter in from the outside? If they were haunting the house, wouldn't they already be inside? Maybe I had suffered from too much anxiety since losing my father. Maybe my mind was finally starting to crack.

There was one thing I couldn't deny, though. The letter that waited before me was a real and tangible thing, regardless of how it had appeared.

I picked the bird up and could just glimpse the outline of words decorating the paper. I considered opening it there, but the light from the window encompassed by the darkness of the attic made me feel too exposed. I stepped back from the pool of moonlight, out of the sight of any watching eyes. I didn't know if the letter writer had stuck around, but now that I had their token in my possession, I felt the sudden urge to get out of the attic.

I tiptoed back to my room as quietly as I had come and eased the door shut behind me. I cringed when it released a loud creak but knew I was in the clear now. If my mom came upstairs to see why I'd been out of bed, and she wouldn't, I could say I had simply gotten up to use the bathroom. The attic door was shut, and there was no evidence that I'd spent the last three hours hiding in its corner.

No evidence, except for the letter I held in my hand.

I turned the lamp on my bedside table on, then crossed the room and thrust my purple curtains together. They wouldn't prevent one from seeing the light beaming out of my room, but at least I was safe from someone watching me. I carried the letter with me to my bed and plopped down on its soft surface. The mattress was heavenly for my sore muscles, and a part of me wanted to just close my eyes, sleep, and forget about the whole endeavor in the attic.

But no. I was committed to seeing all of it through, wherever the mystery might take me.

The wings of the bird opened easily, revealing its master's beautiful, curling words. I leaned back against the headboard and read.

> I know you must think I'm crazy.
>
> But I would be crazier not to acknowledge my feelings for you.
>
> I promise I mean you no harm, I wish only to explain what you have done to me.
>
> A week ago, I thought my life was complete.
>
> I breathed, I spoke, I moved. I did what I was told.
>
> But it wasn't until I laid eyes on you that I realized I had been dead.
>
> Lifeless.

I thought I could ignore your presence, return to the life I knew, but it proved to be impossible.

There is no life, not without you.

I don't want to scare you, because I know these words are deep.

I will keep my distance indefinitely if that is your desire.

But I will continue to write until the day you drive me away.

Until then, sweet dreams, Cami.

Love,
Z

By the time I read the letter a third time, my eyes had welled up to the point where I couldn't make out the words. I could still feel them though, a warm presence poking hesitantly at my heart. As the tears finally fell, I brought the letter to my chest and allowed myself to cry.

My reaction was so different from when I found the second letter, I had to take a moment and reflect on my feelings, the emotions that were wracking my body and leaving my mind so blank. I had been such an emotional wreck lately; it was hard for me to know where to start.

I wasn't hyperventilating and freaking out like the last one. I wasn't terrified that I was about to be attacked. (Okay, maybe closing the curtains proved I was a tiny bit afraid.) Discovering the second letter had thrown me off guard, but this one I had been expecting. I had waited up all night just to receive it.

I thought back to when I found the first letter. The first bird. Even though I'd believed it to be a hundred years old and the writer long dead, hadn't I been slightly jealous of the girl he wrote to? I'd wanted that love to be expressed for *me*. For those words to be mine. Why should I flip out and lose my mind when I actually received my wish? All of those words were meant for me.

Because it's creepy, the voice in my head hissed. This guy had obviously spied on me countless times and never showed his face. Now he was leaving me letters to profess his love for me. Wasn't this how all stalker movies began? If the movie progressed like it should, I could very well be dead in the next scene.

He says he means you no harm. Oh, yeah. Like I should believe that. The guy that offers free candy to kids probably has a very innocent smile on his face before stuffing them into his kidnapper's van and they're never seen again. Why should I trust anything this "Z" person wrote to me?

Because you want to.

I realized I'd finally landed on the truth. I really did want to believe it. All of it. Because the part of me that had been bullied, treated like trash, and abandoned by my father desperately wanted to believe that someone in this world truly thought I was special. That someone could look at me and be amazed by what they saw.

Isn't that what all girls wanted? To be loved?

There was still so much left unexplained, though. Even if I could trust that the words were true and the letter writer posed no threat to me, I still didn't understand how they accomplished the unbelievable acts I'd witnessed. How had the window opened on its own? And how on earth had the bird been made to fly through it? I felt the letter in my hands again, but it was just an ordinary piece of paper. An old sheet, not like the pages in my lined notebooks, but still nothing that should possess the ability to take off and fly.

My mind was reeling with the mystery of it all.

I folded the letter into a square and opened my nightstand drawer, stowing it away with the others. For the second time since moving to Green Peaks, I made a decision. A reckless one, most likely.

I was going to write back to my secret admirer. I would learn the identity of my letter writer, for real this time, and find out how they were messing with my house. I was going to be ready when the next night came.

I didn't care if it was stupid, or if I was playing right into the hands of the famous stalker movie I seemed to have found myself caught in. I was going to write the lines that made up the next scene and take my fate into my own hands.

I turned the light off and allowed the darkness to embrace me. In the seconds that passed before my eyes could adjust, I watched as shapeless creatures flitted in and out of the shadows, observing me from their distance but never quite approaching me.

I tossed and turned for hours but eventually fell into a troubled sleep, where my dreams taunted me with their endless questions and lack of answers. Paper birds flew above my head, blocking the sun and making it as dark as night. I stared up at my new home, to the attic window that was standing wide open. I could feel the pull behind me, toward the trees of the Cursed Woods, but I took my time in turning around. At the edge of the trees, where I had seen him my very first day, I caught a glimpse of dark eyes, barely visible in the shadow of a man. Then the figure shifted, disappearing into the trees once more.

Chapter Seven

Last night's dreams left me drained and on edge. My body seemed to have gained a hundred pounds of weight overnight, or at least it felt that way with the effort required to move my limbs. I could see the light filtering in through my eyelids, suggesting it was at least late morning, but my eyes were glued shut. It wasn't until my cell phone began to ring that I even thought about moving.

I let a moan escape. When did I set my ringer volume so *loud?* And why did my nightstand have to be so far away? I crawled across the bed and grasped at the table blindly, sighing when I finally got a hand on my phone.

Not bothering to open my eyes and see who it was, I hit the button to answer the call. "Hello?"

I yawned as I waited for a response. I decided I couldn't keep my eyes closed any longer, so I forced them open and rubbed away the sleep with my knuckles. The clock on my nightstand read eleven thirty a.m. I had apparently managed to get *some* sleep, despite the tossing and turning I did all night.

Sleep had evaded me until dawn allowed a bit of light to spill in through the curtains. Maybe I'd have to start sleeping with a nightlight again, like after I watched "It" with my father when I was six. I had needed the light to sleep for the next several years, and my mother forbade the watching of any scary movies until I was twelve. It looked like my current predicament was having all sorts of effects on my well-being.

The seconds ticked by, and there was still no response on the other end.

"Hello?" I repeated. My voice was still thick with sleep, but I was finally starting to wake up. When the other line remained silent, a cold chill trickled down my spine. My heart rate was picking up—a result of my already shot nerves combined with the adrenaline my body had begun to pump through my veins—and I was wide awake in no time.

"Is anyone there?" I could hear the fear in my voice as I waited for an answer. I untangled myself from my flower-stitched comforter and made my way across the room, the hardwood icy on my bare feet. Standing at the edge of the window, I pulled the hem of the curtain back slightly and peeked out at the backyard below.

The sun was shining brightly on the weeds and grass that could sincerely use a cut, and I squinted my eyes against the assaulting rays. There was nothing suspicious in the backyard, and even the trees of the Cursed Woods looked a little more innocent this morning. But my heart continued to hammer in my chest the longer I waited for a response.

Maybe my stalker was continuing to the next stereotypical scene of the movie I seemed to be starring in. First he sent me the letters, and now he was calling me and listening to my frightened voice, staying silent and breathing into the phone while he got his weird stalker kicks. I didn't think I could hear anyone breathing, but my paranoia was spiking quickly. What was that rustling noise in the background? Could it possibly be the sound of a letter being folded meticulously into a paper bird?

"Cami!" The sudden burst in my ear caused me to swear and drop the phone. I knew that voice, and it definitely didn't belong to a stalker. I scrambled to pick up the phone, my heart still beating a mile a minute.

"I'm so sorry!" Natalie was going on. "I called you and then had to drop the phone and chase my little sister around the house." She sighed, and I could almost hear her eyes rolling in her head. "What's up, girl?"

I closed my eyes and breathed, trying to compose myself before answering. I didn't know how perceptive my new friend might be, but I didn't want her to know how freaked out I'd been. I wasn't ready to talk to anyone about my situation yet.

"Hey Nat," I said cheerfully. I was surprised by how normal my voice sounded, considering my heart was still beating out of my chest. "I just woke up. What about you?"

She sighed dramatically. "Well I'm *trying* to work on our history assignment that's due tomorrow, but my sister has some friends over and they're being brats. Quit it, Molly!" There was a chorus of giggling, followed by more of Natalie's yells. Something made a *thump* as it was thrown against a wall.

"Anyway," Natalie said, "I was wondering if I could come over and we could work on our homework together, maybe hang out for a bit. I can be there in twenty minutes?" The hope in her voice was evident.

I always assumed that Natalie had a million friends outside of our group because of her outgoing nature. I figured she hung out with other girls all the time. But something in her voice made me reconsider those assumptions. Maybe her loud volume and energy were a turn off for most of the kids here. She had Carly, but Carly didn't strike me as someone who would like to hang out, gossip, and do each other's nails and makeup. Maybe Natalie was as excited about our new friendship as I was.

"Sure!" I said. I realized the excitement in my voice was real. I needed some girl time to get my mind straight, and Natalie was the perfect girl for the job.

I felt my hair and cringed. I was a total mess from my sleepless night. "Make it thirty minutes though, I have to get ready."

We said goodbye and ended the call. I grabbed a pair of jeans and a T-shirt and headed to the bathroom. The hot water loosened the knots in my back and brought some life back to my frozen toes. I could have spent thirty minutes in the shower easily, but I forced myself out after ten and dried my hair in a towel before throwing it into a high, messy bun. I decided to forget the makeup and headed down to the kitchen instead. Caffeine took priority.

My mom sat in one of the stools at the bar with her own mug of coffee, laptop open in front of her. The circles under her eyes suggested she got as much sleep as I did. But when she saw me enter the room, her smile warmed her face and made her look much younger.

"It's alive!" She chuckled at my heavy steps and looked pointedly at the clock, which was nearing noon. I returned her smile, glad that my mom was back to her cheerful self. I knew we still had plenty of tough days ahead of us, but together we would manage to make it through.

I started boiling some water and grabbed my mug and infuser. While I waited for the tea to brew, I hopped up on the chair next to my mom. She had Pinterest open and was browsing for Fall activities to do with her class.

"Natalie's coming over soon to work on some homework. Is that okay? We'll probably just hang out in my room." I knew she wouldn't care, but years of asking for permission had stuck with me.

My mom looked at me out of the corner of her eye and smiled. It was a knowing look that said she had always expected me to fit in here, and here I was doing just that. It appeared that she was finally over her tears of joy and had come to accept that I was going to be okay.

"That's fine, honey." She took another drink of her coffee, draining the cup in one gulp. "Let me know if you get hungry and I'll make you guys some sandwiches."

Despite the random displays of emotion, my mom was possibly the easiest parent to live with.

My tea was half gone when I heard the knocking at the door. "I got it," I said quickly. I jumped up and poured the rest of the cup down the drain. My mom hadn't moved from her seat, and she smiled wryly as I left the room.

I answered the door and found Natalie waiting on the porch, her floral Vera Bradley backpack slung over one shoulder and a small pink tote hanging down by her waist.

"I brought the provisions!" she announced before opening the bag in my face, revealing what had to be several pounds of candy. I raised my eyebrows at her questioningly. "Stole it from the brats." She shrugged and walked through the door. I laughed at her expression, wondering what it would be like to have a sibling to fight with and steal from. My parents had never shown any interest in growing our little family, and now the option was off the table. I snagged a piece of chocolate and followed her up the stairs.

Natalie remembered the way to my room easily and wasted no time in making herself comfortable on my bed. I was glad to see she was also wearing jeans and a graphic tee with no brush of makeup on her face.

Natalie extracted her history book out of her backpack, followed by a notebook and worksheet that we were supposed to have filled out by tomorrow.

"Please tell me you've already done the assignment and I can just copy your answers." She made a puppy dog face and brought her hands together, pleading.

I laughed and grabbed my own textbook and worksheet off my desk. The truth was, I had been way too distracted by the idea of my mysterious letter writer to even think about doing homework. Natalie might have saved me a failing grade by showing up and forcing me to work on it.

"Well, I wrote my name at the top. Does that count?" I showed her the blank sheet and she pretended to faint at the sight of it, laying back on my bed with a hand pressed against her forehead. We both laughed and got our pencils out.

"I'll start at the top and you start at the bottom. We can meet in the middle and share each other's answers for the rest," she said, and we both got to work.

It seemed like a good idea to knock the assignment out quickly, but after a few questions I could tell we were both getting distracted. Natalie had stopped flipping through her book for answers and was instead sitting with her chin in her hand as she stared off into space. My attention kept getting drawn to the window, where the curtains were opened wide to allow natural light in and give me a perfect view of the Cursed Woods. Each time I began writing an answer I found myself glancing up at the trees, expecting to see a person standing there, watching my window. The worksheet was twenty questions long, and neither of us was getting any closer to the middle.

After what could only have been ten minutes, Natalie huffed out a breath and stood up. "I need a break," she stated and began walking around my room aimlessly. I gladly dropped my own book and leaned back against the headrest. I grabbed a couple of chocolate pieces from the pile that had spilled out of the bag and onto my bed. Shooting the tin foil balls into the trashcan by the door, I relaxed and let the chocolate melt in my mouth.

Natalie was taking in the details of my room as if she were about to be quizzed on it. Her hands lightly skimmed over the books scattered across my desk, the mess that I had forgotten to tidy up, but she obviously didn't have a problem with. She picked up the framed picture of Michael and me dressed as Arya Stark and the Night King for last year's Halloween party at school.

"Is this your boyfriend?" she asked, giggling at the horns taped to his forehead. I allowed my face to demonstrate my horror and pretended to gag on my chocolate.

"Um, no." I laughed as she set the picture back down. "That's just Michael, my best friend from Plainfield." I'd already told her a little about him, and she nodded as she remembered my stories.

Moving on from my desk, Natalie walked over to my dresser and began to open the drawers. I tried to hide my shock at the sudden invasion of my privacy. I had never been friends with a nosy person before. But the way she inspected the contents of each drawer with the same indifferent look on her face suggested this was the most normal thing to do in the world. I guessed I didn't really care if she wanted to check out my clothes and underwear, but my discomfort turned into fear as she moved further around the room. She was heading right for my nightstand, where my three letters were tucked not so safely inside.

I held my breath as she reached the nightstand and opened the drawer. I squeezed my eyes closed, hoping she wouldn't see them, or simply ignore them. They were just three folded up sheets of paper, after all. They couldn't look that interesting. But I knew I was in trouble when she gasped.

"What's this?" She exclaimed. *She found one of the letters and is already reading it,* I thought sadly. I opened my eyes slowly, trying to come up with an excuse that would explain the letters without launching into a spiel about mysterious stalkers and a possibly haunted attic. I was getting ready to spout something about a stupid role-playing game but stopped when I saw what she was holding.

It was the leather-bound book my parents bought me for my birthday three years ago when I started showing a real interest in art. I sighed as she plopped onto my bed with it, knowing there wasn't anything incriminating within the pages.

"You have an art journal?" she asked, flipping through the sheets. After three years I hadn't filled it completely, but there were still plenty of sketches to look through. I didn't keep a traditional journal, instead choosing to fill the pages with whatever pictures popped into my head at some of my most emotional moments.

"I keep one too," Natalie said. She nodded at many of the drawings and raised her eyebrows at some of the others. "These are really good, Cami. I'm impressed."

I smiled at her interest. "Thank you." Discreetly, I closed the drawer and pretended to be looking at the pictures over her shoulder. A bead of sweat ran down my forehead. I felt like I had just dodged a serious bullet.

Part of me wondered if I should just go ahead and share my secret with her. Maybe it would be better for me, safer, if someone else knew what had been happening. If I did wind up missing or dead, the letters would certainly be a key item in bringing down my murderer. But as much as I was referring to the letter writer as a "stalker" in my head, I really didn't believe he had intentions to harm me. His method of reaching out to me might have been slightly creepy, but I also couldn't deny it was a little romantic. And maybe there was a reason he couldn't approach me yet.

The bottom line was that I wanted to see this mystery through. Right then, I felt like I had a little bit of control over the situation. But as soon as I shared it with someone, I would lose that shred of control. Natalie would tell me not to go through with the plan I'd been strategizing for that night, and who knew what she would do with the information. She didn't have the tightest mouth, and if she let my secret slip to our friends or, heaven forbid, my *mother,* I would never hear the end of it. I would never uncover the truth behind the letters or be able to see it all play out.

I steeled myself and made the decision to keep my letters a secret for as long as possible. Until I could figure out exactly what was going on, I needed everyone to stay out of my way.

We spent the rest of the afternoon gossiping about nothing important, and eventually we managed to scrape together answers for all the questions on our worksheet. By the time Natalie left, my stomach was bloated with half the bag of candy and I had a serious sugar high.

Fueled by the sugar and the newfound confidence I always received after hanging with a friend, I sat at my desk and prepared for whatever the night would bring. Gingerly, I set my pen to a piece of notebook paper, smiled, and began to write.

Chapter Eight

Hi. It's me, Cami.

I just wanted to let you know that I've been reading your letters. They're beautiful.

You're obviously way better at this than I am.

I want to learn more about you.

If you're reading this, please give me a sign that you received this letter.

I have to know that you're real.

Love,
C

I read over my letter for the hundredth time. My words weren't poetic like my secret admirer's had been; they were very straightforward and to the point. I'd concentrated on making it look as legible as possible, but my handwriting still didn't hold a candle to his loopy calligraphy. My notebook paper also looked out of place next to the old, fancy-looking pages that had been left for me. But I didn't have anything else to work with, and I had to communicate with him *somehow*.

The chair in front of my table was much more comfortable than the spot I had inhabited the night before. I didn't want to hide from him exactly, but I wasn't sure if I wanted to make my presence known just yet either. The candle sat unlit before me, and I considered lighting it to let him know that I was there, but I didn't know if my presence would scare him off. I needed to give him my letter and let him know I wasn't interested in turning him in for trespassing before I did anything else.

My watch face glowed in the darkness, informing me that it was just after eleven thirty. I was too wired over the fact that I was about to communicate with my secret admirer. I had no fear of falling asleep on the job tonight.

I gave my letter one last glance, the words barely visible in the moonlight, and then began to make the folds necessary to deliver my correspondence. Michael and I had made enough of them over the years that I could probably fold the paper in my sleep. In only a few moments, my letter was transformed into a perfectly aerodynamic paper airplane.

There were more clouds out tonight, making it harder to see my backyard below. I had taken the liberty of cleaning the dirt smudged window a few hours before, so only the darkness stood as a barrier now. The moonlight broke through the clouds intermittently, giving me a few minutes at a time where the yard was just visible for my straining eyes.

My eyes were beginning to water from the force of my staring when the sky suddenly opened, casting illuminating rays and scattering the shadows across the grass. With the arrival of the light, I could just make out a dark figure moving quickly away from the Cursed Woods, in the direction of the back of my house. Directly towards me.

I held my breath as he drew closer and attempted to get my heart rate under control. If it didn't settle down, my heartbeat alone would give me away. Surely every creature within a mile radius could hear it pounding in my chest.

The figure showed no signs of stopping, and I wondered if he would run all the way up to the house and begin climbing up the side of it. He appeared to be nimble enough for the job.

Just before reaching the flowerbed that ran the perimeter around the porch, though, he stopped in his tracks. I imagined that I could hear his heavy breathing mixed in with the crickets, owls, and other country noises that made up the soundtrack of my new home. He had moved so quickly, and the length of our yard made for a very long sprint. I was surprised he wasn't bent over double, trying to catch his breath.

But he wasn't bent over. The figure stood tall, his shoulders squared, portraying the perfect picture of confidence. Or what I could only assume was confidence with the limited lighting and distance separating us. I knew without a doubt he was intent on the mission set before him.

The figure was just lifting his face to look up at my window when another cloud rolled across the moon, cloaking him in darkness once again. I silently cursed the clouds for their terrible timing. Couldn't they have waited a few more seconds before blocking my view? I just wanted to finally see his face. And get an idea of how he delivered his birds to the attic, of course.

I picked my letter up and prepared myself for what came next. I knew my window of opportunity would be small, so I held the paper airplane in my right hand, aimed at the currently closed window. Ready to launch as soon as it opened.

The seconds ticked by as I waited, frozen in my ready-to-throw pose. I knew at the back of my mind that very little time had passed, but it seemed like hours since he had arrived at the flowerbed below. I reminded myself to breathe again. That would just be perfect if I passed out due to lack of oxygen and missed my chance.

A minute after he arrived, the attic window finally eased itself open. I waited as patiently as I could for the bird to invite itself inside, its wings flapping happily, excited to deliver its message. Then I launched my paper airplane out into the night. Two seconds passed, and the window closed behind it.

The bird lay on the table in front of me, still at last, but I ignored it for the time being. I didn't dare move, not in the precious moments following the delivery of my letter. He was supposed to give me a sign that he received it. I didn't know what kind of sign he might choose, but I wasn't about to miss it because I was fumbling around with the paper bird.

What if he didn't receive my letter, though? It was so dark out, even the white of my paper airplane could be swallowed up in the darkness. I had a sinking feeling I might sit here for hours, waiting for some sign that was never coming, my poor letter laying unseen in the flowerbed where it had crash-landed below. It would lay there collecting dew until morning, and by the time I had retrieved it, the letter would be soaked through, my words unreadable and utterly useless. Just like my plan had been.

I was watching the scene unfold in my mind when a surge of movement in front of me brought me back to the present. The window opened wide, closed, and then opened again, almost playfully. The candle on the table flickered to life, blinding me momentarily in the sudden burst of light. If those acts alone didn't warrant enough evidence that my letter had been received, then what happened next would lay all doubts to rest.

A voice spoke out of the night, carried to my ears through the open window, like it was riding on the wind.

"Good night, Cami." The voice whispered in my ear. *"I'll be back at the same time tomorrow."* The voice was rich, textured, and distinctly male. It was deep, but not too deep. I felt for certain that the speaker was close to my age.

Almost as an afterthought, the voice added, *"Bring more paper. We can talk."*

And with that, the window slid closed once again. The candle flame was driven to the right before being extinguished in a puff of smoke, a phantom breath blowing it out. I tried to see what was happening in my yard, but my eyes couldn't adjust to the abrupt darkness fast enough. Even so, I thought I could feel the presence of the boy stop just before he reached the woods and turn to look back at my window.

By the time my eyes could make out the shapes lit by the now unshaded full moon, the ground was empty once again.

Hours after sharing words with my secret admirer, I found myself waiting on the front porch as Natalie pulled up in her truck. The morning had passed in a blur, and I didn't fully remember how I came to be sitting in one of the rocking chairs by the front door. Sleep had evaded me once again, and it looked like it would be a very long day if I continued to struggle to focus. At least the zombie version of myself that had carried me to the porch had somehow remembered my backpack.

"You look like crap," Natalie said as I opened the door and climbed in.

I yawned. "I didn't get much sleep."

Natalie rolled her eyes and pegged me with a look that said, "Obviously." She turned the truck around and headed for the road that would take us to school.

We quickly fell into our normal school day routine. Natalie launched into a rant about Monday mornings and how they should be outlawed by the federal government, and I stared out the window and *mmh'*ed and *yeah'*ed at what I hoped were the correct places in her one-sided conversation.

The truck's seats had never felt so soft before, and the bumps we hit in the outdated roads were almost soothing as they tried to rock me to sleep. I dozed undisturbed for a few minutes before Natalie pulled into the parking lot of the school. I jerked awake when she drove the tires into the parking curb.

Natalie laughed at the state I was in. "That's the last time I let you eat so much candy before bedtime," she joked before grabbing both of our backpacks and headed towards class. I smiled back and fell clumsily out of the truck behind her.

It was times like these that I wished I could somehow bottle her endless supply of energy and drink it. *Maybe they should use her face as the logo for Monster Drinks*, I thought tiredly.

Once I got my legs moving and blood flowing, I felt myself wake up a little bit. But the drone of Mr. Angle's voice did nothing to help keep me there. The lecture on Westward expansion wasn't stimulating enough to hold my interest, and I grasped at any thoughts that would prove loud enough to keep myself awake.

There was only one thought that could keep me awake after staying up all night, and it was the very thought that had kept me awake in the first place. What was I going to do about the mysterious Z?

I could feel his last letter digging into my jeans pocket, already folded into a crumpled square after having been read a dozen times. It seemed that every letter gave me another piece of the puzzle that was my secret admirer, but I had no idea how to put them all together. I let my eyes glaze over as I thought over his most recently written words. I already had them memorized, of course.

> I have yet to see any policemen combing the attic or trees.
>
> I hope I'm right to assume that means you haven't written me off completely yet.
>
> Or, at least, you aren't afraid enough to call for help yet.
>
> I really hope you can come to trust me, Cami.
>
> I know in my heart there is a link between us, binding us.
>
> I might be coming off too strong, but trust me when I tell you that your presence only makes me stronger.
>
> I cannot lie to you, just as I cannot lie to myself.
>
> I must return home before anyone realizes where I've been.
>
> Just know, Cami, that I shall always return for you.
>
> Love,
> Z

I knew there were details about my secret admirer hidden within the lines, and I spent the rest of the school day trying to uncover them. He had a curfew, apparently, because he had to get back home before anyone realized he'd been gone.

Was he a student at my school? That idea made the most sense, but I never noticed anyone watching me during class or in the cafeteria. I never felt that presence either, the one I had experienced in the woods. In the trees, I'd felt someone watching me. And it was the same feeling that had pulled me toward the trees the closer I got to my house. I never experienced the same sensation while at school, and I determined that to mean my admirer wasn't a fellow classmate.

He's from the woods, that quiet voice whispered in my head. I knew at once that it was right. If there was some kind of spirit haunting me, it didn't originate from my house. It was from the Cursed Woods. It probably lived there, or resided there anyway, as spirits weren't exactly living. Maybe with other spirits that it needed to return to before they realized he was gone.

I wanted to bang my head on the desk as my thoughts returned to ghosts once again. I knew in my heart that my mystery guy was still alive. He had to be.

I attended each class in a stupor, my mind reeling with all the possibilities of what could be going on. Eventually I grew exhausted from mulling over the same ideas and getting no closer to discovering the truth. At that point my head seemed to fill with a sort of fog, numbing my thoughts and leaving me in a daze. I recognized the zombie version of myself when she appeared, and I let her take over my body as my mind tried to recover in the background.

It was out of this stupor that I found myself pulled from in the last class of the day. English and Literature had always been one of my favorite subjects, but even the discussion of Mr. Darcy's character couldn't pull me out of the fog.

"Ms. Stone?" Mrs. Lathrop asked from the front of the room. I had a feeling it wasn't the first time she said my name, because at that moment I looked up to see ninety percent of the class staring back at me, most of them smirking.

The teacher was looking at me expectantly, and I knew I had missed something. "I'm sorry, what was the question?" My voice was rough in my ears—from lack of use, no doubt.

Mrs. Lathrop rolled her eyes in a way that suggested she didn't get paid enough to deal with teenagers like me. She turned away from me and asked one of the goody-two-shoes in the front row the same question I had failed to hear. Normally I would have been embarrassed, guilty even for not paying attention in class. But all I felt as Erin York answered the question intended for me was relief that I was off the hook.

I looked down at my desk to find that I'd been doodling in my notebook without realizing it. In the middle of my notes on Pride and Prejudice, I had drawn the attic window as I'd seen it the night before. The table was sketched lazily below it with a lit candle on top. The part of the picture I'd spent the most time on, though, were the eyes.

Two dark eyes stared up at me out of my notebook, from outside the window. They stared through the glass, and I felt as if they were really seeing me, as if they were alive. I brushed my fingers over them lightly and could feel the weight I had pressed into my pencil. I must have traced over the eyes a dozen times, as they seemed to be etched into the paper now.

I glanced around to see if anyone had noticed my drawing. Most of the students were quietly taking their own notes, others staring off into space. A few were fixed on the clock as it ticked sluggishly towards three p.m.

Natalie was the only one looking in my direction, scrutinizing me in a concerned way that reminded me of my mother. She was several seats away because Mrs. Lathrop was one of the few teachers who still believed in alphabetical seating charts. It was a subject we had complained about together on many occasions, but at that moment I was grateful not to be seated next to my best friend. I tore the sheet out of my notebook and crumpled it into a ball, relaxed in my knowledge that no one had seen it.

I knew there would still be questions about my odd behavior that I would have to answer on our drive home. I also knew that Natalie's attention span was about as long as Dory's from Finding Nemo, and I could direct the conversation away from myself pretty easily. I would let her in on my secret as soon as I figured out exactly what my secret entailed.

For now, I just had to follow through the motions and hope that whatever roller coaster I'd found myself strapped to would end safely on the ground and not at a broken piece of track that would launch me into space. I supposed I would make it to the ground either way. I just hoped I would still be in one piece when this ride ultimately reached its end.

Chapter Nine

I survived the ride home by asking Natalie questions about her family, boys she had dated in the past, and embarrassing moments she could never forget. My newly sparked interest kept her talking about herself for the duration of the ride and achieved the goal of keeping the conversation away from my odd behavior.

Unfortunately, the conversations and attention required on my part depleted my already meager supply of energy. By the time we arrived at my house, I was struggling more than ever to hold my eyes open.

While Natalie had been easy enough to distract from my appearance, my mother was a different story. She barely made it through the door before she took one glance at me, dropped her books on the table, and rushed to my side.

"What's wrong, honey?" She felt my forehead and cheeks, searching for a fever that wasn't there. I fought the urge to swat her hand away.

I leaned my head back against the couch and closed my eyes. I might as well take the opportunity and run with it.

"I don't feel so great." I didn't have to try very hard to make my voice come out weak and wavering. I was already a walking zombie, after all, and I hadn't been this tired since I contracted Mono three years before. I knew my mom was flashing back to that week, where I had spent twenty hours a day in bed, only getting up to stretch and go to the bathroom.

My mom frowned at the lack of heat she found in my face, but she couldn't deny that I looked sick and exhausted. I could almost hear the gears turning in her head, trying to decide if I was faking an illness to avoid some kind of test at school tomorrow or if I was actually sick and needed to be sent to bed.

In the end, her nurturing mother instincts won out.

"You head on up to bed and get some rest." She ordered with a squeeze of my shoulders. I nodded submissively, as if I'd been trying to avoid bedrest all day. In reality, I'd been fantasizing about the softness of my bed and the warmth of its covers on and off for the past several hours.

"I'll run to the store and see if I can find some Campbell's. I'll check up on you around supper time."

With that, my mother turned to grab her purse. She came back to kiss my forehead before heading out to the car, its engine still warm from her recent trip home.

I sighed and closed my eyes. Free and alone, at last.

I couldn't deny that I was in dire need of sleep. Sighing again, I mustered up the strength to shuffle my way up the stairs and into my room, where I collapsed in a heap on my bed. I moaned at the softness of the pillows and comforter. They were even better than in my fantasies.

Before I could pass out completely, I set my phone alarm for eleven-thirty, taking a moment to switch the sound to vibrate so that my mom wouldn't hear a screeching alarm in the middle of the night. I knew I should shed my clothes and find my pajamas, but the mattress was so *soft,* hugging my body in its embrace and eliminating any motivation to move. The world went black and I left my fully clothed body, curled into a ball on top of my bed, behind.

It seemed like a year had passed since I had managed to get any dreamless sleep, so I was surprised when I opened my eyes and discovered it was already dark outside. I must have slept for hours without a single dream or thought to disturb the deepness of my slumber. The edges of my mind were still a little fuzzy from the lingering sleep, but I felt more rejuvenated than I had in a long time. I was revived and ready to take on the world.

I hadn't bothered to turn on a light when I came into my room, and the moonlight streaming in through my window cast shadows that crept across the floor. I turned to my nightstand and found my phone sitting next to a glass of water and a bottle of Ibuprofen.

Something scratched my cheek, alerting me to the fact that I was cocooned under a thick, crocheted afghan, a gift from my grandmother before she passed away. My mom must have snuck in here while I was asleep and covered me up, leaving the water and medicine behind for when I awoke. Normally I was a very light sleeper, so I must have been in a serious coma for her to have accomplished this feat despite the creaky door and floorboards.

The clock on my phone read ten p.m. I still had plenty of time. A loud grumbling rumbled from beneath the blanket, and I discovered what must have woken me. I was starving.

I opened the drawer of my nightstand to search for the snacks I usually kept hidden for my late-night hunger pains, but it was empty of anything edible. I remembered I had eaten the last granola bar two nights ago and never bothered to replenish my stock. If I wanted food, I was going to have to brave it to the kitchen.

Grabbing a pair of thick, fuzzy socks, I covered my feet to help muffle my footsteps. The house seemed to take pity on my tired, hungry state, because it stayed mostly quiet while I made my way carefully down the stairs.

With only my cell phone's light to guide me, I tiptoed into the kitchen. On the counter sat two cans of chicken noodle soup and a glass bowl, ready to microwave them in. Not wanting to risk the sound of the zapper, I hunted down a box of Ritz Crackers and stole a sleeve to take with me. I paused at the bottom step, listening. I could just make out my mother's even, heavy breathing coming from behind her bedroom door.

With the coast clear, I climbed the stairs and pulled my bedroom door closed behind me. I still had almost two hours before I needed to be in the attic, so I took my time eating my way through the sleeve of crackers. They weren't much, but they quieted my growling stomach for the time being.

My backpack was propped up on my desk, carried up here by my mother while I slept, I assumed. I'd slept through my usual homework time, and I had few other things to do while I waited for midnight to come. I tried to read the assigned chapters of Pride and Prejudice, but I was still too edgy. The hours of sleep had given my body the rejuvenation it needed, but the blanket of calm I'd woken up with was quickly disappearing as the night progressed. I read an entire page of the novel before I realized I hadn't taken in a single word of it. How could I concentrate on Eliza's boy problems when I was still trying to come to terms with my own?

Frustrated by my lack of productivity, I shoved the books back into my bag with a growl. If I couldn't knock out my homework, perhaps I could try writing another letter to my secret admirer. I found a notebook and pen and opened it to a blank page. But as the minutes ticked by, the page remained blank. No string of words sounded right. With a sigh, I gave up on that task as well.

It was eleven o'clock and I didn't expect my letter writer to appear until closer to midnight. Even so, I was bored with my room and figured I might as well make my way up to the attic. I grabbed my notebook and pen and crept into the hall.

Before heading towards the attic, I stopped at my bathroom and peered beneath the sink. Just as I'd expected, it was stocked with candles and lighters ready to be lit in case a heavy storm took out our power. I balanced a lighter on top of my notebook and proceeded down the hall.

Once I made it up the stairs, I ignored the light switch and hit a button on my phone, causing its flashlight to flare into life. There was something comforting about the boxes of herbs and other random objects littered about the area that I hadn't noticed on my first trip up here. The attic had grown on me and was quickly becoming as comfortable as the treehouse I'd used as my getaway spot while growing up. I felt at peace in the small room, like it was as much my home as it was the miscellaneous items that spent most of the last century boxed up here in storage.

Taking a deep breath, I approached my table and set my things down. He was expecting me to be here, so there was really no point in trying to hide. Before I could stop myself, I flicked the lighter on and set the flame to the candle's wick. The candle bathed the room in light instantly, its flame sending shadows that bounced playfully around the room. I turned my flashlight off and sat down.

As I waited for my secret admirer to show up, I reveled in the fact that I was finally getting somewhere with him. He said we could talk, and I understood that to mean he was going to answer some of my questions. My mind reeled with all the things I wanted to ask him. Who was he? How did he manage all the impossible tricks I'd witnessed in the attic? Did he actually live in the woods, and if so, how many more like him were there?

I was contemplating how I would word all my questions when the window opened in front of me. The air that swirled lazily inside was comfortingly warm, probably one of the last warm nights of the year. I was suddenly grateful that it wasn't raining. Wet paper would make our correspondence much more difficult; not to mention the rain would be miserable for my secret admirer to stand in.

I looked at my phone and smiled, my heart already accelerating in anticipation of our meeting. It was only eleven fifteen, but the mysterious Z had arrived.

On cue, a familiar shape fluttered through the window and landed delicately in my outstretched palm. I wasted no time in opening the bird tonight.

The words on the page were still written with a beautiful hand, but they slanted in an almost rushed fashion, like my letter writer was as excited for this conversation as I was. My eyes read swiftly over the short note, made easy by the light of the candle.

Good evening Cami. I'm here, as you requested, ready to divulge the information you seek. But first, how are you? You can send your replies like you did last night. I'm ready to finally talk with you.

I smiled at his greeting and quickly tore a sheet from the notebook. Now that the time had finally arrived to talk to him, the right words seemed to come to me easily.

Good evening, Z. I think you have me at a disadvantage. You know my name, but I don't really know yours. I'm doing great, by the way. How are you?

In a matter of seconds, I had the note folded into a paper airplane and launched it out the window. I didn't bother aiming anywhere in particular. If he had a way to control his paper birds, surely he was able to direct my airplane as well.

His reply was quicker than I would have believed possible. It took less than a minute after I sent my letter flying. But I was starting to believe that many impossible things were achievable when Z was involved.

My name is Ezekiel Rivers, but my family and friends call me Zeke, or just Z. I'm glad to hear you are doing well. You could say that I'm in a better mood than I've been in my entire life, thanks to you.

I read over his words twice before responding. *Ezekiel*. It was a pretty name, but not a very common one. Certainly not the name of anyone attending my school. I bit my lip as I considered how to respond.

Okay, Zeke. It's nice to finally sort of meet you. I have to confess, though, while I've been enjoying your letters, I've also been slightly frightened by them. It sounds like you've been stalking me. Am I wrong in that assumption?

There. Acknowledge the elephant in the room right away. I wanted to learn more about Zeke, but first I needed to know that he wasn't a danger to me. I only had to imagine his response for a few minutes before the next bird flapped its way inside.

Me, stalking? I can see why you would think that, given some of the things I've written about you, but the truth is that I have never followed you anywhere. I have observed you from a distance, but only because you were where I was already looking.

You see, on the day that you moved into your house, I was visiting it as well. The house once belonged to my family, and we've made a point of looking after it over the years. The job currently falls on me, and when I saw you and your mother arrive, I couldn't help but observe you. I feel drawn to you in a peculiar way, one that I struggle to describe.

Every time I came to check on the house, you were there, and the pull only grew stronger. I felt like I would burst if I didn't share my feelings with you, and so I wrote the letter, knowing in all likelihood you would never find it. But you did. Despite all the odds, you found me and have continued to seek me out.

Do you believe in fate, Cami?

The long response left me breathless. I mulled over his words, trying to understand them quickly so he wouldn't be waiting hours for a reply. His family once owned my house, and they'd been keeping an eye on it over the years. But I knew that the house hadn't been owned in a century. Did that mean they were ghosts, after all? I needed to put that theory to rest.

I don't know if I believe in fate. I've never really thought about it. But I am still confused. You say your family has watched over the house for a hundred years. Are you dead?

Okay, so my question might have been a little blunt, but I was never very good at sugar coating things. I just needed to know the answer before I drove myself crazy wondering about it. I threw my airplane outside, and a few moments later I thought I heard quiet laughter coming from below. When the bird arrived this time, it circled around my head playfully before stopping to land in my hands.

No, Cami, I am very much alive. I'm eighteen years old, scheduled to turn nineteen in six months. My great-grandparents, along with the others in my community, escaped into the forest one hundred years ago. We've been living there ever since.

We have no contact with people outside the forest, and I could get in a lot of trouble if they found out I was talking to you. It is our biggest rule. Keep hidden and remain safe.

I puzzled over his words, trying to make sense of what he was saying. There was a whole community of people, cut off from the rest of the world, living secluded within the Cursed Woods. I knew the area of trees had to be huge, but I also found it hard to believe that no one had discovered them yet. How had they stayed hidden for so long? And why were they hiding in the first place?

I'm glad to hear that you're not a ghost. I've been a little worried.

Why are you living in the woods? What made you "escape" there?

There was a longer pause following the delivery of my last question, and I had a feeling he was contemplating telling me something. When I opened the next bird, I held my breath, anxious to uncover more of the mystery surrounding Zeke.

This isn't a topic I feel comfortable writing about. I would rather discuss it with you in person.

It's getting late, and I need to get home before anyone discovers I've been gone. Would you be interested in meeting me tomorrow? I can come around midday, if you like. When the sun is up.

I'm sure you still have some reservations about me, as you should. I encourage you to bring a weapon or anything that makes you feel more comfortable. All I ask is that you be alone. I can't risk sharing my secret with anyone else.

I'm trusting you, Cami. I hope you can trust me too.

As I read his parting words, a thrill shot through me. Whether it was fear or excitement, I didn't know. He was willing to meet me in broad daylight, here, at my house.

I knew I was being reckless and breaking every rule in the book when it came to online dating and chat rooms, but I really wanted to meet him. More than that, I wanted to hear his story. I was ensnared by his mystery, and I was finally presented with the opportunity of uncovering all of it.

I'll be behind my house at noon, and my mom will be at school. Just don't try anything funny. I'm feistier than I look.

It was a pleasure talking to you, Zeke. Good night.

I knew he had read my letter when a voice spoke quietly in my ear, carried on the wind just like it had been the night before. *"Until tomorrow, Cami. Sweet dreams."*

The window slid noiselessly shut and the candle blew out in a wisp, leaving me alone in the darkness once again.

Chapter Ten

It wasn't hard to convince my mom that I needed to stay home the next morning. I laid awake at the crack of dawn, listening for her careful footsteps. When my door creaked open, announcing her arrival, I curled myself into a ball under my covers and made myself look pathetic. She took one look at my shivering, exhausted form and announced that I was in no way going to school today.

I nodded my head and did my best to hide my smile. It was a little concerning how easily I was getting my way lately.

After my mom left for work, I stared up at the ceiling as time ticked away, my mind numb with what I was about to do. Maybe I'd made a mistake in telling Zeke I would meet him. I still had no proof that he wouldn't hurt me. I could stay inside and watch from my window, hand on my phone in case he decided to break in. Or I could avoid him altogether and go to school, claiming I was feeling much better. At least I knew I'd be safe there.

Perhaps I was foolish for wanting to go through with this plan, but I wasn't a coward. I could take care of myself, after all. I bent over the side of my bed and extracted the heavy little box from its hiding place. I cradled the pistol against my chest as I gazed out the window at the Cursed Woods, knowing the trees housed more than just the animals I heard each night. I wondered if Zeke was still asleep and if any of his people realized he had exposed them all to a stranger.

I got out of bed and went through my morning routine in a daze. The gun accompanied me everywhere I went, like a pet that needed to watch my every move. It waited on the dresser as I got dressed, the bathroom counter as I brushed my teeth, and the kitchen bar as I sipped my tea. Even though I had hours before Zeke would arrive, I was comforted by the gun's presence. If my father wasn't here to protect me from my bad decisions, at least his weapons could act in his place.

As the sun rose higher in the sky, I made my way to the back porch to wait. It was seventy-five and sunny, a perfect day to spend outdoors. I sat in one of the cushioned chairs, the gun waiting patiently on the table beside me. As the morning breeze swirled my hair around my face, I let my mind wander.

If you could look past the fact that he lived in the woods, my relationship with Zeke really wasn't all that different from the other boys I'd talked to over the years. He was still just a boy, assuming he wasn't lying about his age.

I got butterflies in my stomach when I thought about seeing him. And the way we had talked back and forth with the letters, waiting patiently for the other to respond, was a lot like the texting conversations I held with my previous crushes. Not to mention that I had always hidden my relationships from my parents until I decided which direction they would go, so the secrecy was nothing new. I may have never taken a gun on a date before, but there was a first time for everything, right?

I don't know how long my teenage brain rambled on, spouting different facts and scenarios that could justify my actions, but when I looked up, he was there.

He stood at the edge of the forest, and the first thing I noticed about him was the color of his hair. It was as dark as the shadows dancing in the trees behind him. His outfit was made of tanned leather pieces sewn together by an expert hand, and I wondered how many animals had given their lives for its creation. Although the leaves and grass swayed in the breeze around him, his hair and clothing remained perfectly still, the elements of this world seemingly lacking the strength to touch him. He belonged in a different time, a different place, but I found myself thanking whatever force allowed him to be here.

The backyard stretched between us, and we gazed at each other silently. I didn't know how long he had been standing there waiting, but when he finally caught my eyes, he smiled. I returned his smile and nodded my head. It was the only permission he needed before breaking into a jog and closing the distance between us.

I stood up as he drew near and hastily shoved the gun into the back of my pants. I didn't want to make a spectacle of myself by brandishing a gun in his face, but I knew when I caught the humor in his eyes that he had seen it. At least he knew I was armed and might think twice before trying anything on me.

"Cami," he said huskily. His voice was even richer than it had been when he spoke on the wind.

I took a few steps off the porch and waited in the grass for him to reach me. He approached me slowly, making no sudden movements as if I were a small animal he was trying not to spook. He extended his hand toward me, his eyes light with hope as he waited for me to accept it.

His eyes were lit with a lot more than hope, I realized as he stood before me. They were the lightest shade of blue I had ever seen in a pair of eyes, almost electric, and striking in comparison to his black hair. It was an odd combination, but seemed fitting for a boy with the name Ezekiel.

I hoped I hadn't been staring at him for too long and knew that I probably looked like an idiot with my mouth hanging open. I grabbed his hand and shook it before he decided I actually was an idiot and started second guessing our meeting.

"Hello, Zeke," I said easily, as if we weren't two strangers meeting for the first time. As he squeezed my hand back, I became aware that he didn't feel like a stranger to me at all. I had never seen his face before, but his features settled in my mind like I had known them my whole life.

I shook my head to clear the fog. If I was going to think crazy thoughts like that, then I probably shouldn't be trusted with the weapon hiding beneath my shirt. *Focus, Camille. You still don't know this boy.*

Zeke allowed my hand to slide out of his reluctantly, and I gestured toward the chairs on the porch.

"Would you like to sit?" I asked. He nodded his head, and I waited for him to climb the steps first. I might have felt unusually comfortable around him, but that didn't mean I was stupid enough to turn my back and offer him an opportunity to steal my gun.

We each took our places in the chairs, our knees only inches apart. His smile was timid and portrayed none of the confidence I'd felt while reading his letters. I realized that he was shy.

I'd had experience with this before, of course. You might text a boy for hours about endless topics, and then meet him in person and discover he was too afraid to open his mouth, let alone tell you about himself. But unlike with some of the boys I had dated in the past, the silence with Zeke wasn't uncomfortable. We stared at each other for a while, simply drinking each other in.

After a few minutes of uninterrupted staring, I decided to break the silence.

"Did you make your clothes yourself?"

What a rude thing to ask! *Stupid, stupid!* I chided myself. My face must have shown the horror I was experiencing, because he chuckled at my expression and shook his head.

"It's okay, Cami, I know I must look ridiculous to you. But no, I didn't make them. My grandmother has a remarkable talent for sewing."

We both admired the handiwork of his clothing in another moment of silence. It was pretty amazing how flawlessly one piece of skin flowed into the next. I couldn't detect any holes or snags that would expose him to the elements.

Without thinking, I reached out a hand and felt the material on his arm. It was soft and smooth, and quite worn in. I was rubbing my thumb back and forth over his sleeve when I noticed his stillness. He was as rigid as a stone, and his eyes stared at me widely in surprise.

"Sorry," I breathed, snatching my hand back at once. Seriously, what was wrong with me today? I normally wasn't this forward. This was the kind of behavior I would expect from Natalie, not me. The lack of sleep over the last several days must have affected my head.

"No, it's fine," Zeke assured me, and his shoulders relaxed instantly. He smiled at my apologetic expression and took a deep breath. There was a renewed confidence in his face now, and I watched his shell crack before my eyes.

"The truth is, I wasn't sure what to expect when I finally met you in person," he admitted. "I was afraid you might take one look at my clothes and rugged appearance and run the other way."

I shrugged. "I'm not a huge fan of running."

We both chuckled, and I admired his smile. I wondered how someone living in the woods managed to keep his teeth so white. Surely they didn't have dentists in his little community. I could just imagine Zeke reclined on an overturned tree with a man dressed in an animal skin apron peering inside his mouth. They'd probably have to use some kind of bone to pick at their teeth. The thought made me giggle even more.

He sighed again, and I could tell he was working himself up to saying the things he'd come here to say. I held my breath and allowed him the time he needed to find the right words. Seconds passed, and he finally met my gaze.

"Okay, so you wanted to know why we live in the forest, why we had to escape. My people are different from everyone else. I'm different." He paused, and I could see the struggle in his eyes. This was hard for him to put into words, but it was also hard for him to discuss with someone like me. An outsider.

Of course, I already knew that he was different. Not just anyone could light a candle without a match or make inanimate objects fly. I was intrigued by the mystery of it all, and knew I wouldn't get another decent night's sleep until his secrets had been revealed. I needed to hear his story now.

I nodded once at his statement, beckoning him to go on.

He paused again, watching my face closely to gauge my reaction. "We have the ability to use magic."

Magic. I didn't know what I had been expecting, but that bold word had never crossed my mind. Aware of his eyes on my face, I quickly composed it into an expressionless mask, determined not to make a fool of myself again. His words were stunning, but I didn't let the shock of them show. I'd known there was something special about him. Was it really that hard to accept that he had used magic to perform those feats? There wasn't another explanation as far as I could see.

After a moment of careful consideration, I smiled.

"So, you're like a witch?" The word tasted funny in my mouth, but my question was still light. I was honestly curious. Weren't witches supposed to be female? But I didn't know the right term to describe a male. Warlock? Wizard? Magician? None of the above?

Zeke let out a breath and smiled back. He'd probably been holding it the whole time I pondered over his confession. Relief that I wasn't running away in fear or, more likely, pulling my gun on him, made his features light up all over again.

"We don't use a specific term to describe ourselves, but yes, you could say we're witches. Magic flows through our veins, and we're taught at a young age to control it."

I nodded my head, pretending his words made sense. In a way, I guessed they did. I'd been close to believing he was a ghost there for a while. Was it that much more difficult to believe he was a witch?

"And the people in your community. They're all witches too?" I asked, interested. "How many of you are there?"

I could see him adding the numbers in his head, his blue eyes squinted slightly in concentration.

"Around fifty or so now. There used to be more of us, but many were killed when we left your town." His face twisted in pain, and the darkness of a time long past painted a shadow on his face. I remained silent as he collected his thoughts.

"We didn't use to hide. We lived among your people in peace, not flaunting our magic but using it for the good of all. But the people feared us, even though we would never harm them. They rounded us up and meant to kill us all.

"A few families were blotted out entirely," Zeke whispered. His eyes were distant, focused on the memory of his people's demise despite the fact that it happened years before he was born. We both looked out at the trees as he went on.

"The ancestors of those of us who remain managed to escape to the forest. We can move quickly when we want to, and it wasn't hard to leave them all behind. The community we have now is well protected by magic. It would take a miracle for humans to find us on their own."

The air was still and quiet, as if the wind and birds had stopped to hear Zeke's tale. I let his words hang in the air for a moment as it all sank in. When I finally tore my eyes away from the woods, I saw that he was watching me.

There were tears in Zeke's eyes as he waited for my reaction. I could feel how deep the pain of his lost people stretched. It was a scar that would never heal, no matter how many generations passed in their absence.

"I'm sorry for your loss," I managed to say. My throat seemed to have closed up. It was obvious Zeke's people had been through a lot. I was no stranger to loss, and I felt the hollowness in Zeke's eyes mirror my own grieving heart.

"If your people have to stay hidden to survive, why would you risk telling someone about them now?" I asked tentatively.

Zeke closed his eyes at my question, and when they reopened the tears had vanished. His blue eyes still sparkled in the sunlight that now made its way onto the porch as the sun followed its downward arc in the sky. His lips curled up as he inspected my face.

"Because of you," he said simply. He leaned back in his chair, as though I might need some distance from him as he spoke his next words.

"I'm risking everything I am, everything I have, because I had to meet you. I can't explain it, but certain forces are drawing me to you. I had to give my feelings a chance, even if you tell me today that you never want to see me again."

He held my gaze steadily, and I could feel the weight of his words as they settled on my heart. I wasn't used to declarations like this, especially from someone I had just met. I didn't know how to respond to such a statement.

"There are more secrets about my family, things I'd like to share with you over time. I'm not going to overwhelm you with all of them today," he began. "I know you need some time to think over everything I told you, and I know there's a good chance you might want nothing to do with me after this.

"I want you to take as much time as you need, and I'm not going to contact you again until I know that you're ready. If you decide you want to continue seeing me, light the candle in your attic at midnight. You could do it tonight, or you could wait two weeks to make your decision. I'll watch for it every night, and I won't contact you until I know that you want me to. The decision is yours."

Zeke stood and walked to the edge of the porch. He bent down to the rose bush and plucked a flower, its buds still closed in slumber. With a wave of his hand the flower opened and revealed the most perfect white rose I had ever seen. He turned back to me and laid it carefully in my lap.

"I'm trusting you to keep my secret, Cami. Even if you decide not to see me again, my fate and the fate of my people are in your hands."

I nodded my head slightly, staring at the boy only a few feet away. I was memorizing his features, and he seemed to be doing the same to me. We were still staring at each other in silence when the sound of crunching gravel had us both turning in the direction of the driveway.

Panicking, I whipped around to look at Zeke, but he was gone. At the edge of the trees I thought I saw a shadow move.

"Until next time, Cami," he whispered over the wind. I smiled and whispered back. "Until next time."

Chapter Eleven

At some point during Zeke's departure, I must have risen from my chair to get a better view of the trees. I was standing on the top step leading up to the porch, my hand resting lightly on the rail, when the red pickup truck came into view at the end of the driveway.

It was only two o'clock, but I wasn't that surprised to see Uncle Peter out before school was dismissed. In my experience, principals seemed to make their own rules. I was just grateful we had such a long driveway and that Zeke could apparently move at the speed of light. I didn't know how Peter would react to seeing a strange boy in animal skins conversing with his niece, but I had a feeling it wouldn't be anything good.

After killing the engine, Uncle Peter spotted me on the porch and made his way around the truck.

"I heard you weren't feeling well today and thought I'd come check on you," he began. His eyebrows were knit together, and genuine concern shone in his eyes. Maybe I should have given my uncle more credit. My father had always believed Peter thought he was better than us, but he could have changed in our years apart. It might have been stellar acting skills, but he seemed like he actually cared about my family now.

I nodded. I was still in a daze from my meeting with Zeke. It was hard to focus on someone as real and mundane as my uncle after hearing Zeke's story of magic and his people's fight for survival.

Peter must have seen something in my eyes, because his expression grew slightly darker. His eyes scanned the trees of the Cursed Woods suspiciously, making me wonder if Zeke's escape hadn't been as clean as I'd previously thought. I held my breath as he finished his search, but when his eyes returned to mine, they were as light as ever. Maybe I'd imagined the whole thing.

"Why are you outside, Cami?" Uncle Peter demanded with a shake of his head. "You should be inside resting, where it's warm."

I was about to exclaim that it *was* warm outside, but that's when I realized the sun had finally descended below the tops of the trees, leaving me in the shadows and cold. Suddenly the breeze didn't feel so warm anymore, and I shivered involuntarily.

"I just needed some fresh air," I said sheepishly. "I didn't realize it had gotten so cold." I was about to turn around and head into the house, but then remembered what was hiding beneath my shirt. Was my shirt loose enough to hide the shape of the gun, or would he see its outline bulging in the back of my pants? That was a conversation I really didn't feel like having today.

Luckily, I was saved from having to find out.

"Go on upstairs and get into bed." Uncle Peter said gently. "Your Aunt Lacey made her famous homemade chicken and noodles, and I brought you some. Go to bed. I'll bring you a bowl."

Once Peter had turned toward the truck, I backed quickly into the house. I did my best to sprint through the kitchen and living room without knocking anything over before ascending the stairs two steps at a time. The box sat on my bed exactly as I had left it, the revolver and bullets shining menacingly up at me. I returned the pistol to its home and slid the box back under my bed with a foot. I was tucked under the covers and catching my breath when Uncle Peter entered the room with a steaming bowl of soup.

My eyes lit up at the sight of the provisions, and I didn't have to fake my graciousness this time. When was the last time I ate a real meal? The smell of the broth made my mouth water as Peter set the bowl carefully on my nightstand and perched on the edge of the bed beside me.

"Your mother won't be home for at least another hour. Do you want me to stay until she gets here?" The concern had returned in my uncle's eyes, and for the first time since this all started, I felt a little guilty for faking an illness. It felt good to know my family cared about me, but I also didn't want them to worry over something that I'd lied about. Everyone was being so good to me, and I knew if I continued down this path with Zeke that the lies would only continue.

"That's okay, Uncle Pete." I smiled. "Really, I'm probably just going to eat the soup and then try to take a nap. Thanks for coming all the way out here to check on me. And tell Aunt Lacey I said thanks for the soup."

Uncle Peter returned my smile, and his eyes crinkled at my appreciation. He grabbed the blanket and pulled it up to my chin before kissing me on the forehead like I was a little girl. The action pressed on my heart, so similar to the sort of thing my father would have done for me. The love in his eyes mirrored that which I had witnessed in my father's eyes on countless occasions, along with something else that I couldn't quite put my finger on.

"Feel better, Cami. And remember, if you ever need anyone to talk to, I'm just a phone call away." He squeezed my knee through the blanket before getting up and taking his leave.

I didn't completely know what to make of my uncle. I'd lived almost eighteen years of my life without him showing much interest in me, but perhaps losing my dad had marked me with a sign that read *needs a father figure*. Peter and Lacey had never conceived any children of their own, so maybe now that I was here they might start viewing me as the daughter they never had. I didn't know how I felt about that, given the clear dislike my dad held for my uncle while he was still alive. How would he feel if he knew that the man he'd always considered to be too stuck up was now filling his shoes as the leading male role model in my life?

I decided to tuck the subject away to ponder over another time. I had too many things on my mind at the moment, the primary one being the emptiness of my gut. My stomach growled loudly, and it took everything I had to eat the soup in a calm enough manner that it didn't splash all over my bed. I gave up on the spoon after a few moments and drank the bowl dry. I could just see my mom cringing at the slurping noises coming from my mouth. The face I imagined her making was too much and I giggled into the bowl, resulting in a line of broth dribbling down my chin and onto my comforter.

I shrugged at the yellow spot on the blanket and proceeded to wipe my mouth with it. I'd get around to cleaning it later. Right then, I wanted nothing more than to turn my mind off and sleep until my mother got home. All of the hard decision making could wait until later.

But my mind wouldn't shut off. Even as I closed my eyes and willed myself to fall asleep, my brain felt like a static filled TV and I couldn't change the channel. It buzzed with ideas of witches and betrayal, random words and images that flashed through my mind one after another but never forming a coherent thought. I was completely wired, and there would be no relief until I faced the worries that plagued me.

I was saved from having to acknowledge those uncertainties by the interruption of a new buzzing, one that didn't exist solely in my head. I grabbed my phone off the nightstand and sat up in relief.

Have you already erased me from your life?

Michael. I really hadn't been the best friend to him lately, but with everything else that had been going on he'd slipped my mind. I felt guilty for a moment before reminding myself that he hadn't texted me since my first day of school either. Friendships were meant to go both ways.

Who is this? I don't recognize the number.

I watched the bubbles spring into life at the bottom of the conversation. This would be fun.

CAMILLE STONE.

I laughed as I typed up my reply.

That's so weird! My name is Camille Stone! What are the odds of another one finding my number?

We teased each other back and forth for a while before getting into a real conversation. Of course he wanted an update on how my new school and life were going.

Well, I joined the art club. Can you believe it?

In Plainfield, I had avoided clubs, sports, and all social gatherings like they were the plague. Art had been my passion for half of my life, but I'd always kept it to myself, only sharing it with those who were closest to me. Leave it to the loudest girl in Green Peaks to finally force me out of my shell.

It's about time you started making friends. You've been there for a couple weeks now, so you've had plenty of time to find yourself a hot boy toy. Am I right?

I sighed dramatically as I stared at the tiny, bright screen. It was too much to ask for Michael to continue distracting me from my problems for too long. Of course he would bring up the one subject I'd avoided thinking about all afternoon. I had to admit that Zeke was cute. Okay, who was I kidding? He was downright gorgeous. There was a wildness about him that could only be produced from an upbringing in the woods, and I'd never met a boy that was more mysterious. The fear I'd felt over the presumed stalking had dulled tremendously after finally meeting him in person, and it seemed to have transformed into a charge that only fueled my attraction even more. But I couldn't tell Michael about any of those things.

You're hesitating. I AM RIGHT!

Crap. I spent too much time fantasizing about meeting Zeke, and now Michael knew something was up. It was a testament to our friendship that he could read me from a hundred miles away, all because I hadn't replied to a text fast enough. I could try to lie my way out of it, claim I'd been in the bathroom or something and that's why I hadn't replied, but I knew that Michael wouldn't let it drop.

A part of me didn't want him to let it go anyway. I needed to talk to someone about this. Even if I didn't give him all the details, it was better than holding it inside me and risk driving myself crazy over the thought of it.

Fine, Varner, I give. I might have met someone.

A kaleidoscope of butterflies took off in my chest, fluttering up toward my throat as I finally told my secret to someone. I didn't realize the weight had been so burdensome until it was released.

SPILL IT NOW. I want to know everything!

Everything? Not a chance. I considered my situation and fumbled to find the right words to disclose just enough of the truth without revealing anything that might harm Zeke and his family. Or, more likely, that might result in my best friend drawing the conclusion that I needed a straitjacket.

His name is Zeke, short for Ezekiel. He's a year older than me and definitely hot. Like a 10 out of 10. But he has a bad boy vibe going on. He might be dangerous. I'm not sure if I want to go for it or not.

There. There was nothing incriminating in that description at all. I mentally patted myself on the back for killing two birds with one stone: finally getting Michael off my back about my boy situation, and sharing just enough of my secret with someone to prevent myself from combusting under the strain of keeping it in for another second.

Honey, you've played the part of the good girl your whole life. You have GOT to expand your horizons. This guy might be exactly what you need.

I wasn't surprised at Michael's sentiment. He was all about the bad boys and taking risks and living life on the edge. But that had never been my way of doing things. I liked structure and making smart, safe choices. Before all of this started, I'd been one of the most down to earth teenagers I'd ever met.

Then I found that second letter in the attic and everything changed.

What if this guy is too much, though? I don't want to bite off more than I can chew.

I gasped and rolled my eyes at Michael's next message that advised me *not* to bite *something*, then waited patiently as the blinking dots informed me he had more to say.

You only live once, right? As long as you don't suspect this guy to be an actual serial killer, I say go for it. If it doesn't work out, at least you'll know you gave it a shot.

I knew Michael's advice might not have counted for much given he didn't have all of the information regarding Zeke and just how much of an outsider he was, but his encouragement to give him a chance made me feel lighter, nonetheless. I was a teenager, after all, and my life had been drastically boring up until this point. Maybe it was about time I took a chance on something and leaped headfirst into the unknown.

I'd planned on giving my decision a lot more thought. I had fully intended on stressing myself blue over the next couple of days, going back and forth over whether seeing Zeke again was a good idea. But talking to Michael had been the fresh breath of air I needed after confining myself to the stuffiness of my own mind for so long. I felt rejuvenated, renewed, and had the sudden resolution that I didn't need to torture myself over a problem that I already knew the answer to.

When my mom arrived home, I met her downstairs and let her see my pink, flushed cheeks and embodiment of good health. It had been a while since I'd appeared in such high spirits, and I didn't bother hiding it from her. I told her Aunt Lacey made us some soup and Uncle Peter had dropped it by, and we shared the rest of it for supper, finally using the dining room for our first meal since moving there. We ate at the unnecessarily large table in quiet peace, neither mentioning what it meant for us. To me, it was a symbol of acceptance. Things had changed for us, would likely continue to change, but everything would be all right.

I went about the rest of my evening as a normal girl should. I called Natalie and got the scoop of what I'd missed at school and talked to her late into the night. My heart already lightened, I didn't feel the need to bring up the details of my own day or how I'd been spending my letter filled nights.

I accepted that from then on, my life would be split in two. I would live the life of a senior girl who spent her time hanging out with her art freak friends and trying to score decent grades before graduation, and the life of a stranger who believed in the mysterious happenings in the Cursed Woods, witchcraft, and the possibility of love at first sight.

It was easy to stay awake with my heart pounding in my chest and my mind racing over the possibilities of my future. So after I hung up the phone and Natalie went to bed, I took the step into the unknown that I'd suspected I would take all along. I made my way up to the attic and lit the candle at midnight.

"*Cami!*"

I jerked awake at the lunch table, scattering a bowl of goldfish crackers and knocking over Natalie's chocolate milk in one sweep of my arm. Had I actually just dozed off in the middle of a crowded cafeteria? My friends' gaping stares and torn expressions of amusement and concern suggested that I had.

My movements were slow and robotic as I collected the spilled crackers, the milk already being sopped up by Jason and Taylor's napkins. It appeared that Zombie Camille had returned for her second act.

"Sorry." I yawned widely. Natalie just shook her head and helped me return the crackers to the bowl.

A week had passed since I lit the candle in the attic, making my statement to Zeke that I wanted to continue our relationship. What that relationship actually *was,* I still didn't know. I'd spent the last seven nights staying up late and exchanging paper airplanes for magical birds, each note revealing more about its sender.

It was sort of like having a pen-pal. I could honestly say that the boy who'd scared me out of my wits, made me question my own sanity, and consider telling the authorities that I had a stalker was now one of my closest friends. We weren't two strangers exchanging letters anymore, but two friends conversing in the only way that seemed safe for the time being.

As much as those letters revealed about Zeke, however, there was still so much left to be said. I felt like I'd been tasked with painting a sunset, but the only colors available to me were black and white. I could produce a grayscale image, but I lacked the most important details, the ones that granted the sunset its beauty.

I knew that Zeke had two loving, somewhat overprotective parents, and a younger sister that he enjoyed picking on, and who he secretly loved more than anything in the world. I knew his favorite hobby was shooting the bow that he'd crafted himself, exhibiting a precision that elevated him as the best marksman in his entire coven even without using magic to guide his arrows.

But despite knowing his interests and dislikes, it was the things that couldn't be said that I craved to learn the most. I wanted to see his eyes crinkle as he watched his sister play, hear his steady breathing just before he released an arrow. I wanted to watch him smile when he didn't know I was looking and hear his laugh when I made a lame joke. I wanted all of the *color* that came with truly knowing someone. The black and white letters weren't enough anymore.

"Is everything okay, Cami?" Natalie's voice was low as we collected our trash, the lunch hour coming to an end. I was startled to learn that she was capable of speaking so quietly. Jason, Taylor, and Carly had moved on ahead of us, and I realized she didn't want the rest of our group to hear her.

I couldn't be honest with her, though. I couldn't tell her that I was losing sleep because I'd been spending my nights getting to know a witch that lived in the woods. A witch whose feelings for me seemed to grow stronger and stronger every night we talked.

Even if I wanted to tell her about Zeke, and a big part of me did, I just didn't see how it would be possible. Telling Michael those half-truths had been one thing. He was a hundred miles away and had no way to fact check my story. Natalie would see through my lies in an instant and then be hurt when

I couldn't tell her more. Above everything, I had to protect Zeke and his family.

Urged on by my prolonged silence, Natalie touched my shoulder gently.

"Is this about your dad?"

Guilt squeezed my chest, its fingers clawing through my ribs and settling around my heart. Or maybe it was my lungs, because breathing was suddenly impossible. It had been days since I'd thought about my father, and those days suddenly felt like years. Was I a terrible daughter for letting a boy distract me from the loss that had turned my life upside down? Or would my dad be happy that I had a reason to feel something other than grief for the first time since he died? I didn't know the answer, and it made me feel even worse.

I didn't realize I was crying until Natalie folded me into her arms.

"It's alright, Cami. I've got you." Her whispered words only made my gut clench tighter. I flashed back to the never-ending car ride with my mother, and all of the necessary stops along the way. I wasn't going to throw up in the middle of the cafeteria. I wasn't.

But I couldn't pretend that my odd behavior was attributed to the loss of my father. Somehow that lie seemed the cruelest of all, not only to my friends but also to his memory. If I let her go on believing that was what this was about for another second, I thought I actually would lose my lunch on the floor.

"No," I said tightly, pulling back from her embrace. I wiped my eyes clumsily with the sleeves of my jacket. I was lucky I'd been in too much of a zombie state that morning to apply any eyeliner. What a mess I had become.

"It isn't about my dad." I gave her a small smile before looking around the room. The cafeteria had cleared out during our scene, and thank goodness for that. I didn't need an audience witnessing one of my rare displays of emotion. But I also didn't need to be the last one walking into class after the bell rang, my face still red and streaked with tears. We needed to get moving.

I gathered up the trash we'd dropped and looped my arm through hers as we made our way towards the door. My mind reeled for an acceptable lie, anything I could tell her that wouldn't result in my guilt growing strong enough to expel my stomach's contents. At least we were nearing the garbage can so I wouldn't make a mess all over the floor.

Then I had it. Another half-truth, but something that needed to be addressed anyway.

"I've just been struggling a lot lately. With my schoolwork, I mean." I met her eyes and gave her a one shouldered shrug. "I'm pretty sure I failed my Calculus exam yesterday. We'll find out when we get them back next period."

It wasn't a complete lie. I really *had* been struggling with my schoolwork in the past week. I was napping during my usual study time so that I could stay up all night writing letters, and my focus had been strained during class too. It was all too easy to tune the teachers out and think about Zeke, replaying some of our conversations in my head and thinking up new topics for us to discuss the following night.

I said I would split my life in two, but my life as a senior in high school was quickly being ignored in the face of my other, more interesting one. I was failing at keeping them separate, keeping them both alive, and I needed that to change. I needed help.

"Oh Cami, you've been such a ghost lately." Natalie squeezed my arm, still wrapped around hers, after dumping the remainder of our lunches in the bin.

"If you've been having trouble, you should have asked for help. I can't say that I completely understand Calc, but I'd be happy to struggle along with you after school. Anytime!"

I squeezed her arm back and brushed away the last of my tears. It was easy to get caught up in the idea of Zeke, the excitement of getting to know a guy for the first time, especially when he was the most interesting person I'd ever met. But I couldn't forget about my other friends. Natalie would keep me grounded, if I let her. She could be my tether to the life I needed to hold onto when the magic and excitement of my other life threatened to sweep me away.

"I'd really like that. Thanks, Nat."

The rest of the day went by more smoothly than I could have hoped. I managed to scrape up a C on my test, a lower grade than I normally scored but still a lot better than the big fat F I'd been expecting. When my eyes began to droop again in English, Jason slipped me a couple of caffeine pills from one of the many compartments of his backpack. They did the job of perking me up, but also caused a tremor in my hands that lasted the duration of the period.

By the time Natalie's truck carried us down my long driveway after school, I was feeling almost like myself again. The cans of Coke I snagged out of the fridge only improved my mental state even more.

We sat on the back porch in the same seats Zeke and I had occupied only a week ago. With our calculus books laid open on our laps, we tried to talk through the previous lesson before the upcoming quiz on Monday. But it was calculus, after all, and sometimes having a second brain only confused things more.

"So basically an invisible number is the square root of a negative number," Natalie mused. She rubbed the end of her pencil against her face as if she were trying to erase an eyebrow.

"Wait, I thought they were imaginary numbers." We both flipped back a few pages before giggling.

"Definitely imaginary. But who's to say they aren't invisible? We can imagine them however we want, can't we?"

We laughed and sipped our Cokes, having a good time despite the boring task at hand. Even if studying with Natalie brought me no closer to an A, I was still glad to be doing it. I just wished I could open up to her about all of my secrets, like normal best friends were meant to do.

After thirty minutes of studying and getting nowhere in our understanding of imaginary numbers, Natalie's phone began to ring. I recognized the song from one of the many boy band CD's she always had blasting in her car.

"What's up, Mom?... Yes, I'm at Cami's, we're doing homework... Yeah, yeah. I'm sorry, I should've told you. I'll be home in twenty minutes."

Natalie rolled her eyes and sighed dramatically as she hung up the phone. "Sorry Cami, I should've known my mom would be freaking out after hearing the news. I'm not saying it isn't serious or anything. I mean, it's scary. But she needs to calm down a little."

I sat forward in my chair. "What news?"

Natalie gave me a strange look as she shoved the textbook into her backpack. "The news everyone's been talking about all day? Like in every class. How have you not heard about it?"

I thought back to my day at school but struggled to remember any announcements or pieces of gossip. Apparently my zombie-self had been in full control, because I couldn't remember talking to anyone all day or even listening in on other people's conversations. I really needed to get my daydreaming under control if I didn't want to gain a reputation like Carly's.

I shrugged and pinned her with a look that said *Well, tell me already.*

Natalie sighed again and dropped her bag before sinking back into the chair. Her movements suggested I was asking a lot from her, but her eyes were bright with the anticipation of being the one to share something with me. It had to be gossip, then, and a juicy bit of gossip by the looks of it.

"Apparently a girl is missing." Natalie's voice was hushed with the severity of her words, but I could still see the light in her eyes that suggested she enjoyed sharing the news with me. It was like the day she and the others told me about the Cursed Woods and the strange history of my house. A town like Green Peaks very rarely saw any excitement, and even a tragedy like this might seem thrilling to some, almost like a ghost story.

"Her name's Heather Reed. She's only a year older than us. I don't know her well, but it's a small town," Natalie went on. I could just recognize the cadences in her speech, as if she really were telling me a ghost story.

"She's a freshman at UW now, but she came home to watch her little brother's baseball game last week. Supposedly she planned on heading back to school as soon as the game was over, but I guess she never made it. For several days her family thought she'd gone back to school, and her roommate thought she decided to spend a few more days at home. But now everyone's comparing their notes, and no one has seen her in a week."

I gasped, my eyes widening. Natalie smiled as if my reaction were exactly what she had hoped for.

"What about her car?" I asked. I couldn't help myself; I was interested. "Surely someone has seen it?"

Natalie shook her head. "No one's seen her or her car since her brother's baseball game. Her mom did watch her leave, but who knows where or when she actually disappeared. She could have gotten all the way to Laramie and been kidnapped there or stopped to get gas or eat along the way and ran into trouble there. No one knows."

I let a soft *wow* escape my lips before shaking my head in awe. It was crazy to think something bad could happen to someone in such a small town, but the reality was things like this happened every day. People went missing, schools had shootings, fathers died while drunk driving. Why was I surprised that a place like Green Peaks would be any different? This town might have been my mother's blank slate, but that didn't make it immune to the same evils we had escaped from. This was the real world, and tragedy could happen anywhere.

"Anyway," Natalie jumped up, her voice back to its usual peppy volume. "My mom's mad I didn't tell her where I was, as if there's actually a serial killer loose in Green Peaks." She rolled her eyes. "I'll talk to you later, Cami!"

With that, she skipped across the yard and into her truck, lugging her flowery bookbag behind her. I remained in my seat and flinched when her truck roared to life with a growl.

If Heather disappeared exactly a week ago, that was the day I finally met Zeke. Was there a significance there that I was missing? But no, that would be absurd. I was looking for elements, connecting factors that didn't exist. My meeting with Zeke couldn't possibly be related to this girl's disappearance.

It could have been Natalie's ominous rendition of the girl's tale, but I was suddenly paranoid that someone was watching me. The hairs on the back of my neck stood straight, as if they were craning to look around me and find the perpetrator themselves. I was being ridiculous though. Just because a random girl I'd never met had gone missing didn't mean that I was in any danger. Natalie's unsettling voice must have put me on edge.

I was just starting to calm myself down when a movement in the trees caught my attention. The woods were dark and too far away for me to see the figure clearly, but something had definitely moved, something big, and I had a feeling it wasn't an animal. Natalie was already too far away for me to call for help, and my mother was at an evening PTO meeting. I was home alone, and if someone wanted to attack me, now was the perfect time.

The figure shifted again, and I could just make out the silhouette of a tall man. My heart pounding in my chest, I jumped up and prepared to run to my room. My gun. I needed to lock the doors and grab my gun.

Then another motion stopped me in my tracks. The figure stayed where he was, but something else continued towards me instead. A bird flapped its way across the yard, closing the distance between us slowly as it struggled to stay upright in the wind. When it finally reached its destination, my outstretched palm, it transformed itself before my eyes into a perfect paper rose. I smiled.

Zeke.

Chapter Thirteen

"What are you doing here?"

My voice was hushed as I glanced back at the house. No one was home, and the trees provided ample protection if someone happened to pull into our driveway at that moment. We were safe for now, I hoped.

Zeke smiled and held my arms, standing back to get a good look at me. His eyes raked over every inch of my body, and I could feel a blush creep into my cheeks as he lingered on my mouth.

"Just wanted to see you," he whispered, and I melted. I pulled him in for a hug and closed my eyes as his scent enveloped me. Smoke, pine needles, and fresh air, a concoction that was distinctly Zeke.

When we finally broke apart, he took my hand and led us further into the trees. His grip was soft and warm, and my hand tingled at his touch. He stopped after a minute of walking and sat down on an overturned tree, patting the spot to his left.

"I thought it wasn't safe for you to come out here during the day?" I asked as I perched on the log beside him. There wasn't much light filtering in through the canopy above us, but in our close proximity I could just make out the circles under his eyes. I knew he was observing the same dark rings on my own face when he brought a hand up and touched them gently with his fingertips.

"You're tired," he stated. It wasn't a question, and I shrugged my shoulders. We were sitting close enough that my arm brushed against his leather sleeve with the movement.

"So are you."

We stared at each other for another moment before he laced his fingers through mine once again.

"Our current method of communication isn't working." Zeke sighed. "I'm dead on my feet during the day, and my mother is starting to take notice. Not to mention," he smiled and squeezed my hand, "I don't like not seeing you."

My chest ached. I was glad it wasn't just me.

"But aren't they wondering where you are?"

I was happy that he was here and I was finally getting to spend some real time with him, but I didn't want him to get into trouble with his family. How did a coven of witches punish a disobedient teenager?

"They think I'm patrolling the grounds, keeping an eye out for potential hunting zones or areas that need more enchantments to keep the humans out." He poked me in the stomach, and I giggled. I was the human that probably needed to be kept out.

"Besides," he added, a mischievous glint lighting his eyes, "I'm thinking I'll bring you to meet them before too long anyway."

My jaw dropped. *"What?"*

I could hear the panic in my voice, knew it was probably echoing in my eyes, but I couldn't reel it in. Forget about what a coven of witches would do to one of their own members who had broken the rules, what would they do to *me?* When they found out I knew about their existence, what measures would they take to ensure I never spoke the truth to anyone? Would they cast a spell to make me mute? Turn me into a frog? Teach Zeke a lesson and silence me forever by simply killing me? The possibilities were endless.

"You can't!" I shouted. I clapped my hands over my mouth and looked around, but the forest was empty.

"Why not?" Zeke laughed. His light voice made me want to believe he was joking, but his eyes were soft and probing as he watched my reaction. They were curious, sincere, and perhaps a little hurt by my sudden outburst.

I forced myself to breathe evenly as I tried to form a coherent sentence. His thumb traced soft circles on my hand soothingly, but I was beyond soothing. The fear of my own death had me choking for air.

"Don't you think they'll hurt me when they find out that I know?" I annunciated each word clearly, like I was talking to a toddler or foreign entity that had trouble comprehending my words. Because how could he not understand my concern?

"They won't hurt you." Zeke sighed. "They can't."

Now I was the one not understanding. I'd witnessed some of the magic he shared with me, the amazing stunts he performed without so much as lifting his finger, and he'd only been skimming the top of his abilities. But if I had an entire coven pitted against me? I was toast.

Zeke saw the confusion in my eyes and leaned his head back, staring up at the shelter of leaves. I waited patiently for him to collect his thoughts and squeezed his hand back. When his eyes returned to mine, they were weary.

"They can't hurt you because they can't harm any human. Not with magic anyway." He shook his head, lost in thought. Sensing there was more, I bit my tongue and allowed him to go on.

"It's a balance of nature, I suppose. It's been like this since the beginning of time as far as we know. Our magic is meant to do good." He paused and sucked in a breath. "When magic is used to harm a human, the wielder forfeits their life as they know it. They lose their ability to practice magic and are transformed into an animal. They live the remainder of their lives trapped in animal form, existing as a reminder to the rest of us of what using our magic for evil will do."

Zeke's eyebrows were drawn together, and I didn't think he realized how tightly he was squeezing my hand. His expression showed the cost of admitting this secret, yet another I was deemed worthy enough to receive.

I mulled over this new piece of information silently. No wonder they preferred to live secluded from the rest of us. We could hunt them down with guns and knives, and they wouldn't even be able to defend themselves with the threat of this curse. It was comforting to know they couldn't hex us as they pleased, but at the same time I couldn't stop myself from thinking it wasn't fair.

"Has it ever happened? To any of your people, I mean."

His eyes on the ground, Zeke nodded. "When the town turned on us, forcing us into the woods, around twenty of my people tried to protect their loved ones and ended up triggering the curse. Another thirty or so died in the escape. The ones who changed helped us start our little community, living as familiars to those of us that remained. But they've all passed on now."

Suddenly the legends around the Cursed Woods made a lot more sense. The sightings of the strange animals had to be the cursed witches that Zeke was talking about. I squeezed his hand again and could see the loss shining through his eyes at the mention of his community's near annihilation.

Seeing the dark place this topic was taking him to, I tried to lighten the mood. "So do you get to choose your animal form? Why didn't any of your people turn into a dinosaur and take out the rest of us, anyway?"

Zeke laughed a deep, throaty chortle. "No, we don't get to choose what animal we become." He bumped his shoulder against mine playfully. "It's thought that our animal form reflects our spirit animal, but no one knows for sure what that will be until it actually happens."

I nodded as if that made sense, as if all of this new information was as easy to take in as one of my school subjects. Actually, I supposed it made about as much sense as the imaginary numbers at that point.

I leaned into him and looked up at his face. With our substantial height difference, I was almost craning my neck. "I bet your spirit animal is a mountain lion. Or maybe a wolf," I said quietly. He was leaning down now, closing the space between us. "Definitely something manly."

His breath was warm on my face, disturbing the hairs that had escaped from my ponytail and tickled against my cheek. My own breath caught in my throat as the final inches between us disappeared. I closed my eyes.

I felt his head jerk up and away from mine, and its sudden absence hit me like a slap in the face. His eyes were wide as he peered towards the entrance of the forest, and I followed his gaze, my cheeks burning.

"You need to go." He jumped up, pulling me off the log with him. I felt the sting in my chest an instant before the hurt painted a shadow on my face. Zeke took one look at me and groaned.

"I'm so sorry, Cami, I didn't realize how long we'd been out here." He hugged me fiercely before half dragging me out of the woods. "Your mother is home."

Fear gripped me as I ran along beside him. It wouldn't be easy to explain to my mother why I had been spending time in the forest so close to dusk. I stepped out of the tree cover and prepared to sprint across the yard before turning back to Zeke.

"When will I see you again?" I didn't want him to leave. The warmth of his body next to mine felt like home.

"I'll be here again tomorrow after you get out of school."

I shook my head. "I have art club tomorrow." I didn't want to think about the things my friends would do to me if I missed it. "Can I see you Saturday?"

Zeke nodded and carefully took my face in his hands. He breathed in the scent of my hair and kissed my forehead gently, sighing.

"Go now, Cami," he whispered. "I'll see you soon."

"What's that supposed to be?"

Natalie pointed to a section on Jason's drawing. We were still in the early stages of our group project, sketching designs and figuring out our interpretations of what the legends surrounding the Cursed Woods entailed.

I looked to where Natalie was pointing and saw a wide oak tree surrounded by smaller, less menacing trees on each side of it. A hole was carved into the tree's body about halfway up, and two red eyes gleamed threateningly out of the pit.

Jason shrugged. "An owl, maybe." He bent over the paper with his black colored pencil, darkening the hole even more.

Natalie rolled her eyes. "An owl?" She exchanged a glance with me and we both giggled at his serious expression. "Why would an owl have red eyes?"

Without looking up from his work, Jason chucked an eraser in her direction. "Because it's in the Cursed Woods, dummy."

I returned my attention to my own work. The trees were swaying in the invisible breeze, some of the leaves detaching themselves and floating on the wind. In the middle of the picture was the form of a giraffe, its features somewhat camouflaged within the cover of the trees. Although its body pointed to the right, its head was turned toward the viewer as if it were inspecting me just as closely.

I stared at the giraffe and let my mind wander. Zeke didn't divulge any specifics on the type of animals his people had transformed into, but the legends said they were species that didn't belong here. I tried to capture wisdom in the giraffe's eyes, a touch of sadness. She'd just lost her family, her magic, and her own beloved body. She gazed out of the forest at the town, at the people who had stolen everything from her.

"Good work, Cami," Taylor praised. I gave him a small smile and peered over at his drawing. His trees seemed more innocent, more forgiving than the ones in Jason's picture. A kangaroo peeked around the edge of one tree, and a monkey hung off the branch of another. I looked over at Carly and Natalie's sketches next. Carly's seemed more cheerful, her animals' eyes soft and childlike and similar to Taylor's. Natalie's drawing was darker, the moonlight gleaming menacingly down on the nearly bare trees. A wolf howled up at the full moon, its haunches raised. Somehow we'd have to make all of our ideas merge into one.

The next several days passed, and my life finally began to develop a sort of routine. Every other day after school, I spent time with Natalie finishing homework and studying for exams. I still didn't know which college I wanted to attend, but I needed my grades to keep the doors open to whichever one I might choose. We switched back and forth between her house and mine, but due to the lack of a distracting little sister, we usually ended up studying in my room. My mom tried to hide her satisfaction that I had a solid friend, one that I spent time completing schoolwork with instead of drinking or doing drugs or whatever other worries kept her up at night.

On the days in between, I devoted my afternoon time to Zeke. My mother was under the impression that I had taken up hiking, which wasn't a complete lie. The clearly marked trails I promised I was staying on might not have existed, but I could hardly tell her that I was accompanied by a wild boy who knew the forest like the back of his hand. That little detail was better kept to myself.

At first I struggled to keep up with Zeke's long legs and instincts that showed him the perfect places to step. I was gasping within minutes of trekking uphill, fighting weeds and brambles the whole way. Zeke was patient with my frequent need to break, and he always held the worst of the obstacles out of the way until I passed.

We talked the entire time, only pausing so I could catch my breath and drink from his leather-made waterskin that had been enchanted to never run out of cold, clean water. Zeke insisted he didn't want to be a showoff, but that didn't stop him from delivering every time I begged him to show me more magic. Blossoms bloomed on the trees before dancing in a pink swirl around me. My shoe and sock were instantly dried after I unwittingly stepped into a hidden puddle. A baby bird was returned to its nest high in the trees with a simple wave of Zeke's hand.

After every demonstration of his abilities, my eyes widened in wonder and I squeezed his hand with reverence. I couldn't help but notice the shy, satisfied grin that erupted on his face every time I gasped in amazement. Perhaps my reactions to his magic were just as stunning to him as his magic was to me. He had been raised to fear people like me, people on the outside, because we would see his abilities as a danger that needed to be eradicated. But with the knowledge that his magic would never be used to hurt me, I could appreciate his powers for what they were: a beautiful gift that the world never should have rejected.

It was on a Thursday afternoon that he again brought up the subject that I'd hoped he'd simply forgotten about. We were sitting in a large bed of weeds bordered on all sides by saplings and brush, creating an intimate space for us to lounge comfortably in.

"I'm still taking you to meet my family." Zeke's eyes were bright and full of laughter, probably because he knew how I was about to react. I groaned.

Zeke smiled and reached forward, tucking a strand of hair back behind my ear. "You're ready for this, Cami. I know you are."

The frightening thing was, I thought he might be right. I'd spent the last two weeks getting to know him, and I wondered if there was any person outside of my family who I understood better. It wasn't just the facts about his life and his upbringing, it was the way he moved and spoke and observed the world around him. I didn't think I'd ever felt so completely at ease with someone I'd known for such a short period of time. When he was gone I felt his absence as a tangible hole in my chest, an aching bubble of space that could not be filled until I finally met him in the forest once again. The strength of our connection frightened me even more.

"Let's say I was ready to meet them," I mused quietly, catching his hand again. "You're absolutely sure they wouldn't hurt me?"

Zeke laughed, and I felt the vibrations as it shook both our bodies. "Oh, they'll do something to you all right." He winked. "They'll tell you stories about me that'll make you wonder why you gave me the time of day. They'll show you I'm really nothing special, not when all of them can do the things I do, and more."

I shook my head and rolled my eyes before grabbing a wandering caterpillar and placing it on his shoulder. "I don't care if they can all wield magic. You'll still be the most special to me."

I blushed and looked down as soon as the words left my mouth. While Zeke had been open from the beginning about how he felt for me, I'd been hesitant in revealing my own feelings, at least through words. I'd never been able to discuss my feelings with people easily. I knew how I felt most of the time, but when I tried to voice my emotions, I could never seem to find the right thing to say.

Thankfully, Zeke had made it clear that he didn't expect anything out of me, and he'd never pressured me into doing or saying something I wasn't comfortable with. He was the most patient guy I knew, and I didn't know if that had to do with his upbringing in the woods or if it was something simply instilled in his character.

From the corner of my eye, I watched Zeke guide the caterpillar onto his finger. He smiled as he considered the insect, and I wondered if he was happy about what I said or thinking about something else.

"Saturday is my sister's twelfth birthday, and we'll have something special in store that night. I want you to come and meet everyone then."

As he spoke, the caterpillar changed before my eyes. Words couldn't describe the beautiful transformation, but within a matter of seconds a butterfly lifted from his finger and flapped around both of our heads. It landed on my wrist and its touch was feather light, as soft as a kiss.

I nodded absently and beheld the small creature. As it took off again and disappeared into the trees, I tried to imagine what it would feel like to have a life changing in my hands. To have the will and control to change someone or something into something new.

But maybe I wasn't destined to bring about this kind of change in another being. Maybe I was meant to be the butterfly.

Chapter Fourteen

It was still light out when we entered the trees, but I estimated that we left the sun behind about a mile ago.

This was deeper into the forest than Zeke had ever taken me before. The trees were so thick they seemed to be growing on top of each other in places, and the canopy over our heads was a living thing whose sole purpose was to prevent us from ever seeing sunlight again. The light of its setting rays filtered in through the foliage, leaving us with a green glow to illuminate our path.

As we drew closer and closer to our destination, I couldn't help glancing over my shoulder at the dark shapes that skirted around the edges of my vision. Each time I turned I was met with the same never-ending wall of green. The shadows here seemed to abide by their own rules.

Zeke squeezed my hand reassuringly while I tried to remind myself why I was doing this. There was a reason I'd lied to my mom and told her I was hanging out with Natalie. Natalie, who had wanted to drive us to Rawlins for dinner and a movie, was under the impression that I was sick and bedbound. After all, there was always the possibility that I'd end up bedbound after meeting Zeke's family. I still had no idea what to expect.

Zeke glanced my way again, his eyes concerned as they traveled over my face. I knew I had to be as white as a ghost, or perhaps a sickly shade of green with the help of the garish lighting. It was cool and damp this far into the trees, but that didn't stop the sweat from collecting on my brow and neck.

"It's all going to be fine, Cami," he said for what had to be the hundredth time. I met his eyes but couldn't return his smile. All of my focus and energy was going towards taking each step forward. And breathing. I continually had to remind myself to breathe.

"Do they know that I'm coming?" I managed to ask. My voice was rough from lack of use. It felt like hours had passed since I'd done more than nod my head and shrug my shoulders. As long as Zeke was telling the truth, I wasn't *really* walking towards a death sentence. But he'd been leading me down this weeded path for quite some time, and I couldn't help viewing it as my own personal Green Mile. Which end would be worse? An electric chair or a coven of angry witches?

Zeke dropped his gaze, his lips pursed into a straight line. "I thought it would be better if we surprised them."

I gulped. I didn't bother asking any more questions after that.

I could tell we were getting close when the trees seemed to thin fractionally. The shadows flitting around the edge of my vision became more frequent, and when a bush shuddered ten feet to my right, I knew we weren't alone. But even as I became aware of the bodies closing around us, none of them bothered to show their faces. It was like they were waiting for a cue, an invisible command to hold off their attack until the right moment. I trembled as I contemplated when that would be.

Zeke slowed his pace to a stop and looked over at me. His expression was carefully arranged, but his calm visage was just a little too forced to be genuine. A muscle in his face twitched, revealing he was just as nervous at our situation as I was.

"Ready?" he asked.

My eyes were wide as I inspected the trees in front of us. Surely we hadn't arrived at his home yet. The patch of forest that lay before me was identical to the one we'd just left behind, unbroken by any signs of human dwelling or evidence of life at all. I moved my gaze up the trees, searching for tree houses or anything that might offer shelter to a group of fifty witches.

Finding nothing, I shrugged my shoulders. "Let's do it."

Tightening his grip on my hand, Zeke stepped forward and pulled me into the heart of his coven.

My body passed through the invisible wall as easily as stepping through a waterfall. It felt like water and air combined into one, washing over my skin while also drying me anew, the sudden breeze lifting my hair into an arc behind me.

I gasped as I took in the sudden appearance of the log cabins, stone cottages, and occasional wigwams spread evenly throughout the wide-open space. Only seconds ago we'd been standing in the center of the forest with no clearing in sight. Now I stood in a perfectly round meadow, the open sky pink from the setting sun hanging beautifully overhead. The sky was just clear enough to display the moon, elegant and full, and waiting patiently for the sun to dip below the horizon.

The people appeared out of thin air.

They stood in a mass before me, some hunched over with wrinkles lining their faces and hands, others mere toddlers hiding behind the legs of their mothers. All wore the leather skins I had grown accustomed to seeing on Zeke. I was transported back in time, no longer standing in the midst of a witch coven but rather a tribe of Native Americans. They stared at me evenly, and their expressions all screamed the same thing: outsider, intruder, threat.

A twig snapped too close behind me, and I knew without looking that we were completely surrounded. It felt like there were thousands of eyes on us, their stares boring into me from every direction. I trembled behind Zeke and grasped his arm tightly, as if my life were hanging on by the thread connecting us. I wanted to hide behind him like the little ones clutching their mothers' legs. Perhaps I was a coward after all.

Only seconds had passed, but it felt like a lifetime before the woman stepped forward, breaking rank from the rest of the group.

"Ezekiel," she hissed. "What have you done?"

The woman's hair was a tangled mass of black curls that fell to lay against her lower back. A single white flower had been weaved into the hair behind her ear, striking against the black waves. Her bright blue eyes were piercing, full of rage, but they slid right past me, suggesting I was too insignificant to be acknowledged. She had eyes only for the boy standing beside me. A boy who glowered back at her with the same icy blue stare.

"Mother," Zeke began, his voice stronger than I'd ever heard it before. "I can explain."

He squeezed my hand reassuringly, and his mother's eyes narrowed. We were in so much trouble.

"I suppose *this* is how you've been spending all your 'scouting' time?" she demanded. Her shrill voice was nearing an octave that only enraged mothers could reach. "I knew you were hiding something, but I never imagined it could be this. Rather than performing your entrusted duties, you've been dabbling with a *human.*" She snarled the word as if I were repulsive. Unclean. Possibly even uncivilized, but I reminded myself that I wasn't the one wearing animal skins.

Anger surged through me at her instantaneous judgment. She didn't know me, didn't know a single human for that matter. It was unbelievable that she would pass judgment on me based on the actions of a group of people long dead.

I squeezed Zeke's arm even tighter and felt my nails bite into the palm of my other hand as I clenched it into a ball. I opened my mouth and sucked in a breath, unsure of what I was about to say but positive that it wouldn't be nice.

"Stop," Zeke shouted. "Just stop!"

For a moment I thought his words were pointed at me, that he knew I was about to say something that would dig us into an even deeper hole. Then I noticed his glare, still pinned on his mother who had taken an involuntary step back. The shocked expression on her face suggested he'd slapped her.

Zeke eased himself out of my vice-like grip, and I was too stunned to stop him. He walked slowly toward his mother with his hands up, a sign of peace. I could feel the space between us growing with his every step as he left me stranded in the circle of his people. I shivered helplessly. I was completely exposed.

When he finally reached her, I became aware of the height difference between them. He had to be a foot taller than his mother, whose head was tilted back to meet his eyes in such close proximity. But despite her small stature, her eyes were glazed steel, and I knew that she was the one with the upper hand. He carefully placed his hands on her shoulders and spoke too quietly for me to hear.

They talked for several minutes in hushed tones, his mother's eyes flickering to mine periodically. I strained to catch their words, and I knew by the way some of the other witches cocked their heads to the side that they were trying to do the same. Could they magically enhance their hearing? Some of them glanced back and forth between us, timed with his mother's stares. I felt naked, the only girl in the entire crowd who couldn't partake in their conversation.

My eyes darted to a young girl with a pretty face who was scrutinizing me silently. Her eyes were curious, devoid of the anger I'd seen in so many of the faces when I first arrived. She stroked the chain of flowers draped around her neck absent-mindedly, the other hand hidden behind her back. She gave me a shy smile. Something told me she couldn't hear Zeke and his mother either, and her blue-eyed gaze put me at ease.

I felt rather than heard a sigh emit from the crowd, as though a universal breath was released that had been tethering them all to their positions. I watched as one by one they turned away from me, moving to attend to some task or another. Some gave me wry smiles before walking away, others raising their eyebrows and nodding once in my direction.

The energy in the small space had shifted. I no longer felt angry eyes boring into me from every direction, and when I did catch the gaze of a passerby, it was polite. It was as if they were accepting me. What had Zeke said to get us off the hook so easily?

"Cami," Zeke called, and I turned back to see my forest boy beckoning to me. His mother stood to his right, and while her expression was still guarded, it held no traces of the outrage that had painted her face only moments before.

I joined their little group and was grateful when Zeke placed a hand lightly on my back. His touch gave me warmth, made me feel stronger. I could do this. The hardest part was already over.

"Mother, this is Camille Stone," Zeke murmured. I held my hand out and she grasped it. "Cami, this is Alexandra Rivers, my mother and the leader of our coven."

My hand froze mid shake, my eyes growing wide. Zeke never told me his mom was the *leader* of the coven! It was bad enough that he had a witch for a mother, let alone one that could order the entire group to attack me. My hand was clammy as I stared up into Alexandra's eyes. She was definitely smirking at me now. I forced myself to finish the handshake, hoping I hadn't hesitated for too long.

"It's so nice to meet you, Camille," she purred. Her voice was deeper than I was expecting, no doubt back to its normal level now that she was finished screaming at her son. I tried to smile back at her, but probably only managed a grimace.

God, I was nervous. Why wasn't there a book I could have read on how to properly meet your sort of boyfriend's witchy mother? How was I supposed to be prepared for this?

"Cami," I spluttered. Her eyebrows rose, and I could feel my cheeks reddening. "You can call me Cami."

Alexandra tilted her head slightly. "Cami." She said my name slowly, tasting it. I smiled and nodded. My eyes were trapped in her bright blue gaze, unable to move as she stared into me, into my soul. I could feel her searching within my being, her presence as light as a feather at the edge of my mind. I didn't know what she was looking for or if she had found it, because the moment was interrupted when an object flew past both our heads.

"Ouch!" Zeke yelped, the stone dropping from his chest and hitting the ground with a thump. He turned in the direction of the assault to find the young girl who had been watching me, a mischievous smile lighting up her face. She held the slingshot down by her side, no longer concealing it behind her back as she had done before.

"June!" he cried, his voice a mixture of amusement and exasperation. June grinned even wider before taking off in the other direction, her short legs unbelievably fast. A sound escaped Zeke that might have been a laugh or a sigh, and he took off after the retreating figure.

"I'll catch up with you in a minute!" he called over his shoulder.

My eyes widened again at the prospect of being left alone in this new place, but my nerves were broken when Alexandra began laughing beside me. "Kids," she said with a shake of her head.

Now that she was smiling and not in danger of hexing me into a frog, I saw that she had a very pleasant face, not unlike my own mother's. Her eyes were bright as she took my arm and led me toward one of the stone cottages. "Come, I'll make you some tea."

The cottage was warm, the already lit fireplace radiating heat throughout the large room. The corner of the open space had to be their kitchen, with wooden cabinets lining the far wall and a stone basin in the center of one that I could only assume was meant to be a sink. There was no spout built into the countertop though, and I wondered where the water would come from.

A large table and six chairs occupied the middle of the room, and the furniture was both modern and ancient. I couldn't imagine that the engravings and swirls etched into the wood were handmade, but I realized they had to be. It wasn't like they could stroll into a furniture store when they had secluded themselves from the rest of the world.

The rest of the room was furnished with a wooden rocking chair, a plump chair with leather stretched over the seat and back, and a makeshift couch. The couch was covered in leather pieces sewn together, with a few gray feathers peeking out of the corners. On its surface lounged an ancient-looking woman, the lines in her face as deep as the etchings on the wooden chairs.

I hadn't remembered seeing the woman in the crowd when I arrived, but still she smiled at me as if she already knew who I was.

"Hello Cami," the woman greeted me. I didn't know if I was more surprised that she already knew my name, or that her voice was almost musical rather than the croak that befit her frail form. "It's about time that boy brought you home to meet us."

I exchanged a glance with Alexandra, but she simply rolled her eyes and strode to a cabinet to grab some mugs. Was the woman expecting a response to that?

"Nice to meet you, er..." The woman smiled widely at me, showing perfectly white teeth that belonged in a body eighty years younger.

Alexandra still had her back to me, but she spoke lazily over her shoulder. "This is my mother, Lucinda." She turned and carried two steaming mugs over to us, handing one to me and setting the other on the tree stump table next to Lucinda's head. I didn't know where the water had come from, or how she had heated it so quickly when it didn't appear they owned a stove.

Magic, I reminded myself. Things were done differently here.

I nodded my head at Zeke's grandmother, trying not to wonder how she knew about me when Zeke said he hadn't told anyone yet. I took my place in the stuffed leather chair after Alexandra gestured for me to have a seat. She lowered herself into the rocking chair, giving us the image of a normal family sitting around to chat. The seat was surprisingly comfortable, and I sipped the steaming tea to give my hands something to do.

After a moment of silent rocking, Alexandra broke the silence. "I suppose he's told you everything then?" Her eyes were tired, her movements slow.

I shrugged my shoulders. "I think so." How would I know if there was more to tell? "He told me what happened a hundred years ago, why you guys live secluded out here. He told me that you all are witches."

Lucinda barked out a laugh and Alexandra pursed her lips, as if she too were trying to reign in her laughter.

"Witches?" She got out, no longer trying to hide her smile. "He used that word?"

I thought back to my conversations with Zeke. He had never explicitly called himself a witch, I reasoned. I had come up with that term myself. Fear shot through me as I considered the possibility that I had just offended them greatly, but Alexandra just chuckled.

"We're magic wielders," she said simply. "You humans feel the need to label everything. We are what we are, and that's that."

There was that word again, *human*, as if she wasn't one. But why wouldn't we try to label or give a name to everything? It made things clearer, helped minimize confusion. I nodded my head at her but held my tongue.

Lucinda worked herself into a sitting position and her blue eyes swept through me. "Did he tell you about the curse?"

I hesitated before nodding solemnly. It was probably best they knew I was aware of their predicament, that I knew they couldn't truly hurt me. Alexandra stopped rocking in her chair and cupped her neck with one of her long-fingered hands.

"I suppose he has told you everything, then," she mused. But there was a twinkle in her eye I couldn't ignore, as if *she* were the one keeping secrets.

The front door opened with a bang and June ran inside, followed quickly by her older brother. Their faces were red and bright and they breathed heavily from whatever chase had just ensued. The girl cornered herself in the kitchen. Zeke grabbed her playfully, rubbing his knuckles over the top of her wavy black hair.

"Mom!" she shrieked, clawing at Zeke's hands. Before his mother could intervene, Zeke laughed and let her go, leaving her hair in a tangled mess.

"If you don't want him to retaliate, don't attack him in the first place." Alexandra sighed. I had a feeling this might be a normal routine for all of them.

"But look at my hair!" she wailed, trying to flatten the curly mess. "The Ceremony starts in an hour!"

Zeke poked her in the stomach, and she slapped his hand away half-heartedly.

"I'll fix your hair, Juniper." Her mother sighed again. "Although I don't really know what the point is. You always look like a wild thing with the way you handle yourself, and everyone's come to expect it."

June stuck her tongue out at Zeke and escaped through a door that I assumed led to a bedroom. Alexandra followed her, shooting Zeke a pointed look. "Behave yourself tonight and try not to torment her anymore. Tonight is meant to be special."

Zeke smiled at me and came over to sit next to his grandmother on the couch. I gazed at the doorway his mom and sister had disappeared through.

"What's tonight?" I asked, interested.

Zeke's eyes were bright. "The Blossoming Ceremony."

The words held a weight to them, an intensity I could feel as a living thing. I didn't know what the Blossoming Ceremony was, or what it would entail, but something told me it was sacred. I couldn't believe he had brought me along to witness it and wasn't sure if I was prepared.

"I suppose he hasn't told you everything then." Lucinda smiled at me and winked.

I absolutely wasn't prepared for this.

As far as I could tell, the Blossoming Ceremony consisted of everyone over the age of twelve gathering in the middle of the meadow to stand around the enormous fire pit. I wondered why they would ever need a fire large enough to burn a small building. They piled enough firewood to create a beacon visible from space, and then added even more.

The darker, paranoid part of me imagined they were making preparations to offer a sacrifice to whatever entity granted them their power. What could serve as a better sacrifice than the unsuspecting human that had wandered into their midst? I shuddered as I thought of the men binding me to the wood, Alexandra smiling as she sparked the flame at my feet. I clung to Zeke and tried to keep my eyes away from the pillar after that.

Before the Ceremony could begin, every face was painted in an array of swirls and colors. The faces of the elderly were brushed with a light hand and left them somehow appearing younger and more innocent. The younger members like Zeke were covered head to toe in angry sweeps of color, the vivid brush strokes transforming them into something fierce and sinister. They looked like warriors, and I couldn't help feeling once again like I was caught within a tribe of Natives.

My face was thankfully spared from the young women running around the camp with their bowls of pigment. The only adornment they bestowed on me was a single white lily to tuck behind my ear. As I observed the colorful faces around me, I noticed all of the women were given a flower to wear. Only June was wreathed in a necklace of flowers, their blossoms layered on so thick that the top petals brushed her chin.

I stood to the side as Zeke's people moved in graceful, fluid movements to build the foundation of the fire. The men handled most of the large pieces of wood, but even the women worked together to carry bundles of sticks and deposit them at the pillar's base. It had to be taxing work, but none of them bothered to use their magic to aid in the process. Perhaps flying heavy logs through the air was more difficult than the feather-like weight of a paper bird, but something told me they were preserving their abilities for a different reason.

I continued to clutch Zeke's arm as if he might float away and leave me with the intimidating faces before me. I had a feeling that the son of the Coven Leader should probably be helping with the preparations of the Ceremony. But as the minutes ticked by, no one looked our way with any signs of hatred or annoyance at his lack of assistance. I wondered again at how easily I had been accepted into their group.

"Zeke," I whispered hoarsely. He turned his head toward me in question. His eyes were bright, almost glowing in contrast to the dark paint coating his face.

"What did you say to your mom when we first got here?" I swallowed as I remembered the tension in the group, the rage that rolled off them in waves with Alexandra riding the crest. After Zeke spoke to his mother in private, it was like a storm had been quieted, returning the water to a smooth, rippling tide. His people had even smiled at me after that.

"How did you get them to accept me?"

Zeke was silent as he took in the curiosity in my eyes, the fear concealed mere inches behind it. The sun was completely down now, and the firelight from the torches encircling us danced across his painted face. I couldn't tell if the shadows beneath his eyes were a trick of the light or something else.

As if making a split-second decision, the shadows vanished. "I told them the truth," he said with a smile. The sudden appearance of his white teeth was a little unsettling. I hoped that painting faces wasn't a routine for them, but at least his eyes were the same. I could focus on them.

I shook my head, bringing myself back to our conversation. What *was* the truth? That he cared about me, possibly even loved me? It surely couldn't be that easy. Zeke was a teenager, after all, and he had brought home the first human girl he'd set eyes on. If it had been me that broke a rule so sacred in our household, I was pretty sure my mom would still be lecturing me now, hours after the fact. Not to mention the possibility of her skinning me alive.

No, there had to be something else going on that Zeke wasn't telling me. I wanted to trust him, but so much of his life remained shrouded in mystery. What if there were more secrets, ones that could impact me, despite Alexandra and Lucinda claiming I knew everything? I couldn't help feeling like he was keeping something from me, something big.

My thoughts were interrupted by a squeeze of Zeke's hand. I looked up and saw that the wooden pillar was complete, finally deemed grand enough by the people who stood around it. The silence in the meadow was deafening, the absence of the witches' idle chatter pressing on my ears and leaving a static energy to hang in its wake.

I followed the eyes that loomed out of the painted faces around me. Their gazes were fixed on Alexandra. She stood at the head of the circle, near the only bare space that prevented the ring from closing. Her hand rested on June's shoulder, whose tiny frame quivered at the massive pillar set before her. It had yet to be lit, and in the growing darkness June's white face stood out from the crowd. The only colors that marred it were the two solid red lines painted just below her eyes.

"It has been three years since our last Blossoming Ceremony. Three years since our own Marcus Wolfe received his rite." Alexandra's voice boomed, slicing through the silence. I jumped next to Zeke, and he squeezed my hand again reassuringly. The eyes of the crowd shifted to a teenage boy positioned a few people to my left. He smiled slightly and bowed his head, his eyes closing and wreathing his face in darkness.

"Now we gather again to witness the Blossoming of Juniper Rivers. She will take her place in our community from this day forward as an equal." Alexandra gazed down at June, pride and admiration brightening her eyes. June lifted her chin slightly, and the flowers on her chest settled as she evened her breathing.

"Juniper, will you accept the inheritance your ancestors have promised you?" she asked. "Will you keep it, nourish it, and wield it only for the good of your people?"

June stared ahead, her gaze fixed on the flameless pillar.

"I will," she said firmly.

Alexandra smiled and let her hand fall from her daughter's shoulder before grasping the torch that was lit behind her. The flame licked at the air as she carried it forward, as if it could taste the fuel of the wood before she set it lightly against the foundation of the pyre.

It took only a moment for the fire to climb up and down the length of the column, growing twenty feet high in a matter of seconds. I squinted my eyes against the burning light but forced them open a crack to watch as the fire roared to life. It was the most magnificent thing I had ever seen. The flames were alive, a power so hot and hungry that I could feel the cracking of the wood deep within my bones. They swirled around the pillar with no regards to nature, transforming into shapes and beings that danced along the wood only long enough to be engulfed by another flame that flourished to take its place.

I stared in awe at the fire's cruel beauty and could feel my reverence echoed in the souls around me. When I tore my attention away from the fire to look up at Zeke, I finally understood why they had taken the time to paint their faces and bodies.

In the light of the blaze, the colors on Zeke's arms swirled and danced in time with the flames. As my eyes traveled upwards, I watched the phantom flames that licked around his neck and face. His blue eyes shone, two solid stones of ice that were impenetrable against the heat of the inferno. I didn't cringe as I beheld the inhuman face before me. He was as magnificent as the fire. He was *one* with the fire, I realized. Just as every person standing in that ring was one with another.

Alexandra reclaimed her place at the edge of the circle, the torch already consumed and contributing to the blaze. As she turned to look back, the ring shifted ever so slightly to fill in the gaps around her and June, adding them officially to our ranks.

"Before Juniper can receive her birthright, she must partake in the Wisdom Revealing." The fire was mirrored in Alexandra's eyes as she spoke. "To prepare for the future, we must acknowledge and accept our past."

Without speaking, Alexandra allowed her arms to fall to her sides before she carefully grasped the left hand of June and the right hand of Lucinda, who flanked her other side. Immediately, all around the circle the witches linked hands. I could see no order in their placements, the old linking with the young in places and the young linking the young in others.

I realized as the circle closed on either side of me that I was the only one left, the only gap preventing the ring from completion. Zeke held my left hand, and to my right a witch reached for me, her blonde hair turned orange in the light of the fire.

I hesitated and looked at Zeke. Surely I wasn't allowed to do *this*? When Zeke said I would watch the Ceremony, I thought I would be standing on the sidelines, observing from afar like the outsider that I was. But here I stood in the middle of all the action, seemingly one of them. Like there truly was nothing he would hide from me.

Zeke nodded his head slightly, and I accepted the witch's hand.

I felt their power immediately. It began as a gentle humming in both my hands, radiating from Zeke and the blonde witch like a quiet sigh of air. It traveled up my arms and down my legs, encompassing my body with its caress. As it moved, it transformed from a dull humming into a solid *thrum,* pulsing through my veins as if charged by the beat of my heart. There was drumming in my ears, and I wondered if it was echoing my ever-increasing heartbeat or if it was somehow placed there by the magic that flowed through my being. When Zeke's hand began squeezing mine gently in time to the beat, I knew everyone must be hearing the same thing.

Through the link of the witches' hands, I could feel the presence of every individual in the circle. To my left, Zeke seemed to emit a woodsy, smoky aura, so similar to his scent that I had come to recognize and love. The presence of the witch to my right felt crisper, like a freshly sliced apple or orange. All around the circle, I could feel the semblance of every person through this strange new connection. I realized that while I might not possess any magic of my own, my body could act as a conductor, allowing the magic to pass through me and enter the next available source.

The magic warmed my body in a way the fire could not. It trickled through my veins like honey, cocooning me in its warm, golden web. I closed my eyes out of instinct, allowing the energy to take over.

I heard Alexandra's voice as if she were calling through a long tunnel. Whether she spoke out loud or directly into my mind, I didn't know. I didn't care. There was nothing in the world at that moment but the thrum of the magic in my veins, the steady beat of the drum in my ears, and the soft pulsing of Zeke's hand that kept me tethered to the earth.

"These images have been passed down, generation to generation. It is our charge to keep them, share them, and remember just how far we've come."

Her voice was melodic, swirling around my head. But I didn't have a head, did I? My body was gone. I was nothing but darkness and heat, the drumbeats filling the void and echoing around my mind until my head contained nothing but its rhythm. A squeeze from somewhere to my left pulled me back, reminding me I was still alive.

Out of the darkness came a vision. A young girl who looked a lot like June, her black hair tied back in a delicate braid. Her nose was a little too long and her eyebrows wider than June's, but they could easily have been sisters.

She was alone in the darkness, but her eyes were focused ahead of her, concentrating on something not too far away. Slowly, she raised her arms, her palms facing forward and revealing long, white fingers. The darkness erupted in light as a fire sparked to life in front of her. It was the first fire, I somehow knew. The first act of magic since the beginning of Zeke's people. The girl's eyes softened, and she smiled shyly before disappearing in a wisp of smoke.

Out of the darkness again came another face. A man, looking to be in his mid-thirties. Unlike the girl's eyes, which had been full of innocence, this man's eyes were cunning, concealing a darkness that rivaled the blackness on either side of him. There was a hunger there, like he hadn't eaten in weeks and was finally staring down a three-course meal.

"No, please. Don't!"

The voice echoed down the tunnel of my mind, its carrier standing just outside of my view, shrouded somewhere in the blackness. The man smiled; rather, he showed his teeth in a malicious grin. If my stomach had been present, it would have clenched at the sight of those teeth, a chill grazing my spine.

The man opened his mouth and spoke in a language I didn't recognize, one that possibly wasn't of this world. There was a cry as something happened to the person who had begged for mercy. I was suddenly thankful that I couldn't see him, couldn't see whatever was causing him to make such a guttural noise.

The man smiled at his handiwork, his cold black eyes satisfied for an instant. And then his eyes widened, and he too was screaming as his body folded in on itself. I could hear the breaking and crunching of his bones as his arms snapped inward, his legs collapsing and bending at odd angles.

My mind flinched as he screamed and screamed, and just when I thought it would never end, his voice vanished. So did his body. The thing that was left in his wake was five feet long and slithered along the ground. Its scales were the deepest blue, almost black, and it opened its mouth to bare its fangs at me. The snake raised itself up and hissed.

And then he disappeared, just like the girl who had preceded him. I embraced the darkness that filled his void, so grateful that the scene was over. But I could feel something else lingering in the darkness. It paused at the edge of my vision, like it was only waiting a moment for me to catch my breath.

I didn't want to know what new horrors might be hiding in those shadows, didn't want to watch another person get disfigured before me. I didn't know if I could handle it. But then there was that pressure again somewhere to my left, a comforting squeeze reminding me I wasn't alone. *Just one more*, it said. *You can do this.*

I nodded my head, or tried to anyway. It wasn't like I had a choice. This "Wisdom Revealing" would run its course, and I would be a prisoner to the darkness and those two hands that held mine until they saw fit to release me.

The final vision took its form around me, this one different from the others. There was no blackness, no single person to dominate the dream. I was looking through the eyes of someone that was much taller than me, the increased distance to the ground at first making me queasy.

I stood in a large house that had been well taken care of. *My house*, I quickly realized. The wallpaper was bright and unfaded, the rich wooden floor shining as I rushed through the living room to grab various objects scattered about. A jacket draped across the couch; a leather bag filled with supplies.

The floorboards didn't squeak.

"Hurry!" I shouted at someone in another room. My voice was deep, definitely male. *"We have to leave now!"*

I heard footsteps pounding down the stairs, followed by the wailing of a baby. I met them at the bottom step. The woman couldn't have been older than twenty, her cheeks flushed and her eyes bright as she bounced the baby on her hip. Her steely blue eyes and black hair were all too familiar, even if this memory was a hundred years old.

I urged the woman in front of me out the door and onto the front porch, keeping pace beside her while we ran straight for the line of trees. Without the walls of the house to drown them out, shouting assaulted my ears from every direction. There were men and women everywhere, some screaming and crying, others pulling children by their arms as they too headed for the cover of the forest.

It was just after dusk, the sky forfeiting the last of the sun's dying glow. In the ever-growing darkness, the torch flames were easy to make out as they chased the people mercilessly into the woods.

"Satan worshipers!" they shouted at us. *"Kill the evil, blot them out!"*

Even louder than the shouting were the gunshots, cracking through the air and filling my nostrils with their acrid smoke. I couldn't turn to see where they came from, couldn't look to see who had fallen. We reached the trees and joined the throng in our flight to escape, the flames of the torches a blur all around us.

I ran deeper and deeper into the woods, shouting at my people to follow me. But the torches were closing in, and we were so outnumbered. We were all going to perish by the hands of people we had believed to be our friends.

They circled around us now, and I knew there was no chance to escape. My head spun as I tried to find a solution, something that would get us all out of here alive. But she had already figured it out for me.

"Take Lucy," my wife commanded. Before I could protest, she was pushing the little crying ball into my arms and turning to face our pursuers. I understood what was happening a second too late.

"No!"

The woman spread out her arms and screamed an incantation that was just audible over the shouts and distant gunfire. All around us the torches dropped to the ground as their wielders gave up their lives. Lucy hushed in my arms, and we both stared at her mother and the sacrifice she'd just made for us. She turned back to look at me, to allow me to stare into her face one final time.

"Go," she breathed, and I knew it would be the last word she'd ever speak.

Clutching my daughter tightly, I gathered the few of us that remained and trekked deeper into the woods. I distantly became aware of the animals that joined our ranks but didn't pause to welcome them. Their sacrifices couldn't be in vain.

I pushed my people onward until the humans held no chance of tracking us. I inspected the faces of those around me, noting the dirt and tears that stained their bodies and faces. I eyed them all gravely as we silently agreed as one. This atrocity would *never* befall us again.

I was jerked out of the mind of Zeke's great-grandfather like being ripped out of the clutches of a nightmare. And a nightmare was exactly what I had just escaped from. I could still feel the ache in my arms and legs from running miles through the forest, could still hear the baby wailing as her mother was left behind to become something else.

Lucinda, I realized. The baby had been Zeke's grandmother. I looked over at her discreetly and noticed a single tear had fallen onto her cheek.

Beside her, Alexandra bowed her head in respect for the ones who had fallen. All around me, the witches bowed their heads in turn.

June lifted her face first and stepped forward into the ring, the hands of Alexandra and the man to her right falling limply to their sides. As soon as their contact was broken, I felt the energy dissipate out of me, its warmth returning to whatever or whoever it had come from. I shivered slightly as the cool night air swept around me.

The fire still burned brightly, towering over us with a height that suggested we had only been in that dark place for a minute. I felt like I'd been standing there for hours, though, and within that time I'd somehow managed to age a few decades.

June approached the fire with determination in her eyes. She walked right up to it, so close I was afraid its intense heat would burn her. Silently, she stretched out her hand, as if she planned on petting the flames.

The fire obeyed her call and fell quietly into a pile of ash at her feet. There was no trace of the wood that had towered above only moments ago, no lingering smoke to scent my nostrils. June clenched her fist, and the flames of the torches around us snuffed out as well, leaving us in utter darkness.

Chapter Sixteen

I slept fitfully that night, my dreams a swirl of painted faces, dancing fires, and screams of people I knew to be dead. I didn't remember Zeke taking me home. I couldn't remember anything after June quenched the fire and absorbed whatever magic had writhed within it.

There was only a breath of a memory—warm hands easing me into my bed before lightly brushing the hair out of my face.

Sleep well, Cami. Then there was a gentle pressure on my hand as something thin and folded was pressed into it.

I tossed back the comforter and searched through the blankets. There, under my pillow, I found the latest letter. The old paper was folded not into a bird this time, but was rounded at the bottom with three uneven spikes pointing at the top. A flame.

Mid-morning sunlight streamed in through the open curtains, and I glanced out at the trees before leaning back and opening it to read.

> Good morning, Beautiful.
>
> I hope you slept well after the adventure you had last night.
>
> I have to say, you are the strongest and bravest young woman I have ever met.
>
> You continue to astound me.
>
> Try to get some rest today. You'll need some time to recover, but after last night's proceedings I

think it's safe to say you can handle almost anything.

I'll be waiting in the woods when you get out of school on Monday.

Until then... :)

Love,
Z

I smiled and hugged his words to my chest. I *astounded* him. Had anyone ever thought of me as astounding? Before I met Zeke, I'd been the most boring teenager on the planet. No one in their right mind would ever have called me special. But now?

Now I was secretly dating a witch who lived off the grid, within a coven in the forest concealed by enchantments. Maybe dating wasn't the right word. We hadn't even kissed for goodness' sake. But it had been clear from the beginning that this relationship would be something more than friendship. It was probably my fault we hadn't progressed into something more yet.

I wouldn't let myself feel guilty for wanting to take things slow. I needed to let my mind handle one new thing at a time. First, that magic existed. Second, that there was a group of witches hiding out in the wilderness a few miles from my town. And lastly, that one of those witches somehow held feelings for *me* of all people. A girl could only handle so much at once.

I thought back to everything I'd witnessed the previous night. It had been shocking, overwhelming even, but I *had* handled it. And perhaps that was why Zeke thought I was astounding. I hadn't turned away from him and run screaming into the woods after all was said and done. I'd held my own, watching those horrific visions along with everyone else.

I could almost feel a trace of the magic that had flowed through my veins, a ghost of the power that dominated the ceremony. It was like a buzz, a weird magical hangover or something. I felt giddy and light, and knew I was probably smiling like an idiot as I emerged from my bed and began dressing for the day.

The stupid grin was still plastered on my face as I skipped down the stairs and glided into the kitchen. My mom was seated at the bar, a mug of coffee in one hand and a book in the other.

"Good morning," I sang lightly, cruising past her. I hunted in the cabinets for my water boiler and favorite mug before brewing the tea. Did I really need caffeine in my already jittery state? Probably not, but I was doing what I wanted to these days.

I heard the book and coffee mug as they were set carefully down on the breakfast bar. I could feel my mom's eyes as she stared at my back, possibly wondering what euphoric creature had possessed her daughter. I tried to reign in my smile before turning to face her.

"Did you have a good evening?" I asked.

She eyed me suspiciously and cocked her head slightly. Obviously, *I* was the one who had the good evening. Her expression was too funny, and I couldn't stop myself from grinning again.

"Yes," she said slowly. Her eyes were narrowed slightly, but I couldn't imagine what she could be upset about this early in the morning. "I take it you had a good time with Natalie last night?"

Natalie? I racked my brain as I tried to figure out what she was talking about. Oh right, Natalie and I had "gone to the movies" last night, and that was why I'd gotten home late. My eyes widened before I hurried to catch up, nodding my head a little too enthusiastically in my attempt to appear like everything was normal.

"Oh yeah, we had a great time!"

She was still looking at me skeptically, and I turned around again as my water came to a boil. Darn my horrible lying skills. She absolutely knew something was up.

"Huh," she said casually, and I heard the mug grate across the bar's surface before she raised it again to her lips. "That's interesting, because I ran into her at G.G.'s Oil last night."

I froze, my hands clutching the steaming boiler an inch from the cup. *Crap, crap, crap!*

"She told me to tell you to feel better."

Why did we have to live in a town with only one gas station? A town so small that it was nearly impossible *not* to run into everyone you know on a daily basis. How was a girl supposed to keep any secrets around here?

"It looks to me like you're feeling *much* better."

She sipped her coffee loudly, obnoxiously. Holding my breath, I set the boiler carefully on the countertop and turned to face her. Half of her face was concealed by the coffee mug, but she had one eyebrow raised and her eyes pinned me with a stare that screamed, *Gotcha!* I was sure my own face resembled a deer in headlights.

"I'm sorry," I mumbled. It was rare that I lied to my mother, and even more rare for me to get caught. How was this conversation supposed to go? Perhaps I should get on my knees and beg for forgiveness now.

Lowering the mug at last, her lips were pressed tightly together, as if she were trying not to smile. She was *smug*, I realized. As if catching me in a lie was an impossible feat, but Super Mom held the victory.

"Are you going to tell me what you did instead?"

I pressed my own lips together to hide my smile. Sure, I could tell her exactly where I'd been. In the middle of the Cursed Woods, meeting a group of magic wielders and participating in an ancient Ceremony as my witch boyfriend's little sister came into her birthright. The story sounded so ridiculous in my head I knew I'd be in even more trouble for trying to tell the truth. But I was exhausted from last night's endeavors, and it was too early in the morning to fabricate another lie anyway. So I stared at her in silence.

She brought her arm up to the bar and rested her chin on her knuckles.

"Were you with a boy?"

My eyes widened a fraction more. *How does she do that?* Super Mom, indeed. Then again, I was a seventeen-year-old girl who had ditched her friend and lied to her mom to free her schedule for something else. If I wasn't hanging out with a boy, then I was probably doing something worse, like drugs. Maybe I should just cut my losses and let her know half the truth before she started demanding that I pee in a cup.

I nodded my head once. Twice. I crossed my fingers that this scrap of truth wouldn't backfire on me, that she wouldn't insist on meeting him and his parents immediately. I wondered who would win the staring match between my mom and Alexandra if no magic was involved.

She removed her hand and used it to take another swig of coffee.

"And I assume you aren't going to tell me his name?"

The coffee mug couldn't completely hide her smile. Her eyes were down, but I had a feeling they were dancing. I shook my head slightly, knowing she'd catch the movement.

After a full minute of hiding behind her mug, she set it down again at last.

"Okay," she said.

Okay? What did she mean by that?

"Next time, at least tell me where you're going, please. And I expect you home before midnight."

I gawked at her, my mouth hanging open. A reprieve. First Zeke's mom and community had let us off easy, and now my own mother. Was there something in the air? Perhaps the universe was finally giving me a break after all I had endured in the last few months. Whatever the reason was, I grabbed onto it like a life vest.

"Thank you," I choked out. I met her eyes briefly before making my escape, before she changed her mind and began questioning me further. I left the makings of my tea behind in my hurry to flee, deciding that caffeine really wouldn't do me any favors in my hyped-up state. I'd go back and clean it up later, when the coast was clear.

I spent the day catching up on homework and studying for the history exam that would be given first thing Monday morning. I texted Natalie and Michael about nothing in particular, enjoying the periodic distractions from my schoolwork. And every so often I found myself staring out the window at the trees, wondering what Zeke and his family might be doing, and imagining that I was there with them.

I woke up early Monday morning, as though my body knew it would be a good day and couldn't wait to jump into it. I was ready for my exam, or as ready as I would ever be. The days of dreading school were behind me. I wasn't the awkward new girl anymore, but a girl with friends and a clique I felt I actually belonged to. I looked forward to Natalie and Jason's banter, Taylor's quiet smiles, and Carly's dreamy and somewhat amusing demeanor.

It was easy to spend eight hours in an environment I was comfortable in, where I could exchange glances with Natalie behind the teacher's back and roll my eyes at Jason when he pretended to fall asleep in a particularly boring lecture. I knew those eight hours would fly by, and then I'd be free to meet Zeke right behind my house.

I wondered what he had in store for us today. Would we walk around the woods and talk like we usually did, or would he take me back to his home? Now that I knew his family didn't want to hex me, I wanted to get to know his sister better, his friends. I wanted to experience more things with him and finally learn all about the secluded life he lived.

I tried to focus on my other life as Natalie and I quizzed each other on the drive to school. I filed Zeke away, shoving those thoughts into a locked section of my mind that emitted a smokey, woodsy scent. Later. I would turn the key to that door later.

Four hours later, I crammed my bookbag into my locker and walked arm and arm to lunch with Natalie. Half of the school day down, and only a few more periods to go. I felt confident I had at least scored a B on my exam, and the rest of the day should have been downhill sailing from there.

Then we walked into the cafeteria, and my stomach dropped.

I could feel the change in the atmosphere immediately. Kids were huddled in groups and whispering rather than laughing and shouting at each other across the lunch tables. There was a weight pressing down on the room, and icy tendrils ran up my spine. Something had happened, something bad.

I exchanged a glance with Natalie, whose eyes were wide.

"What's going on?" I whispered. I kept my voice low, mimicking the hushed tones of my classmates and even teachers who were huddling quietly at their own tables.

Natalie shrugged her shoulders, and we unlinked our arms. The food line was silent as we accepted our burgers and fries, but I thought the lunch lady's eyes were sad as she handed me the meal. Jason motioned to us from across the room and we hurried to join the rest of our friends.

We had barely taken our seats when Jason launched into an explanation.

"Another girl's been murdered."

My blood ran cold at Jason's words.

Another girl killed only three weeks after the disappearance of Heather Reed. We all leaned across the table, mirroring the huddles of students that populated the lunchroom.

"Who was it?" Natalie whispered. In my already shocked state, I barely recognized how softly she spoke. My obnoxious, loud friend was gracing us with her rarely used quiet voice. I knew then that she was scared.

"Jessie York," he breathed.

Natalie and Carly gasped. I didn't know this girl, of course, but I'd heard the name York mentioned before. I followed Jason and Taylor's eyes to a group of seniors sitting a few tables away. It was the brainy group, the handful of kids I'd seen eating their lunches absently while they read huge novels under the table. There were no books to be seen now, though, and a few of the girls appeared to be crying. I counted their number and noticed someone was missing.

"Erin York's older sister," Jason went on, and I realized who the vacant seat must have belonged to. Her table of friends seemed too dark, almost drab looking without her mass of red curls lighting up the group. "She was pulled from P.E. last period. Apparently the body was found this morning."

The body. Jessie York, Erin's sister, wasn't found this morning. Her body was. That was what happened when someone died. You began to talk about them in the past tense, and eventually accepted the fact that your loved one was no more.

It wasn't Jessie they would bury in the ground, it was her body, her husk. Jessie was already gone. *Just like my father.*

I steered away from that thought, focusing on the matter at hand.

"Where did they find her?"

Jason grimaced at my question, and I knew he found no enjoyment in sharing this news with us. Natalie had reveled in sharing the story of Heather's disappearance when it was new and exciting, but based on the green shade of her face, I had a feeling she wouldn't be talking about either girl for a while. Not now that there were two. Not when she realized the danger was *real*.

"She's a sophomore at the Community College, but she works part time at G.G.'s Oil. Apparently she was working there late last night and never came home." He took a steadying breath.

"They found her in the dumpster behind the building."

My stomach flopped again. *Tossed in the dumpster like a piece of trash.* What kind of monster did that sort of thing? I didn't want to think about what state her body might have been in, what sort of things were done to her before her life was finally snuffed out.

There would be no lingering doubts regarding what had happened to Heather. She was dead, most likely discarded in the same way Jessie had been. It was only a matter of time before her body showed up too. Her parents would refuse to accept it for a while, clinging to the hope that she'd simply run off or had amnesia like in some cheesy soap opera before remembering who she was and finally finding her way home.

But she wasn't coming home. I knew this because I'd come to know the world we lived in. It was dark, it was ugly, and it didn't hesitate in ripping our loved ones away from us.

For the rest of the lunch period, I listened to people reminisce about Jessie. *She was such a quiet girl. Always minded her own business. She was the perfect daughter and sister. Remember when she gave that freshman her lunch because he didn't have any money? She was good. She will be missed.*

When the bell sounded, I followed Natalie out of the cafeteria and down the hall that led to our lockers. I felt like I was in a trance, and just focused on placing one foot in front of the other. I was dimly aware of the sluggish movements of the students around me. We were all zombies today.

As we neared the row of navy-blue lockers, Natalie nudged me with her elbow and brought me back to reality. I looked up to see a large group of kids huddling around one of the lockers. The murmuring of the students was a low buzz in my ears, and I watched as newcomers pushed past each other to get a look at whatever was holding everyone's attention. I realized with a start that they were looking at *my* locker.

Natalie must have noticed it at the same time, because at that moment she grabbed my arm and began pushing her way through the throng. As we waded through the sea of students, I felt them go silent around me. It might have been my imagination, but I swore a few of them cringed away from me when they recognized my face.

At last we reached my locker, and I froze with Natalie's arm around mine. I didn't have to turn around to know we weren't in the middle of the mob anymore. I could feel the empty space around me like an electric field, could hear the unified breaths of the students hovering six feet away, giving me a wide berth. Like I had the plague.

Newspaper clippings were taped all over my locker door, adorning the blue metal in an array of gray. My heart stopped in my chest as I recognized the articles cut straight out of the Plainfield Daily Post. I felt them then, the eyes burning into me from every direction. They stared out of the student body I'd finally been accepted into, my best friend who had dropped my arm, and also out of the flat, black eyes of the victims who smiled upon my locker door.

I took in the faces of Amelia Piper and Nathan Miles, their junior yearbook photos a grainy blur. And then there was my father, his photo taken from a fishing trip we went on just last summer. His eyes were somehow warm, as if the black and white photo had failed to leach all the life out of him. As if the article below his gaze stating exactly what he'd done was no more than a bad dream.

This was a bad dream. This had to be a nightmare. Because my past was supposed to be behind me, was supposed to stay in Plainfield where it belonged. I hadn't received any hateful text messages in weeks. I thought my old classmates had gotten bored, had perhaps moved on to bullying someone else since I was no longer around. I was so wrong.

Hands reached out and began clawing at the locker door, ripping and shredding at the evidence. My hands, pale white against the gray, inky paper. They shook in my struggle to hide the articles, even as bits and pieces clung to the cold metal as the tape held on.

My fingernails scraped against the blue paint. I had to get rid of all of it. There couldn't be a single piece of gray left to remind me of what I was, what my father had made me a part of. *Worthless, alcoholic family*.

I was down to a single piece of tape that was refusing to let go. The papers were balled in a fist I had pressed against the cold steel, but that stubborn piece of tape was laughing at me, just like the students were probably laughing at my back from the safety of their group, the safety of their numbers.

Quietly, another set of hands began working away at the tape. Her hot pink fingernails made quick work of it, and then they were around me, pulling me in for a tight hug. It was only then that I realized I was crying.

I couldn't hug her back, though. Even as the bell rang again and the students behind us dispersed, I stood rigid and unmoving as she squeezed me to her chest. I couldn't look at Natalie, at my new best friend who'd accepted me without question. She had a normal life in this tiny town, had normal parents and a sister and a family that would never be broken. How could she continue to hug me with the new knowledge that I was tainted?

Shame washed over me, hot and familiar. I was going to ruin her social standing, just like I ruined Michael's. Destroying things was a skill my family excelled at.

Footsteps echoed down the now vacant hallway. It was probably a teacher, ready to hand out detentions for hanging around my locker when class had already started. That would just be the cherry on top of my perfect day. It was mere hours ago I had risen from bed with the foresight that today would be a good day. How naive I had been. You weren't allowed to have good days when your father was a murderous drunk. Somehow, I'd forgotten that.

"Cami?" A male voice called. The footsteps picked up as the caller jogged to my side.

I was shaking at that point, my sobs stuck in my throat. I scrunched my eyes closed tight, believing for a moment that if I couldn't see the papers and the judgmental faces of my peers then they didn't exist. Like a toddler, if I couldn't see them then they wouldn't see me. And that was all I wanted at the moment, to never be seen again.

There was whispering as Natalie spoke quietly over my shoulder to our new arrival. A calm, breathy reply. I didn't try to make out their words, knowing they were surely discussing me and my pathetic state. When would I stop being a burden on everyone?

"Go on to class, Miss Morgan. I'll take it from here."

It, like I was simply a situation that needed to be handled. Natalie squeezed my shoulders one final time before releasing me. Through my tears and running nose I could barely make out the scent of my uncle's cologne a moment before I opened my eyes and peered up at him.

His face was thick with sympathy, and something else I had to squint my eyes to make out. Determination, I thought. But at what?

"Come on, hun." He said simply.

His hand was warm and firm on my back as he led me through the school and into the principal's office. I wasn't going to fight the special treatment this time, not when the alternative was attending class in my puffy eyed state, where more probing eyes awaited me.

His office was small and neat. A white, L-shaped desk took up half of the room, its surface covered in neat stacks of paper, a stapler, and a cup holding an assortment of boring black pens. A laptop was open on the far side of the desk and I was startled to see my own face staring out of it.

The picture my uncle had chosen for his background image had been taken five years ago, back when our families still visited each other a few times a year. My twelve-year-old self was sandwiched between my aunt and uncle, my wet hair dripping onto the purple polka dotted bathing suit I'd decided was my favorite that summer. My mother stood on the other side of my aunt, wrapped in a blue cover up and an unnecessarily wide straw hat. My dad must have been the one to take the picture because he was nowhere to be found. His absence in yet another family moment had my eyes streaming all over again.

Uncle Peter led me to the wooden chair in front of his desk and motioned for me to sit. I silently obeyed, my tears now running freely down my face and splattering onto my jeans. With my head down, I could just catch his movement from the corner of my eye as he sank into the office chair on the other side of his desk.

We sat for a moment without speaking. My occasional sniffle and hiccup were the only sounds to break the silence. I could feel his eyes on my face, but he gave me time to pull myself together before sighing quietly.

"Do you want to talk about it?"

Why did adults always think that talking about something would magically make it better? I didn't think my throat could open wide enough to let a single word out, let alone try to explain the situation I had just been in. But my uncle had rescued me, had saved me from walking into class and enduring the stares and whispers that would inevitably follow me everywhere for the rest of the day. The least I owed him was an explanation.

I looked down at my hand and realized I was still clutching remnants of the evidence. Wordlessly, I dropped the ball of wadded up newspaper on the desk and allowed my uncle to sift through it in silence. I watched his hands unravel and smooth out the articles, his deft movements somewhat soothing as I tried to catch my breath. I kept my head down, afraid to meet his eyes and whatever emotion would be displayed there.

"Camille," he said at last.

My eyes finally flicked up to his, but the emotions I saw there weren't the ones I'd been expecting. There was sympathy, yes, but something stronger burned behind it.

"Who the hell did this?" he demanded.

Anger, I thought. The other emotion was anger. I'd steeled myself for the pitying leer I'd come to expect from adults ever since my father died. I hadn't expected him to get angry on my behalf. My chest swelled in appreciation. In my current dejected state, anger was an emotion I could handle.

I shrugged my shoulders. "I don't know." I mumbled. The clippings were taped up during lunch, so anyone could have done it. Perhaps one of my classmates had a friend who went to Plainfield and had waited until now to share the knowledge with the school. I was pretty sure a tiny place like Green Peaks didn't have cameras in the hallways, so unless someone fessed up to the crime it would most likely remain a mystery.

My uncle shook his head.

"I'm going to get to the bottom of this, Cami." He said firmly. "I don't tolerate bullying in my school, and I certainly won't allow it to happen to my own niece."

His voice held the resolve I wished I had in my own heart, and I couldn't help feeling grateful for it. I may have felt defeated, but perhaps I could let my uncle be strong for me. Maybe I didn't have to carry the burden alone.

Uncle Peter sighed again and sat back in his chair.

"This isn't your fault, you know."

His eyes held mine and I felt myself nodding at his words, whether I believed them or not. It wasn't my fault my father had killed those kids, but that didn't stop me from feeling guilty just the same.

I still had two periods left before the final bell would ring, but Uncle Peter didn't make me go back to class. I sat across from him for the remainder of the school day, talking when I felt like it and simply enjoying the silence in between. It was the break I needed and might have been the only thing keeping me from having an actual meltdown in the middle of school.

He offered to drive me home, but I just shook my head. Natalie would be waiting for me, and I knew I couldn't avoid her forever.

When the final bell rang, I nodded at my uncle in thanks and made my way out to the parking lot to wait. It was easier in the open air to pretend people weren't looking my way. The hallway had been suffocating, but out here I could breathe. Natalie never locked her truck, so I sent her a text and climbed into the cab where I could hide.

She must have sprinted across the parking lot, because in thirty seconds she was opening the driver door to join me. Her face was a mask of worry and tears sparkled in her eyes as she drank me in.

"I'm so sorry, Cami." She whispered. Leaning across the cab, she grabbed me in another bone crushing hug, and this one I returned. I should never have doubted her loyalty. It was going to take more than a drunk, dead father to turn Natalie against me. Still, even as I gripped her back, I knew she wasn't the one I needed to be with at that moment. As she drove me home, I felt the pull towards the forest once again, stronger than it had ever been before.

When we arrived in my driveway, I didn't hesitate. I slammed the door behind me and hurried to the back porch where I dropped my backpack in a heap in one of the chairs. I didn't bother going inside, and I didn't care if Natalie was still watching me from the truck. I didn't care about anything except getting to the one person who had the ability to erase everything else from my mind.

I ran towards the tree line, feeling my worries and fears leave me with every step I took. When I finally broke into the woods, he was there waiting for me. My one constant in this relentlessly messed up life of mine.

I didn't stop running until I slammed into his chest, didn't bother to breathe until I felt his arms around me.

"Cami?" Zeke asked in alarm.

There were no words to describe what I was feeling, no way to explain my sudden need to keep him in spite of everything else that was going on. And so I didn't speak as I pulled away just enough to look into his eyes. I didn't say anything before standing on my toes and pulling him down to kiss me.

Chapter Eighteen

I breathed in Zeke's scent, wondering if it was possible to be intoxicated by a person's fragrance.

We were sitting on an overturned tree, my back pressed up against his chest. The bark was covered in a layer of spongy, green moss that created a soft blanket to relax on. I never imagined I could be so comfortable, so at ease in a forest called the Cursed Woods. I also never knew a witch could be so easy to talk to.

"Do you miss him?"

He twirled my hair around his fingers, brushing my shoulders and back lightly. How could someone's touch be so warm and at the same time send goosebumps racing across my skin? If I was a cat, I would have purred.

"Yes," I whispered. His hand made soothing circles on my back, and I leaned into him further.

"Sometimes I wake up smelling coffee and I think for a moment that he'll be waiting at the kitchen table." I shook my head slowly. "But it's always just my mom."

Somehow, it was easy to talk to Zeke about my dad. Painless, even. He had led me away from the forest entrance, down a path only his eyes could see, and eventually eased me onto that log in the heart of the trees. When he brushed away my tears and asked me what had happened, I told him everything. I spilled my soul. I wasn't sure how he understood half of what I said amidst my blubbering, but somehow he caught every word.

"He would have liked you." I said with a smile.

"Oh?"

I turned to look at his face and saw bewilderment there. How could Zeke not know that he was an amazing guy?

"He loved the outdoors. Fishing, camping, hunting. He was a firm believer that when the zombie apocalypse came, our family would know how to survive the elements. You know how to take care of yourself, and that's something he would have respected."

Zeke's eyebrows drew together. "Zombie apocalypse?" He said the words like they tasted funny in his mouth. Of course he had no idea what I was talking about. It was easy to forget that he wasn't a part of my world, that he was secluded from all the pop-culture and references that were created in the last hundred years.

I laughed at the expression on his face. "Don't worry about it."

It was difficult to keep track of time in the woods, where the light filtering in through the leaves always made you feel like it was just after dawn. I didn't know how long we'd been sitting there talking, and a part of me didn't care if I stayed there all night.

This was what I needed. *Zeke* was what I needed. I took another deep breath and relished the air filling my lungs, unburdened by the weight that had pressed on my chest mere hours before. I held onto that moment with Zeke with everything I had left, knowing that when I returned to reality the weight would likely return as well.

Zeke broke the moment by stating what I already knew.

"It's getting late," he whispered into my hair. "You probably need to be getting back." His voice was thick with regret, and I knew he dreaded my departure as much as I did.

I heaved a big sigh and extracted my phone from my jacket pocket to check the time. The screen lit up and displayed the block numbers brightly: 7:05.

Crap. Had we really been talking for three and a half hours? My mom was going to freak. I sat up with a jerk as I noticed the ten text messages and six missed calls. My phone was still set to silent mode from the school day, and my mom was already freaking out. *Double crap.*

I jumped to my feet and spun around to Zeke. "I have to go now." I choked.

His eyes widened as he took in my frantic state. "I'll lead you back."

He gripped my hand and turned towards the direction of my house, but before we could take so much as a single step the shouting reached our ears.

"Ca-mi!"

"Camille!"

"Cami where are you?"

Three sets of voices, one male and two female. I could hear them tromping through the leaves and debris, their steps coming directly at us. I whirled toward Zeke, panic illuminating my face. "My family."

He nodded and pulled me close, crushing me to his body in one final hug. I breathed in his scent again and willed it to be enough to keep my chest and airways open after he was gone. He pressed his lips against my forehead and I shuddered, savoring their softness and warmth.

"Go," he breathed.

Then he was gone, his warmth ripped away from me as painfully as a bandage being removed. My chest tightened immediately, and I stared at the swaying plants and leaves he'd disappeared into. A part of me ached to follow him, to simply leave my family behind and never look back.

"Cami!"

My uncle's voice broke through my pondering and I listened to his heavy breaths as he approached me from behind. I finally turned when he reached me, taking in the relief in his eyes that was only marred by the lingering fear of not knowing where I'd been. He sighed as I faced him at last.

"What are you doing out here?" He heaved between breaths. He had obviously been running, and I felt a twinge of guilt at his distraught state.

"Just hiking," I shrugged.

Uncle Peter finally caught his breath and eyed me suspiciously. "Hiking?"

He inspected the forest behind me, the trees that Zeke had disappeared into seconds before. I kept my gaze on my uncle, forcing myself not to turn and look for Zeke's footprints that might be visible in the soft ground. *There won't be footprints,* I promised myself. Zeke was made from the forest, and he knew how to navigate through it without leaving any traces behind.

I nodded my head, bringing my uncle's attention back to me. He scrutinized my face slowly, his gaze lingering just above my eyebrows. As if he knew Zeke had just kissed me there. *Don't be crazy, he can't know that!* I shook off the thought before paranoia could really set in.

Uncle Peter stared at me a moment longer, searching for an answer to some unspoken question. Then he closed his eyes and sighed, shaking his head slightly.

"Come on Cami, let's get you home."

I gripped the steaming mug of tea, willing it to bring life back into my numb hands. There was nothing to be done about the numbness in my mind, though. The only cure for that was making its way deeper into the Cursed Woods as we spoke.

"What were you thinking?" My mother huffed for what felt like the hundredth time. She had collapsed into the oversized armchair after working a visible path into the carpet by her pacing feet. Her head was in her hands, as if she couldn't stand to look at me now that she knew I was safe.

Aunt Lacey rubbed her shoulders soothingly and pegged me with a glare that said, *this is why I didn't have kids.* I couldn't blame her. Guilt squirmed in my stomach once again for being so selfish as to not consider my mom before disappearing into the woods for hours. I didn't even have the decency to leave a note.

"I'm sorry," I whispered again. It was all I had managed to get out since we'd arrived home and settled into the much-neglected living room.

"You're sorry?" She boomed, finally looking up at me. Behind the well of tears flowing down her face, her eyes were crazed. "I thought you were dead like the others!"

I stared at the floor and tried to breathe around the hole in my chest. From his seat beside me on the couch, my uncle leaned over and placed a soft hand on the back of my neck, squeezing gently.

"She's right, you know," he said in a low voice. "You shouldn't be out in the woods with a killer on the loose. And you certainly should have told your mother where you were going."

I couldn't help hearing my father's voice behind his words. If only my dad had been there, maybe I wouldn't have felt the need to run off after a bad day. Maybe I would have confided in him instead. But, of course, I wouldn't have been bullied in the first place if it wasn't for my father.

I met my mother's gaze again and flinched inwardly. She was *so* mad. I hadn't seen her this upset with me since I'd snuck out when I was fifteen, driving after curfew without a valid license. There had been a boy involved then, too, although I could hardly compare that ember of a relationship to the growing inferno I shared with Zeke.

As if reading my mind, my mom narrowed her eyes at me. "Is this about that boy?" she demanded. "Were you with him in the woods?"

I felt my uncle's hand tighten momentarily on my neck, his nails biting into my skin fractionally. Had he caught a glimpse of Zeke's retreating figure after all? I couldn't afford to have my family digging into the secret of what lived in the middle of the Cursed Woods. I had to protect Zeke and his people at all costs.

I tried to breathe evenly as I met my mother's glare. "No, I wasn't." Surprisingly, my voice sounded convincing even to my own ears. I guessed it was true when they said practice makes perfect. Soon I'd have an Olympic medal in the sport of lying.

I forced myself to maintain eye contact as I went on. "I had a rough day at school and thought a hike would make me feel better. I didn't realize how late it had gotten."

My uncle's hand relaxed and paused for a moment before moving down to rub my back. I didn't need to examine his face to know there was sympathy there. I watched my mother's eyes leave my own and focus on his. A heartbeat later, I felt rather than saw his solemn nod.

My mother stood slowly, and I imagined her joints creaking like the hinges on the ancient doors of our house. Her body seemed to have aged decades in the last few hours. She was silent as she crossed the large room and settled into the other place beside me on the couch. Carefully, she grasped the hand I had clenched into a fist on my knee.

"Has the bullying started again?"

My eyes darted to hers. There was a hollowness there in her eyes that I suspected could only be present in a mother who felt like she was failing her child.

I had done everything I could to hide the fact that I was being bullied after my father's demise. Always being careful to lock my phone and close my laptop, I thought I had successfully hidden the incriminating messages from her. It was instinct to try to hide that torment from my mother, to prevent her from feeling obligated to help me when I knew there was nothing to be done on the matter.

I wondered how she had learned the truth, how long she'd known I was suffering more than a teenager who'd just lost her father ever should. Something in her eyes told me she had known for a while. A part of me wanted to be angry that she never reached out, never asked if things were getting better if she knew what was going on. But mostly I just felt defeated. I never wanted her to share that pain with me.

I couldn't look her in the eyes anymore, and I couldn't bear to explain what happened at school one more time. I listened in silence as Uncle Peter described the incident and discussed it with my mother in hushed tones. They spoke like I was a wild animal, incapable of hearing voices uttered above a whisper without getting spooked. Maybe they were afraid that if they spoke too loudly I would take off for the woods again. It wasn't that bad of an idea, honestly.

In the end, I didn't cause another scene by taking off again. My aunt and uncle stayed for supper: lasagna that had to be nuked in the microwave because it sat on the counter all evening while my mother lost her mind looking for me.

There was no more talk of bullying, and, much to my surprise, my mom didn't bring up the fact again that I had spent time with a boy recently. It was one of the most normal suppers we'd had in a while, despite the darkness outside the windows that betrayed the late time.

For a single evening, I could pretend I lived in a normal world. Nothing might ever fill the void of my father, but my aunt and uncle were a warm presence I hadn't taken the time to fully appreciate until that night. We joked and laughed and filled our stomachs, all while the real nourishment was taking place in our hearts.

It wasn't until the next morning that I was forced to remember this wasn't a perfect world.

Green Peaks High School did not have an assembly hall, or even a theater with a stage to feature the drama productions. In a school that taught only two hundred students, the gymnasium held everything from basketball games, to plays and musicals, to student pep-rallies. It made sense that the gym would be used to house yet another assembly, the subject of which had the whole town in a panic.

The bleachers that were usually folded against the wall to accommodate more activities had been pulled out, suggesting we were about to watch the Green Peaks High basketball team get pummeled by a rival school.

Upon entry, we were sorted into our graduating classes, the freshmen and sophomores taking up the bleachers on the visiting side and the juniors and seniors grouped in the home side bleachers.

Within the senior body, I stared across the gym at the freshmen squirming in their seats. Had I really been that young, that innocent looking, when I began high school three years ago? I couldn't imagine my frame ever being that small, my eyes that wide. Perhaps in the wake of the town's tragedy we all seemed a little smaller, a little more innocent. More vulnerable.

I held Natalie's hand as more seniors filled in the seats around us. Or rather, I offered my hand as a sacrifice to keep her comfortable. I did my best to keep a straight face as she squeezed the life out of it.

The whole bench shook as Natalie's knee jumped up and down in rhythm to my racing heart. I hoped the screws holding the bleachers together could make it through the entire assembly. Listening to the steady creaks, I cursed myself for not choosing a seat in the bottom row.

"I wish we could get this over with already." Taylor murmured from my other side. Carly nodded beside him as more students trickled in and joined their waiting classmates. Jason hadn't made an appearance yet, which wasn't at all surprising. I wished for once that Natalie and I didn't always arrive at school twenty minutes early, that we were like Jason and had to sprint through the halls every morning to beat the tardy bell by seconds. The anticipation of this meeting was killing me.

I closed my eyes and focused on my breathing. In and out, I dragged the air down into my lungs and pushed it back up again. Since I moved to Green Peaks, my life had been nothing but ups and downs. The highs I achieved through my time with Zeke were always shattered by the darkness of reality and reminders of my past. I wondered how many more downs I could survive before the hypothetical roller coaster in my mind would finally snap, breaking me with it.

"Did I miss anything?"

Jason's voice pulled me out of the depths of my mind, and I turned to watch him settle onto the bench beside Natalie. He took her other hand without being asked and began making small soothing circles with his thumb. I watched as both of their faces softened fractionally, then noticed how Natalie's breaths evened and relaxed, her leg finally growing still. Maybe it was the stress of the situation at hand or something that had been years in the making, but I couldn't stop my smile as I witnessed what I hoped was the beginning of something great between two of my closest friends.

I turned my attention to the rest of the gym and found that the bleachers were full at last. I recognized a few of my teachers sprinkled in throughout the faces of lower classmen, their expressions grave. I forced my lifeless hand to squeeze

Natalie's back, not for her comfort but for mine. If my teachers were this somber, the news had to be even worse than we'd thought.

"Good morning everyone," a disembodied voice rang out. I quickly found the source of the sound—four large speakers hanging from the tall ceiling and pointing to every corner of the gym. As I examined the black, felt covered boxes, a high-pitched wailing assaulted the room. I joined in the scramble to cover my ears as someone made an adjustment to the volume.

"Sorry about that," the voice laughed. "Testing, testing, one, two, three."

Principal Morse made his way across the court, stopping when he reached the jump circle in the center of the gym. His brown hair was in its usual combed back style, and his khaki pants and black polo shirt suggested he was ready for a normal, dull day at the high school. But normal days didn't begin with a school assembly, and there was nothing dull about the subject he was about to broach.

"Can everyone hear me?" Uncle Peter spun in a circle as he regarded the serious faces of the students and faculty. Those that still had their hands over their ears put them down at last and nodded their approval.

The silence that fell over the room was deafening as we waited. What news was so important that it required an interruption in classes? Were they letting us have an early fall break? Was there a problem with the plumbing, causing the halls to be filled with sewage and therefore unfit for classes? Endless possibilities buzzed through my veins as I waited for my uncle to steel himself for the speech he had prepared.

Uncle Peter covered the microphone with one hand as he breathed a deep sigh. He lifted his chin and gazed upward for several seconds, as if he might find the courage to get through this meeting carved on the ceiling tiles. After what felt like an eternity, he took another deep breath, uncovered the microphone, and began.

"As all of you are well aware, tragedy has plagued the community over the last few weeks." His eyes darted to my corner of the gym, the seniors, where Erin York huddled in a group of her friends a few rows below me.

"I wish I had better news to tell you." Peter sighed. "I wish I could tell you that the killer was found, and we can finally wake up from this terrible nightmare. But the only thing we've continued to find are the bodies of his victims."

Another sigh as Peter closed his eyes. Every fidget in the room stilled as we steeled ourselves for his next words. *Please,* I thought, *just get on with it.*

"Early this morning, one of our own was found dead in the woods."

My breath caught in my throat as my uncle turned slowly on the spot, surveying all of us. Another. There had been *another?* And so soon after Jessie! Weren't serial killers supposed to space their murders out more? *And* it was someone from our school. In a community this small, there was no doubt everyone in attendance would know the victim.

The gym quickly filled with the whispering of students: the same hushed question repeated a thousand times. Who? Who was missing in the assembly of two hundred students? It felt like a game of Clue as I watched my classmates crane their necks around, searching for the faces of their friends, relaxing when they found them. I couldn't stop myself from following suit, regardless of the fact that I barely knew a quarter of the students at Green Peaks High.

Peter put us out of our misery by revealing the young woman's identity at last.

"The latest victim of the Green Peaks Serial Killer was our own Penny Carson."

Gasps rang out across the assembly. My own breath still stuck in my throat, I watched as Taylor and Carly shook their heads in denial. They searched the crowd once again, trying desperately to find our beloved art teacher's face. I could feel their anger and despair radiating in my own chest. I knew they wanted nothing more than to call my uncle out for telling such a cruel lie and stop this never-ending nightmare.

But it wasn't a lie, and this nightmare was real. I could see the evidence just by examining the faces of the teachers and faculty present. They had known, I realized, well before we began this assembly. They'd probably had their own meeting before any of this started, because they were the adults here and would need to be prepared to handle our adolescent grief. But how could you prepare yourself to handle the grief of two hundred students when you could hardly handle your own? When the victim was not only a beloved teacher, but also a dearest friend?

As the gym filled with crying students, all I could do was squeeze Natalie's hand on my right and Taylor's on my left. I didn't know when I had taken his hand or if he had taken mine, but I was grateful to have one more tether to the earth. Natalie shook beside me as she sobbed into Jason's shoulder.

I felt Taylor's other arm move and turned silently to see him grasping Carly's hand on the other side. We were a joined force, sharing our emotions through the bond of physical contact with me in the center. I couldn't help remembering that bond I shared with Zeke's coven. Was it my imagination that I could feel my friends' energies now, just as I'd felt the energies and minds of those witches? Even if that was the case, I didn't feel powerful or in possession of any life changing abilities. I felt small and useless and overwhelmed in the wake of this tragedy.

I thought my uncle would give us more time to recover, more time to process this new piece of information before charging on with the next bit of bad news. But like ripping off a Band-Aid, maybe it was for the best that he inflicted all the pain on us at once rather than dragging it out.

"Ms. Carson was found at the edge of the Green Peaks Forest closest to the school, discovered by an early morning jogger."

Natalie flinched beside me, but Principal Morse went on, no longer pausing to compose himself between statements.

"I also feel obliged to tell you that Ms. Carson's body wasn't the only one found last night. The body of Heather Reed was also recovered, officially marking her as the first victim of the Green Peaks Serial Killer. Her car and her remains were found stashed in the forest just off the highway."

There were more murmurings from the students, but I didn't bother opening my mouth to whisper to my friends. Perhaps some of Heather's friends and family had continued to hope that she was alive and well, but I never held such delusions. Jessie's murder had been the nail in Heather's coffin for me. If a person could be capable of murdering one girl, what would one more evil deed be to his already blackened soul?

"For those of you keeping a tally, that's three young women dead. Two of them were found in the 'Cursed Woods' as you kids call it."

My eyes narrowed slightly. Where was Peter going with this? Of course we were all keeping a tally. You could hardly ignore or forget the name of a person who was taken from this world so cruelly.

I zeroed in on my uncle, still standing in the center of the court with his back to my side of the gym. As if he could feel my eyes on him, he turned and gazed at my section of the bleachers. At *me*.

His posture had changed in the last few minutes, his shoulders now straight and his head held high. I felt his eyes burn into mine, knowing I'd seen this steely expression on his face before. He'd worn it in the principal's office just the day before. Could that really have been only yesterday? He'd been determined then, and he was determined now. For what, I didn't know.

My uncle went on.

"For those of you who grew up here, whose families have grown up here, you'll know there are interesting stories surrounding the forest we call the Cursed Woods."

I held my breath again, not liking where this was going.

"There have been rumors, legends passed down about what kinds of things might be lurking in the depths of the forest. Some of your grandparents or even great-grandparents might know what I'm referring to, although no one likes to discuss it."

Uncle Peter scanned the faces of the students again before settling back on me.

"This town has seen more evil in the past month than it has suffered in the last one hundred years. Two lives have been taken on the fringe of the forest, and a third at a building just outside of it. I think it's time we start listening to the stories of old, the ones that speak of evil living in our very own Green Peaks Forest."

There were more gasps as students looked at each other, the whispers growing louder as they shared their own rumors about the Cursed Woods to anyone who would listen. I glanced over Natalie's head at Jason. He met my eyes and gave me one of his one shoulder shrugs before turning his attention back to wiping Natalie's tears.

This could not be happening. My uncle couldn't be suggesting that Zeke's people were responsible for these murders. It was inconceivable. The group of witches who had taken me in and accepted me so easily wouldn't harm a fly. They couldn't use magic to harm people, not unless they wanted to spend the rest of their lives in the body of an animal.

Unless, of course, they hadn't used magic to kill them. I didn't think there were any curses connected to hurting people the old-fashioned way.

What if Zeke wasn't the only member of his coven that liked to frequent the town they'd been shunned from? I had a hard time believing any of its members would murder someone in cold blood, but what if they'd been caught performing magic? What if *Zeke* had been caught performing magic by someone less understanding than me? How far would he go to protect his people's secrets?

I tried to wrap my mind around the possibility, but my thoughts were a muddled mess. I knew my face must have been a white sheet of confusion, my eyebrows drawn together as I tried to process my uncle's implications. Now wasn't the time for me to consider that I might be dating a serial killer. Not here in this school, surrounded by people grieving for the victims and calling for the killer's blood.

"I've already spoken to the city council, and the town will be implementing a curfew of nine o'clock every night, effective immediately."

There were cries of outrage and actual boo's thrown at my uncle as he went on. I tried not to laugh at the fact that my fellow classmates were more upset at being given a curfew than they seemed to be about the deaths of their friends. But with a killer on the loose, surely they would come to see the logic in it. Did they want to be next on the growing tally of victims?

I closed my eyes, hoping the assembly was nearing its end. I never thought I would miss attending my morning classes, but I'd gladly welcome three straight periods of calculus if it got me out of that gym a second faster.

Over the roaring of disgruntled adolescents, I almost missed my uncle's next words.

I shouldn't have judged my classmates so quickly. I might not have cared about a nine o'clock curfew, but there was one thing I did care about.

"In addition to the curfew, the city is also banning all entry into the Green Peaks Forest."

My eyes flew open. *What did he say?*

"No more parties in the woods, no taking shortcuts to friends' houses, and absolutely no hiking."

The roaring in my ears had nothing to do with my fellow students' complaints. As I stared at the back of my uncle's head, I mentally threw daggers at every inch of his body, praying he would take it back. He couldn't do this. He *wouldn't* take away the biggest happiness I had found since learning about my father's death.

Uncle Peter turned toward me once again. For a fleeting moment, I caught a flash of steel in his eyes so cold that it cut through to my very bones. Then they returned to their normal warm chestnut just before he gave me a tight-lipped smile.

Chapter Twenty

I was *banned* from entering the Cursed Woods. Banned from my meetings with Zeke. Even as I packed my bookbag after the final bell rang, I had trouble wrapping my head around the thought.

After Principal Morse released us from the gym, the school day seemed to pass by in a single breath. Every time I opened my eyes I was transported into a different classroom with no memory of the changing periods. Calculus. Blink. Physics. Blink. English. Blink. And then I was slamming my locker closed and following Natalie out to her truck.

Natalie had been silent for most of the day. Everyone seemed to deal with the news of Ms. Carson's murder differently. Taylor, who was usually polite if not a little quiet, ignored everyone around him and stared at the ceiling for the duration of the lunch period, never once touching his pizza. Carly, on the other hand, talked constantly, as if trying to make up for the lack of Natalie's gossip. I swore her voice was hoarse by the end of the day from blatant overuse.

Jason was quieter than normal, only joining in the conversations to make jokes that were too good to pass up. I caught a glance of the notebook he was doodling in and thought I could make out the features of a certain blonde actress. There was no nudity that I could see, thank goodness, but perhaps the face of Marilyn Monroe was a welcome reminiscence of the art teacher who had laughed at his unruly behavior despite her attempts to be stern with him.

I wasn't exactly sure how I was handling the latest death. It pained me to admit it, but I was having an easier time blocking out all thoughts of Ms. Carson and the other murdered girls than should be possible given the circumstances.

I should have been crying and grieving with the rest of the school, but instead I'd wiped my mind clean. Like an out-of-range radio, I filled my head with the sound of static and white noise and refused to let a single thought penetrate the wall. It was the only way I could make it through the school day without having another melt down.

If I thought about the murders and their proximity to the Cursed Woods, I would also be forced to think about my uncle's accusations of who was responsible for them. It was best if those speculations were saved for my bedroom with the door locked and the curtains drawn. I wanted no witnesses if there was a chance I might fall apart.

Natalie didn't utter a single word on the drive home, but her face was easy enough to read. Pain from losing one of her favorite teachers, fear that she could be next, and guilt that she was worrying about her own life when the lives of three innocent women had already been taken.

I wished I had the words to console her, but my mind was still a blank canvas. I knew that she would bounce back eventually, though. We all had our breaking points, but I was confident that Natalie had yet to reach hers.

When we pulled up to my house at last, I gave her a quick hug across the cab and scooped up my bag to leave.

"Cami," she said, causing me to pause with the door half open. She was staring out the window, past my house and at the woods, as if they were alive.

"Be careful." She breathed.

I stared into her eyes for a long moment before nodding. Maybe I was wrong about her reaching her breaking point. Before I could contemplate saying something in return, she forced the truck into reverse with a groan and backed down the driveway, disappearing from sight.

I *hoped* that she would bounce back. I'd have to see if there was anything I could do to help her regain that loud, exuberant demeanor I'd come to know and love.

Our teachers had been gracious to us in light of everything that was going on, so I didn't have any homework to distract myself with when I finally made it to my room. My mom wouldn't be home for another hour, so I had nothing but the empty house and my swirling thoughts to keep me company. Thoughts that were gaining strength and momentum and would quickly turn into a raging cyclone if I didn't address them soon.

Could there be any merit to my uncle's allegations? Could Zeke's people actually be responsible for the murders? My heart screamed no, a steady beat in my chest that sang of the goodness I'd seen in his people, in Zeke himself. Surely a guy that would stop and exert some of his precious magic to help an injured bird wouldn't turn around and murder an innocent woman in his next breath. It just didn't make any sense.

But as much as my heart said no, the more my head wondered if it wasn't completely impossible.

They had survived this long in the Cursed Woods by laying low and keeping their existence a secret. What if, after all this time, the younger generation decided to relax their rules, and had become more lenient with what they believed they could get away with? They might start to stray further and further away from their community, even going so far as to enter the town that had exiled their ancestors a century before.

Zeke had made a bold move by coming to my house and interacting with me. Someone else in his community could have done the same thing. And if that witch had been caught performing magic, who knew what they might have done to cover their tracks?

I pictured Heather standing in the woods with her hands raised, a group of leather clad teenagers closing in on her from every angle. I saw Ms. Carson running through the trees, tripping on some vines before turning over to stare at Zeke, his bow and arrow aimed steadily at her chest.

I shook the visions off quickly. I was letting myself get carried away. I needed to focus on the facts at hand.

I thought back to what Uncle Peter said in the gym, about the "evil" living in the forest. What exactly did he know about the tribe of witches hiding in the Cursed Woods? Did he know the whole story, or just the rumors about the strange lights and animals that gave the legendary forest its nickname? If I was going to figure this all out, maybe I needed to hear the story from another perspective.

Before I could convince myself it was a bad idea, I grabbed my phone and pulled up the contact list. He answered on the first ring.

"Hey Cami! Is everything okay?"

I could easily recognize the concern in my uncle's voice. Maybe I should have been annoyed that he thought the only reason I might call him was if something was wrong, but to be fair I couldn't remember a single time I'd called him in the past. My mother had always made sure my aunt and uncle's numbers were present in my emergency contact list in case something happened, but I'd never needed to use them. It would have taken a catastrophic event for me to bother my aunt when she lived a whole state away.

If I continued to think in circles without any outside advice, this could very well turn into a catastrophic event when I completely lost my sanity.

"Hey Uncle Pete! No, don't worry, everything's fine." *Lie*. Things couldn't be less fine at the moment. Hopefully he couldn't hear that in my voice. "I was just calling to ask you something."

My uncle's voice brightened after learning I wasn't in trouble. "Sure! Do you want me to come over? I can be there in a few minutes." There was a metallic jingle on the other line, as if he was already grabbing his keys to leave.

"Oh no, that won't be necessary!" I said quickly. "My mom will be home in a bit, and I was hoping to just talk."

Perhaps I should have just texted him. I hated the awkwardness of phone conversations. But I had a feeling if I'd sent him a message asking him to spill everything he knew about the Cursed Woods he would show up at my house and demand to know why. With my mediocre lying skills, it was in my best interest to have this conversation over the phone where he couldn't see my face twitch.

"Sure hun, you know you can talk to me about anything."

I flashed back to our meeting in his office when he encouraged me to come to him any time I needed to talk. I wondered if he was remembering the same conversation.

"It's about the assembly we had earlier." I paced the length of my room, a habit I had no doubt picked up from my mom. "You said something about the Cursed Woods. About something evil in it?"

I bit my lip, letting him read the questions in my silence. My room really wasn't big enough for this kind of pacing.

"I did," my uncle said slowly, his voice changing once again to be deep and serious. "There are a lot of things you don't know about this town, Cami. Things we keep hidden from outsiders."

He paused again, and I could hear his breath becoming unsteady over the line. "Are you sure you don't want me to come over? I don't know if this will be easy to discuss over the phone."

I shook my head, then remembered he couldn't see the gesture. I sighed and focused on keeping my voice even and convincing. "No, Uncle Peter. I just want to understand. Why can't I go into the Cursed Woods?"

Tell me what you know about the witches, I wanted to scream. I waited in silence, trying to reign in my impatience.

My uncle breathed deeply several times before responding. "If I tell you this, you have to promise to keep the information to yourself. I don't want you texting any of your friends from Plainfield or making a post on Twitter or whatever." I rolled my eyes. "Because you're my niece, and because you're a resident of this town now, I'll tell you about the history of Green Peaks. But be warned, it isn't pretty."

I held my breath and gave him the floor to go on. I imagined him licking his lips and wondered if his face resembled Jason's just before describing the bizarre occurrences around the Cursed Woods.

"Many years ago, Green Peaks had a larger population than what we keep nowadays. The town thrived, and much of that was due to the *gifts* of some of our residents." He spat the word, as if it was something dirty.

"There were people that could perform miracles, they say. They could make crops grow in abundance, heal the sick, and grant a life that was easy and comfortable for all who accepted them. My grandfather witnessed some of the acts himself. But he also learned how they acquired all that power."

Wait, what? I had never thought about Zeke's people needing to acquire their magic. I just thought it was a part of them, something they were born with that came into fruition at a certain age. At the Blossoming Ceremony.

My uncle's voice dropped another octave.

"They were Satan worshipers," he whispered. I couldn't stop the chill that ran down my spine, covering my bare arms in a sheet of gooseflesh.

"Their performances may have seemed miraculous, but the people eventually caught on to what they were doing. Young women went missing, and their powers grew stronger." He paused, letting his doctrine sink in.

"They were performing sacrifices."

I stopped my pacing and peered out the window, at the trees that were eerily calm despite the whirlwind that blew through my mind. *Sacrifices?* It couldn't be. Zeke would never participate in something as dark as a sacrifice. And Satan worshipers? I tried to imagine frail, old Lucinda butchering a goat and praying to the devil to grant her a long life. The thought made me laugh out loud.

"Sorry," I said quickly, stifling my laugh. "But this all seems kind of ridiculous, Uncle Pete."

He sighed into the phone, as if he had expected this reaction from me. "I know it seems crazy. This is part of the reason we keep the stories a secret in this town. Outsiders wouldn't understand."

I felt the jab but tried not to let it sink in too deeply. I had always been an outsider, a loner on the fringe of every social hierarchy since I'd been old enough to know there was one. I seemed to fit into this school now, but I had yet to see if the emergence of my past would turn me into an outcast once again.

"Our children are told stories of what happened all those years ago, but even some of them refuse to believe." He went on. "My grandfather helped lead the eradication of those evil-doers, and it was thought that they had all been run off or killed. We assumed the Green Peaks Forest had been cursed when they were wiped out. But it's becoming clear now that they never left us, not completely."

My uncle's grandfather is responsible for the death of Zeke's great-grandmother. Perhaps I should have been more concerned with the possibility of the old coven leader performing sacrifices, but all I could think about was a screaming child, her mother carrying her through the woods while the torches and gunfire closed in on them.

If the witches truly had sacrificed innocent women all those years ago, were the townspeople's actions justified? *Children* were killed in that massacre. Did they deserve to die for the sins of their parents? Blood had been shed on both sides. Would the cruelty of this world never cease?

"It doesn't matter if you believe it or not," Uncle Peter sighed. "Just promise me you'll stay out of the woods?" It was phrased like a question, as if he knew ordering me to obey would likely result in the opposite outcome. I still didn't know if I believed Zeke's people were responsible for the murders, but it would be smart to keep my distance until I knew for sure.

"Okay," I agreed reluctantly.

"Good girl. Is there anything else you wanted to talk about?"

I shook my head again. "No, I think that's it for now. Thanks uncle Pete."

I could hear the smile in his voice when he replied. "Anytime, Cami. I'll see you at school tomorrow."

I set the phone down on my desk and returned my gaze to the window and the silent trees beyond. I said that I wouldn't enter the woods. I didn't say anything about talking to one of the witches myself. After weeks of not being used, it looked like the attic would be our medium once again.

Dinner was quiet that night, the silence only broken by our forks and knives grating against the glass plates as we cut into our chicken.

It was evident that my mom had been informed about the latest death. When her hands weren't busy dicing the chicken into perfectly even cubes, they were wringing the napkin in her lap or tapping an uneven beat on the table. Her eyes swept the room constantly, darting towards every creak of the house like she was expecting the killer to drop in and join our evening meal.

When our plates were finally empty, I all but ran into the kitchen to clean up the mess. I was ready to escape to my room and prepare myself for a midnight meeting with a possible murderer.

I had almost made it to the staircase before my mother stopped me.

"Camille, wait."

Great, she used my full name. Here comes a serious talk. I turned around and raised my eyebrows. She stood in the doorway to the kitchen, her red fingernails flashing as she continued to worry away at the napkin.

"I heard about your art teacher."

Obviously, I thought dryly. *Just look at the state you're in.* She continued to shred the paper into little pieces, seemingly oblivious to the mess she was making on the floor.

"Are you okay?" She finally asked, looking away from the remnants of the napkin to meet my stare. The hollowness was back, her eyes as deep and empty as a freshly dug grave. I had to avert my gaze, afraid that yawning pit might swallow me whole too.

I shrugged my shoulders. "I'm fine," I lied. I wasn't in the mood to get into it with her. I had too many other things on my mind to want to stop and talk about my feelings.

I watched her cross the room from the corner of my eye. "I'm here for you honey," she whispered, pulling me into her arms.

Her warmth pressed against me, and I realized how cold I had been. A part of me wanted to break down and cry, to let loose everything I'd kept bottled up inside and give the burden to my mother to carry. She'd never been the one to take the burden from my back, though. That had been my dad. My mother had shouldered enough burdens on her own lately, with the loss of her husband and most of our money, and I knew she couldn't handle both our weights on her own.

Maybe she felt guilty for never asking me about the bullying and was trying to make up for it now. But I wasn't going to cry into her arms to make her feel better. I wasn't ready to give up my burden yet.

I pulled away and looked into her eyes. "It's fine, Mom." I said gently, trying to communicate everything I felt in those three simple words. *I'm not okay, but it's fine. I have some things I need to deal with, and I can't tell you about them. I need you to trust me to figure it out on my own this time.*

My mom nodded and her eyes softened fractionally. "Okay," she agreed, as if she understood.

I left her at the bottom of the stairs but stopped when I reached my room, listening. After a few moments I heard the floorboards creak as she made her way to her room, then the click of the door as it swung shut behind her.

I didn't know if this would work or not. The other times I waited for Zeke in the attic I'd at least suspected he'd be visiting my house each night. But ever since we started meeting after school there had been no reason for him to send me letters. I just hoped that his magic and whatever bond seemed to stretch between us would be strong enough for him to receive my call.

I sat at the little wooden table, watching the moonlight stream in through the already open window. My father's pistol was hidden beneath my jacket, loaded and ready to go once again. I sincerely hoped I wouldn't need it, but I couldn't ignore the fact that three women were dead, and *someone* had to be responsible.

There was no point in waiting around, so I grabbed the lighter and closed my eyes. I thought about Zeke, focusing on the pull that had tugged me towards the Cursed Woods time and time again. I opened my eyes and gazed at the candle, imagining that my eyes were Zeke's, that he was the one watching as I carefully lit the wick and illuminated the attic. I stared at the flame, watching it dance as the air swirled in from the open window. *Come here,* I thought clearly, practically shouting the words in my head. *Zeke, come to me!*

I sat and waited. And waited. Every minute that crawled by left me more convinced that I was an idiot for even trying this. I wasn't a witch. I had absolutely no power in my blood that could make telepathy possible. Zeke was probably asleep, miles away from my useless attempt to contact him.

After thirty minutes of sitting in the same spot, my bottom was sore against the unforgiving wood. I shivered against the early fall breeze and pulled my jacket tighter around my torso. I had been stupid to think this would work.

Leaving the pen, paper, and lighter in place, I blew the candle out and closed the window as gently as possible. Making my way across the cluttered space, I stepped carefully over boxes and discarded items, their dusty surfaces lit only by the light of my phone. I paused when I reached the door, and I almost didn't hear it.

The window opened behind me, emitting a sound that was more of a sigh than a creak and letting loose a gust of cool air that tickled the hair around my face. I was turning to face the night when the candle erupted to life, blazing remarkably bright for its tiny wick and sending shadows to dance around the room. I dropped my phone and hurried to the table, arriving just in time to catch the paper bird that flapped determinedly through the window.

I barely waited for the wings to stop moving before I ripped the letter open and took in the familiar cursive.

What's going on? Are you okay??

The words were smudged and messy from writing in such a hurry, but there was no need for him to sign it. I had called for Zeke, and he answered.

I'm fine, I wrote quickly, **but I can't meet you after school tomorrow and I need to talk to you.**

I threw the airplane out the window and watched the darkness swallow it whole. I looked down at the yard below and could barely make out the dark shape of a figure huddling in the garden bed. The second bird appeared a moment later, its white outline emerging from the darkness like a star that had finally broken through a cover of blackened clouds.

I thought something had happened to you. Do you want me to come up there to talk? Or would you like to sneak down here?

Oh. I never even considered waiting for him on our back porch. I had needed to talk to him, and the attic was where we talked. This dusty, neglected room would always be our place in my mind, even if it wasn't necessary now that we were meeting in person.

I knew I could easily sneak outside, especially if Zeke used magic to muffle the creaks of the old house to prevent it from alerting my mother. But the weight of my father's pistol pressed against me, a silent reminder that Zeke might be dangerous. If I was about to address the possibility that Zeke's coven was performing human sacrifices, I might want to keep some distance between us.

Can't risk it, I wrote, omitting the fact that his unpredictable reaction was the thing I'd be risking. **Can we talk like old times?**

When the next bird swooped into the room, I immediately noticed it was different from the others. Its wingspan seemed wider, its head all but nonexistent, and thick black lines marred its white surface and stopped me from ripping it open.

Hold to ear, the scrawled words read. Curious, I lifted the bird to my ear and listened, like I was searching for the ocean in a seashell.

"Hello, beautiful." Zeke whispered. I jumped and almost dropped the paper, cursing quietly. I examined its elongated wings, looking for a microphone or speaker, but of course there were none. I slowly brought it back to my ear like a telephone, trying not to feel like an idiot. He chuckled, and I swore I could feel his breath caress my skin.

"Letters are overrated, don't you think?" He asked quietly. "I want to hear your voice."

Unlike a phone that distorts the caller's voice and carries an all but unnoticeable stream of static, Zeke's words rang through the messenger bird clear and true with none of technology's interference. He could have been standing right behind me.

"Hello Zeke," I responded softly. I hoped he couldn't hear the hitch in my voice or my uneven breaths. Now that he was here and I was finally about to accuse him of murder, a new wave of fear washed over me, trickling down my spine in a chilling torrent. I didn't think the height of three stories would save me from his wrath if it turned out my accusations were true. I imagined him sending a whole flock of paper birds after me, slicing through my skin with their razor-sharp wings until one of them found their mark.

I took a deep breath and forced myself to begin. It was only a matter of time before my courage failed me.

"Something's happening Zeke. People are dying, and I have to ask you about it."

I told him about Heather disappearing the first day we officially met, and how her car and body were found in the Cursed Woods weeks later. I told him about Jessie, the quiet, sweet girl who had been murdered after finishing her shift at G.G.'s. She died the day after Juniper's Blossoming Ceremony. The wheels in my head spun as I realized this would've been the perfect time for a sacrifice, right after such an important ritual, but I kept the thought to myself and went on.

As I recounted the most recent death, my favorite teacher, I couldn't stop the tears from running down my face. I'd done a good job of reigning in my feelings up to this point. Too good, I decided. My bottled emotions had finally reached their peak, spewing out in a river of pain and tears that refused to be kept inside a moment longer. I hoped the dampness of the paper wouldn't interfere with Zeke's magic.

"Shh, it's okay Cami," he whispered soothingly. The bird warmed against my ear, and my face dried in a gentle brush of heat. Of course he could find a way to wipe away my tears without actually touching me. *Over competent witch*, I thought wryly.

I sniffed and sucked in a breath, steeling myself to ask the crucial question at last. "Do you and your coven know anything about the murders?"

I hadn't accused him, not yet at least, but the real question was evident in my tone. *Are you responsible? Did you murder my art teacher?*

Zeke went silent. I felt the air still around me, as if the night was holding its breath. His reply came a moment later, and I couldn't ignore the hurt in his voice. "You think we had something to do with it?"

I closed my eyes. No matter how many times I imagined the conversation in my head, nothing was harder than the real thing.

"All of the bodies were found in or around the forest." I hedged.

A sigh reverberated out of the bird, tickling the hair around my ear. "No, Camille," Zeke said firmly. "My people had nothing to do with this."

I waited, unsure of how to proceed.

"But," he added finally, "I have known about the murders for a while now."

I sat in the chair and listened as Zeke recounted his story. As magic wielders, Zeke's people were acutely aware of the energy around them. Over the hundred years of living in the Cursed Woods, they had become one with the forest's energy, their awareness stretching as far as the trees spanned. On the day of Heather's murder, the witches felt the energy in the forest shift. Something evil had encroached on their land.

"It took us all night to find the body," he said heavily. "We're all experienced hunters, but finding the source of that pain was something none of us had done before. By the time we arrived, the killer was gone."

His voice was rich with regret. "We couldn't move her body to a place she'd likely be found, although many of us wanted to try. It would have been too risky and moving her from the place it happened might have prevented the killer from being identified. We had to leave her there.

"We've been trying to track the evil presence ever since, but it's difficult. They could be in the woods right now, but unless they're committing an act against nature we won't even know they're there. It felt different after your teacher, though. It's like every time they take an innocent life their beacon becomes stronger, easier for us to track. I just hope next time we're able to stop them before it's too late."

Zeke ended his narrative with another remorseful sigh. He had known about the murders even longer than I had. Why had he kept them a secret from me? How could I trust he was telling the truth now?

"Why didn't you tell me?"

"I didn't want you to think we were responsible, not when I'd finally convinced you to meet me. You were everything to me. You still are. I didn't want to ruin it."

I thought about that for a moment. Certainly if he planned on murdering me he'd had plenty of opportunities to do so. If they needed a sacrifice for June's Blossoming Ceremony, wouldn't it have been easier to use me? I'd walked right into the heart of their coven, a much easier sacrifice than sneaking into our town to find Jessie.

My uncle could have been wrong. In a town where rumors and legends were passed around as frequently as favorite recipes, it was more than possible that he'd been fed false information.

"So, you don't perform sacrifices?" My voice was small as I anticipated his reaction.

Zeke laughed in my ear, and I unclenched the fist I'd been holding.

"Of course not," he managed to get out. Then, with a little less humor, "Did you really think we were capable of that?"

"Of course not," I mimicked quickly. "But my uncle told me some things and... well, it doesn't matter. I just had to be sure."

I tried to ignore the voice in my head telling me he could still be lying, manipulating me into believing him. But this was Zeke. After all the times I'd questioned him, believed him to be a stalker or even a ghost, he had always turned out to be exactly what he said he was.

He was a boy, a magic wielder, who happened to have very strong feelings for me. Perhaps even *love,* although neither of us had worked up to using that word yet. After all the craziness that went into this relationship, I couldn't stop myself from trusting him. I wanted, *needed,* to trust him. While I wasn't looking, Zeke had become an irreplaceable person in my life. I would follow my heart where he was concerned, even if it ended up getting me killed.

"I'm glad you're not a murderer." I whispered with a smile.

"I'm glad you no longer think I am." He whispered back.

A thought occurred to me and I paled slightly. "What will happen if you catch the real killer?"

Zeke was silent for a moment, but I felt the bird buzz with a sort of electricity, as if it couldn't contain the fury of the witch who had created it.

"They killed on our land," he said softly. "We'll make sure they pay for the lives they stole."

I blanched slightly at the coldness in his voice, but I couldn't disagree. Whoever killed those women deserved every ounce of torture the witches of Green Peaks Forest could deliver them.

"I think your uncle's right about one thing, though." Zeke added, his voice back to its normal smooth timbre. "I don't want you going into the forest again until this is all sorted out."

I felt my lip jut out. "If you're with me I shouldn't have to worry about any serial killer trying to do me in."

There would just be the task of explaining to my mother why I was still hiking in the woods when the whole town was forbidden from entering its depths. Not to mention I'd promised my uncle I'd stay out of there, but that was before I knew Zeke's people weren't to blame. We had to find some way around this nonsense.

"No," he asserted, his deep voice taking on the quality my dad had always reserved for ending arguments. "I won't risk you getting hurt. We'll have to come up with another way to meet."

I pouted as I once again imagined how my life would be if Zeke were suddenly ripped from it. I remembered the depressing days after my father's death, the fear of never fitting in, the way I had come to loathe myself. Zeke had lifted me up out of that dark place, had helped me realize I wasn't the despicable person I'd painted myself to be. I needed him in my life, and I'd hunt the killer down and bring him to justice myself if that was what it took.

I thought of Ms. Carson and was hit with a sudden inspiration.

"I think I know of a way we can see each other."

Chapter Twenty-Two

A whole week passed without anyone dying.

It was one of the most boring, uneventful weeks since I first moved to Green Peaks. Students still whispered behind cupped hands, but by the end of the seven days the fear that had been spreading like wildfire throughout the school quickly turned into brushed off humor.

Rumors were passed from class to class, each one more ridiculous than the last. The killer was spotted on school grounds. He'd leaked his plans of who his next target was, the name changing from the cheerleading captain, to the first chair trombonist, to the lunch lady in a matter of seconds. There wasn't a killer at all, and the girls were victims of a secret government cover story.

Each time a new rumor was started, the reality of the situation moved even farther away from home. Perhaps that was why the rumors were started in the first place. No one wanted to believe any of this was real.

While I may not have agreed with the rumors themselves, I had to admit I was grateful for the effect they invoked on my friends. Just as I hoped, Natalie bounced back from the edge she'd come so close to sailing over. She smiled and joked with the rest of us, and I could have sworn I caught her making eyes at Jason behind his back. Her voice hadn't reached its crescendo of a volume yet, but I knew it was on its way. Despite the threat of the serial killer at the backs of our minds, things were returning to normal.

The cafeteria was as loud as ever when we sat down to eat that Friday. Jason crunched his potato chips noisily and had to shout to be heard over the other conversations. "I heard Harvey Waldrop is having a bonfire tonight. Anyone want to go?"

Carly's fork dropped into her tray with a clatter, splattering spaghetti sauce all over her denim jacket. I openly gaped at him as well.

Jason brushed the long locks of hair out of his face, revealing a smirk that said, *I always knew you both were goodie-two-shoes.*

It was Taylor that gave words to our obvious discomfort. "We have a curfew, dummy. Does 'killer on the loose' ring any bells to you?"

Carly and Natalie laughed, and I snickered in sync with them. I couldn't agree more. The fact that things were returning to normal wasn't necessarily a good thing, not yet anyway. We still needed to make safe decisions, and I'd made a promise not to enter the Cursed Woods until all of this was resolved.

Jason rolled his eyes. "No one's actually taking that curfew seriously. I have a reputation to keep. If I start following the rules now, what will all of you think of me?"

"That you're not a complete idiot?"

"Exactly." Jason winked.

Natalie shook her head, exasperated. "The Fall Art Show is tomorrow evening, or did you forget about that too?" Jason's face fell slightly. "If you get yourself in trouble and miss it our senior year, I won't just be thinking you're an idiot."

Jason's eyes turned soft as he peered at her questioningly. He placed his elbows on the table, resting his chin on his raised knuckles that held remnants of blue and yellow paint once again. I'd never seen him look so torn, as if choosing between his bad boy reputation and the opinion of a girl he might secretly like was the most difficult thing he'd ever done.

After a moment of unbroken staring, he dropped his gaze and muttered, "I'll think about it." Natalie took a long drink of her apple juice, unsuccessfully hiding her smirk.

She was openly smiling as the two of us walked through the bustling halls to our next class. The halls were filled with slamming locker doors and the squeak of shoes on linoleum as we strode away from the cafeteria. I decided it was as good of a time as any to enact the first phase of my plan.

"Hey Nat, are you doing anything after school?"

Natalie started slightly, as if I'd broken her out of a particularly engaging daydream. No doubt her mind was still back in the cafeteria, telling Jason off and reveling in her win again and again.

She shook her head, bringing herself back to the present. "Not yet, I don't. Did you have something in mind?"

I took a deep breath, steeling myself for her reaction. I could feel a blush reddening my cheeks already. "I was wondering if you'd want to go shopping. I sort of met this guy-"

Natalie stopped in the middle of the sea of students, forcing them to change directions to avoid running straight into our backs. A shriek split through the bustling noise, silencing all conversations around us. I slapped a hand against her mouth and pulled her quickly toward the classroom, my face reddening further as everyone in the hallway stopped to stare at us.

Oh, the joys of befriending the loudest girl in school.

"Why didn't you tell me sooner?" Natalie demanded in her truck after the final bell rang.

It was a miracle she made it through the rest of the school day without spontaneously combusting. Within the short walks between classes and the few notes she managed to pass without our teachers noticing, I'd given her very little information about Zeke. Of course, what information I had given her was total bogus.

I shrugged my shoulders at her question. Where to begin? Because he was a witch living on the outskirts of society, who blamed the citizens of our town for the deaths of his ancestors? Or maybe because up until very recently I thought he had something to do with the murders, might have even been the Green Peaks serial killer himself? The list was endless. The truth was, I'd needed time to come up with a valid story that might explain away some of Zeke's weirdness. Not to mention all the time I needed to hone my lying skills.

"I guess I was embarrassed," I mumbled sheepishly. My face still burned from her overzealous reactions, making my act more believable. "We met on Facebook and I didn't know how you'd feel about me talking to a guy I met online."

"You have him on Facebook?" She squealed, bouncing up and down in her seat and making the already rickety truck shake even more on the bumpy road. "Show me a picture now!"

Crap. I'd have to come up with better lies if I didn't want my story to immediately crumble apart.

"I can't," I sighed as dramatically as possible. "His sponsor family made him get rid of it because they're so strict. I didn't save any of the photos before he had to take his profile down."

Natalie made a sound that was something between a groan and a plea. "You said he's a foreign exchange student from Canada? Which school is he going to?"

"Saratoga." I quipped, grateful she'd accepted my excuse so easily.

"I can't believe you're dating a *panther*." She groaned again. The known rivalry between Green Peaks and Saratoga was one of the reasons I'd chosen it to be Zeke's fictional home. I knew Natalie wouldn't have any friends over there to fact check my claims.

"They're not all bad." I winked. Natalie giggled again, and I knew she was enjoying our conversation immensely. She was in her prime, talking about boys with her best friend. I almost felt bad for leaving the juiciest details out, for robbing her of such a fantastic story. But Zeke's secrets weren't mine to share.

We were still laughing when we pulled off the highway and turned into Rawlins, giving me my first look at the town my mother claimed held everything I'd ever need. To put it mildly, I was unimpressed. I had to admit it was larger than Green Peaks (there were stoplights, after all), but aside from a few hole-in-the-wall restaurants and moderately priced hotels, the town had little to offer in terms of recreation. We passed a Walmart on our way into town, so at least my mom wasn't lying about that. If the clothing store Natalie mentioned turned out to be a flop, I could always fall back on saving money and living better.

"Here we are!" Natalie exclaimed as she directed her truck to the curb outside a building called Windswept Goods. The shop was small and homey looking, with cute bookshelves, vases, and flowers adorning the display window. It gave me the feel of a Pottery Barn or IKEA store. The right window held a few mannequins sporting flowy dresses, ripped jeans, and an off the shoulder shirt. Natalie was right; the clothes were exactly the style I loved. There was only one problem.

"Hold on," I held my arm out to prevent Natalie from jumping out of the truck. "Does this store sell men's clothing?"

Natalie's eyebrows pulled together. "Why?" She looked me up and down, pausing to scrutinize my face. "Don't tell me you're thinking about cross dressing! Sorry, girl, but I don't think you could pull that look off."

I laughed and shook my head. "Of course not. I'm not shopping for *me;* I'm shopping for Zeke!"

"Oh," Natalie's face fell, and I knew she was disappointed in what our girl's trip was turning out to be. She undoubtedly thought I wanted to buy some cute outfits for myself to impress this new boy in my life.

If Zeke was a normal high school boy, I might have spent all my savings on clothes and accessories I thought would impress him. But as it was, I could probably show up in a potato sack and Zeke wouldn't know the difference. All my outfits seemed alien to the leather skins he was accustomed to wearing.

"There's a thrift store a couple blocks down. Want to try there?"

I nodded enthusiastically and the nearly empty wallet in my lap breathed a sigh of relief.

"A thrift store would be perfect."

The dull, brick building was certainly harder on the eyes than Windswept Goods had been, appearing almost industrial from the outside. But as we neared the front door, I could make out men's jeans, T-shirts, and a few shabby looking suits through the darkly tinted windows.

"Why are you buying Zeke clothes, anyway?" Natalie asked as we walked through the front door. We were blasted with a rush of air that smelled like old books and a scent that reminded me of my grandmother. "Didn't he bring plenty of clothes from Canada?"

My mind started scrambling once again. Why did Natalie have to be so inquisitive? Normally she was happy to talk my ear off in a constant stream of stories and gossip, barely giving me time to get a single word in. Of course she'd pick today to ask a million questions.

"It's his birthday this weekend," I stuttered lamely. "And—Canadians regularly give clothes as gifts." My cheeks were heating under the pressure of the ill-concealed lie. I quickly changed tactics, lowering my head and lifting my shoulders slightly, trying to make myself look smaller in embarrassment. "I just... thought it'd be nice to find him something."

I peeked up at my friend and relaxed when I saw her ear-splitting grin.

"You've got it bad, don't you?"

I blushed even more and allowed her to pull me deeper into the store. My subconscious wiped the bead of sweat away from her brow. *Crisis averted.*

Despite smelling like an old lady's parlor, Rawlins Thrift was very forthcoming in the men's department. I managed to find three plain T-shirts in red, green, and black, and a couple pairs of jeans that looked to be about his size. Erring on the larger side, I stopped at a spinning rack of belts and grabbed one at random. The black leather was soft in my hands, and I smiled when I noticed the buckle. Silver and probably too big for anyone north of Texas, its saving grace was a line of trees engraved with fine detail into the metal. For my forest dwelling witch, it was perfect.

Determined to make something out of our shopping trip, Natalie's mood improved when she found a flowery dress and a pair of long white gloves. She claimed they made her feel completely Gatsby and couldn't wait to wear them to the art show tomorrow. I was on cloud nine too, each item of clothing bringing me that much closer to executing my plan. We swung our baskets of goodies dramatically as we headed to the back of the store to get the last item on my list.

The shoe department had to be larger than the men and women's clothing sections combined. It seemed that everyone had shoes to give away. Running shoes, church shoes, sandals. There were shoes for every occasion possible, in every color and size. As I ran my hand over a pair of loafers that appeared larger than my forearm, a thought suddenly occurred to me.

"Oh no."

I stared at the giant loafers, then at the kid sized tennis shoes placed carelessly beside them. My eyes raked up and down the rows of shoes, taking in the vastness of sizes. How was I supposed to know how big his feet were? All that time I spent staring at him, memorizing the lines of his face and admiring the bulk of his muscles, I'd never once stopped to examine his feet.

"I'm guessing you don't know his shoe size?" Natalie laughed as she came over to join me. I looked at her questioningly, and she pointed at my hands. I gripped a giant loafer in one hand and a tiny sneaker in the other, squeezing them like a lifeline. I swallowed.

"Why didn't I ask him his shoe size?" The question was more for her benefit than mine. Even if I'd thought of asking Zeke, it would have been a waste of time. He wore the size of shoe his grandmother made for him, shoes that were measured not in numbers but specifically to fit his feet alone. Even if I could somehow ask him right then, he wouldn't be able to tell me a number.

"What do I do?" I asked Natalie, panicking. "I never look at his feet!"

Natalie cocked her head to the side, thinking. After a moment her eyes sparked, and a mischievous smile spread across her face.

"Well, how big are his other body parts?"

Confused, I shrugged my shoulders. "Normal, I guess. His arms are pretty big..." I faded off as her smile grew wider. She raised an eyebrow and glanced pointedly at the loafer in my hand, smirking. I dropped the shoe with a gasp.

"I haven't seen *those* body parts!" I pretended to chuck the sneaker at her as we both dissolved into a fit of laughter. I was aware of people staring at us openly. An old lady in a uniform pursed her lips at us, but it only made us laugh even harder.

My face was beet red, but I didn't care. Tears streamed down my face, and my chest ached painfully as I tried to breathe around the uncontrollable spasming in my diaphragm. I was the happiest I'd been in weeks, draped over my best friend and laughing on the floor of a thrift shop.

Chapter Twenty-Three

I stood at the edge of the Cursed Woods, listening to the trees as they swayed behind me in a gust of October wind. Their leaves rustled like a chorus of whispers, effectively preventing me from hearing anything else. I wondered if the sudden blast of air was occurring naturally, or if a certain witch didn't want me listening to his ongoing struggle.

"Do you want some help?" I asked for the third time. Patience had never come easily to me, but I was genuinely trying. I resisted the urge to tap my foot and tried to be sympathetic. *Remember, this is new to him.*

I glanced at my phone again. We'd been out there for almost twenty minutes, and my mother was expected to come home at any time. What was that boy doing in there? Wrestling a bear?

"No, I think I've got it."

Zeke's voice was uncertain, but it came from directly behind me. The leaves tittered in the breeze once more, as if in nervousness or excitement. I steeled myself for a moment, and then turned to appraise my work.

I gasped.

The boy standing before me belonged on the cover of People magazine. The stonewashed jeans brought out the brightness of his electric blue eyes, and the plain black shirt was a perfect mirror to his slightly disheveled black hair. As my eyes raked over the bulges of his bare arms and the faint stubble lining his jaw, I realized "boy" couldn't be a more improper term. This was a man, through and through. A man who wanted *me*.

"Um," I swallowed. I continued to gawk at him like an idiot, as if I'd never seen a member of the opposite sex before. Who knew a set of everyday clothes could have such a monumental effect? My goal was to make him fit in, but I'd missed the mark entirely. It didn't matter what clothes he wore; Zeke would never fit in. I had taken a wild, primordial being and transformed him into an Adonis.

"You clean up nice." I managed to whisper. His eyes softened and then glittered with something that might have been humor.

"Thanks," he whispered back. We stared at each other for another minute, drinking in every detail in this stolen moment we had to ourselves. I knew we were wasting time, but I couldn't force myself to end it.

After what could have been seconds or minutes, Zeke shifted and looked down, alerting me to the fact that he still held the belt in his hands.

"I don't know what to do with this." He said apologetically.

I tried and failed to hide my smile. My uncultured witch. I took the belt and began threading it through the loops of his pants. My hands lingered on his waist longer than necessary, and I breathed his scent in deeply. It was intoxicating at this proximity, and I forced myself to step back after securing the buckle, before my hands decided to travel somewhere else. We had a plan to follow, and I couldn't risk blowing everything because my raging hormones got the best of me.

"It's called a belt," I said with a smirk. "It keeps your pants from falling down."

He arched an eyebrow and looked down at his jeans.

"I would never let my pants fall down. That would be embarrassing."

It was his turn to smirk as I realized that so many of our everyday objects could be done away with in the presence of magic. If his pants started to slip, he could magically pull them up and keep them there. Suddenly the belt seemed like a really stupid purchase.

"I like it, though." He said quickly, reading the dejected expression on my face. He ran a finger over the metal trees and smiled to himself. I relaxed slightly.

Preventing pants from falling wasn't the only way magic could aid in apparel. I knew as soon as I handed him the pair of Nikes that they weren't going to fit. His feet *were* big, much bigger than I'd anticipated. But instead of handing them back and asking for a larger pair, he sat on the ground and brought the left one up to his foot. As he slipped his toes into the opening, I watched the shoe grow before my very eyes, stretching around his foot until it fit as snugly as if it had been tailored for him. He proceeded to do the same with the other, and just like that he had a perfect set of shoes.

My mind jumped back to our joking the day before. What other "things" could he magically enlarge if he wanted to? I choked down the bubble of hysterical laughter and turned towards the house.

As I slipped my hand into Zeke's and led him up to the porch, I wished for the hundredth time that I could share my secret with someone. Natalie would absolutely lose it if she heard my absurd speculations. I wanted to talk about Zeke's magic, joke about the possibilities, and have a normal female conversation about the guy I was falling for that wasn't threaded with lies.

I knew I was being selfish, though. The safety of Zeke and his people was infinitely more important than my desire to gossip with a friend.

"My mom should be here anytime," I murmured. The porch steps creaked beneath our feet as we climbed slowly up to the house. "Do you want to wait inside or stay out here?"

Zeke's throat bobbed as he glanced back and forth between the house of his ancestors and the forest he called home. The smirking man from a moment ago was replaced with a trembling child, all evidence of the prior confidence leached from his bones. His eyes settled on the trees and he took a steadying breath.

"Out here. Please."

I hoped his desire to remain outside was because the woods made him feel secure, and not because they offered a quick escape route.

I squeezed his hand and led him to the wicker chairs to wait. As we made ourselves comfortable, I couldn't help smiling in remembrance of that day not so long ago when we'd sat in these same seats, meeting for the very first time. Now there was no gun in my pants, and Zeke was the one who appeared to be praying for his life.

"She's going to love you."

Zeke tore his gaze away from the trees to examine my face. I couldn't help noticing the way his eyes held mine. They were starving, desperate eyes, the same ones that had fed on the presence of the forest just a moment before. It was as if I was as much of a lifeline as his home was.

"She knows she's meeting me then?"

I bit my lip. "Not exactly."

He flinched, and I grabbed his hand before he could bolt for the woods.

"If I'd told her she was finally going to meet the mysterious boy I've been talking to, she would've skipped running her errands to clean the whole house. I needed enough time to make you presentable before she got home, and that required leaving out the fact you were coming at all."

I didn't know if he could see the logic in my decision or not. His eyes still looked like if they opened any wider he'd pop a blood vessel.

"Besides," I purred, "this will pay you back for that stunt you pulled with your own parents." He looked at me questioningly. "At least you don't have to worry about my mom hexing you. The worst thing she can do is cry on your new shirt."

Zeke held my gaze for a moment longer before letting out a sigh. He had to know he was getting off easy. He didn't even have to worry about my father chasing him away with a gun. Of course, I'd almost used that tactic on him myself.

We didn't have time to deliberate on the matter more, though, because at that moment my mom's car turned onto the long driveway. The tires crunched over the gravel in a popping rhythm, echoing the quick beats of my heart. I might not have been as terrified as I was meeting Zeke's parents, but I had to admit I was still nervous. I wanted my mom to like Zeke, even if she couldn't know everything about him.

The SUV pulled to a stop next to the house, the engine dying in a low choke. I squeezed Zeke's hand again as my mother stepped out.

As she grabbed the grocery bags out of the back and started towards the house, her dark hair swirled around her face, preventing me from reading her expression to know if she'd noticed us on the porch. I didn't have to wonder for long, though. I realized the exact moment she spotted me sitting there, next to a *boy*, when she dropped the grocery bags on the ground.

Her breath escaped in a high-pitched gasp just as the wind shifted, blowing her hair back to reveal her face once again. Her eyes popped as they swiveled back and forth between Zeke and me, and I smiled invitingly before motioning her over to join us. *Here we go.*

Forgetting the grocery bags, she stumbled the last few steps to the deck and used the railing to pull herself up to our level, as if she were too weak to ascend the steps on her own. I smirked as she finally approached, wondering silently how much she would embarrass me today.

"Mom, this is Zeke."

Her eyes latched onto Zeke, and I felt him tense next to me. I gave his hand one more pump and nudged him forward.

"Zeke, this is my mother, Terri."

Zeke jumped up on cue and extended a hand toward my mom. I sighed internally, grateful for whatever universal force that allowed my wild boyfriend to act like a proper gentleman.

"Pleased to meet you, Terri."

She accepted his hand and shook it robotically, all while her eyes roved over him from head to toe. I knew what she was seeing. A tall, muscular hunk of a man that couldn't possibly be interested in her quiet, awkward daughter. I wondered if his scent was as intoxicating to her as it was to me, or if she could even detect the pine and woodsy aroma mixed in with the lingering perfume of a campfire. When her eyes glazed over and she started to sway, I decided that she could.

After a full minute of staring, it became evident that my mom was incapable of speech. I grabbed her by the elbow and led her through the door, gesturing towards the forgotten groceries behind her back. Zeke jogged down the steps to grab them before following us into the house.

I deposited my mother onto a barstool in the kitchen, then flitted around the room, acting as host in her stead. I grabbed a pitcher of lemonade from the fridge and poured three glasses, the silence growing more and more awkward by the second.

Zeke unpacked the groceries onto the counter curiously, examining each can of vegetables and box of processed food with undue caution. I steered him into a seat on the other end of the bar before he could give away his cluelessness. Although, perhaps allowing him to shove the gallon of milk into a random cabinet would be enough to jar my mom out of her catatonic state.

As I put away the groceries, I filled the uncomfortable void by babbling about Zeke's made up history. I fed my mom the lies I'd rehearsed about Zeke's life in Canada, how he'd always wanted to come to America as a foreign exchange student and had finally gotten his wish in his senior year. The more I talked, the more she loosened up, occasionally nodding her head until she finally joined in on the conversation and spoke.

"It sounds like you're a very interesting young man, Zeke." My mom smiled. I released a sigh of relief, which was echoed quietly by the boy beside me.

"You have no idea." I chuckled.

Overall, I had to admit that the awkward "meeting of the parents" ordeal had gone as smoothly as possible considering my mother's personality. She didn't cry (*thank goodness)* and after moving past her uncomfortable ogling she barely stared at him at all.

During the next hour, we picked up an easy cadence of conversations that mostly centered around Zeke's love for the outdoors. I made him out to be a real woodsman, chopping firewood for his parents' woodburning stove and hunting wild game with his stellar archery skills. The best part was that most of the narrative we spun was based on the truth. Zeke could talk for hours about hunting down twelve-point bucks and the satisfying feeling of letting an arrow fly.

The longer we talked, the more I realized how much more there was to Zeke than just his magic. I knew this, of course, but it was a refreshing reminder that I could share plenty of details about Zeke with my friends without ever crossing into dangerous territory, the subject of magic. With this realization in tow, I rode in the backseat of my mom's car with confidence that we could pull this off.

I held Zeke's hand as we neared our destination, his thumb making small circles on my palm that sent warm tingles all the way up my arm. He squeezed my hand harder every time we hit a bump, and I realized with belated interest that this was probably the first time he'd ever ridden in a car.

His eyes were glued to the window and the line of trees that flashed by in a blur of green. When he squeezed my hand again, I allowed him to tether himself to me, to be the anchor he needed in this new experience of my world.

In a flash I felt that connection take hold of us again, similar to the warmth I'd felt as his magic flowed through me during his sister's Blossoming. It wasn't telepathy, of that much I was sure, but something so old and carnal I didn't have the words to describe it. It washed over me in a wave, a unique feeling that this was *right*. Zeke met my eyes and grinned sheepishly, as if he knew exactly what was happening but wasn't ready to spill the secret yet.

Under normal circumstances, I would have demanded he tell me what he knew right then and there. But I didn't want to break this moment, whatever *this* was. So I smiled back at him shyly and allowed the warmth to fill my body and soul.

The moment was broken all too soon when we finally pulled into the parking lot of the school and joined the swarm of students and parents filing inside like an army of ants entering its nest. Zeke eyed the dozens of people with a reserved expression on his face, probably wondering if they would chase him into the woods with pitchforks and guns if they knew what he truly was.

We followed an elderly couple into the gym and finally got a glimpse of the art show Ms. Carson had worked so hard to put together before she was murdered.

A sort of memorial had been set up along the first wall of the gym. Three long tables were arranged against the wall, loaded with the paintings and projects the art teacher had poured her heart into over the years. There were black and white sketches, watercolor, charcoal drawings, and several impressive sculptures.

We followed the line inching along, and I spotted a small caricature of a boy laughing, his eyes closed as he leaned back in his seat with his feet on the desk. It could have been anyone, if it wasn't for the striking blonde hair and dimples. Ms. Carson put on a good act of hating Jason, but here was proof that she didn't mind the boy's joking and attitude as much as she wanted us to believe. I didn't see any other students displayed in her work, which spoke more than the stern looks and trips to the principal's office ever could.

"Cami!"

I spun around and saw Natalie standing with Jason, Taylor, and Carly, the whole posse together and waiting for me to join them. Natalie was bouncing in place and staring at Zeke, and I was surprised she hadn't attacked us already. Jason had probably held her back.

My mother smiled in their direction and drifted off to admire the artwork on her own. I had to give her some credit. Even if she wasn't the coolest mom, she at least knew when to stop hovering and leave the teenagers to their own devices.

I found Zeke's hand and looked up to find his electric blue eyes fixed on mine. "Ready to meet my friends?"

We made our way across the gym, walking around the tables laden with student artwork and dodging children running from one end to the other. The whole town seemed to be out that evening. Maybe in a time of sorrow and fear everyone could use a little beauty through art to lighten things up.

Finally reaching my friends, I pulled Zeke in to close the circle. "Everyone, this is Zeke. He's a foreign exchange student from Canada. Zeke, this is everyone."

Taylor and Jason reached out and shook Zeke's hand, while Natalie looked like she might actually start drooling. Carly smiled politely and then went back to staring vacantly out across the gym.

"So you're from Canada, *aye?*" Jason snickered.

Zeke obviously missed the joke, so I rolled my eyes on his behalf. "Yeah, yeah. Let's skip the rest of the Canadian jokes you have prepared. He doesn't speak French, he doesn't like hockey, and he *has* wrestled a bear."

I laughed at their awed expressions and was about to drop a "just kidding," but then I noticed Zeke's indifference. He shrugged. "Only once."

The boys whooped and clapped him on the back. Any fear I'd been holding onto that Zeke wouldn't fit in with my friends or that they wouldn't think he was cool dissipated. We could do this. We could *actually* pull this off. Everything was going to be fine.

We walked towards the closest table to begin our inspection of the art projects. Natalie pulled me ahead of the group, and I heard Zeke fall behind with the boys who were demanding details on the bear fight. Content that he could handle himself for a few minutes without giving anything away, I gave Natalie my full attention.

"W-O-W," she somehow managed to drag the word into three syllables. "You didn't tell me he was hot. Like *hot,* hot. Like, you're going to need a fire extinguisher if you don't want him to burn the whole school down, hot."

I punched her arm playfully and then shrugged. "I guess he is pretty hot."

That was the understatement of the year. But I didn't want to risk Zeke hearing me gush about him and wind up embarrassing myself. I could do that easily enough on my own.

"He smells nice," Carly commented beside us. I figured that was about the best compliment you could get from her. The fact that she noticed something about him at all spoke wonders. Natalie and I both nodded in agreement.

We passed a table full of painted fall leaves and jack-o'-lanterns, and moved on to the next that held large canvases butted together to make even larger works of art.

"Our group project!" Natalie squealed.

Five canvases stood side by side, and I couldn't believe how well it came together. Carly's portion was on the far left and made up the lightest, cheeriest part of the Cursed Woods. A rabbit hopped between lush trees, full of orange and yellow leaves that created a beautiful canopy. An eagle soared out of the picture, its wings continuing into the next canvas, which was Taylor's. His forest showed a few less leaves and a slightly darker sky. A couple of monkeys hung from the branches, and a kangaroo hopped playfully towards the next painting.

My rendition of the Cursed Woods sat in the middle. The sky peeking through the forest reflected that of a cloudy sunset, with shadows beginning to creep out from the trunks of the trees. There were just as many autumn colored leaves on the ground and in the air as there were sprinkled throughout the branches of the trees.

I'd spent most of my time perfecting the giraffe, and looking at it now I knew I'd gotten it right. There was just the right amount of camouflage to make it appear the creature was hiding, but its eyes were fixed on me, the viewer, with a depth I had no idea I was capable of capturing. The giraffe was hiding, yes, but its eyes somehow conveyed the fact that it was hiding from *me.* A human. Just as Zeke and his people were hiding from us now.

Moving on from my painting was Natalie's, the background a little darker yet and her trees even more naked than mine. A wolf howled at the full moon just visible through the dark blue clouds, and a tiny trail of mist began on the right edge of the picture and continued on into Jason's.

Jason's painting was the darkest of them all, with bare trees and no leaves in sight. That giant oak I remembered him slaving over stood in the middle of the picture, its arms reaching out to either side, as if it would grab anyone who dared come too close. Red eyes peered out of the tree hauntingly. It could have been an owl, a squirrel, or a demon, whatever your imagination made it. The mist that started in Natalie's picture grew into a thick layer of fog that concealed the bottom third of Jason's trees. Any manner of animal or beast could be hidden in that fog, and the more I stared at the swirling layers of paint, the more I thought I could see them.

Altogether, our paintings showed the gradual transition from fall to winter, day to night, and peacefulness to fear. It reflected the evolution of the Green Peaks Forest into the Cursed Woods, the creation and cultivation of a legend that was still told around campfires one hundred years after its birth.

A piece of that legend materialized behind me, the warmth of his chest radiating through his brand-new shirt and into my back. He leaned forward to get a closer look at our work, his chin brushing against my hair. Instinctively I began to curl into him, then fought the urge as I reminded myself where we were.

"The middle one is mine." I whispered.

Hair tickled my cheek as he nodded, disturbing my dark strands with his chin. I felt a smirk stretch across his face, and suddenly I was very self-conscious of what we'd put together. Was he offended at our interpretation of his home? I was still proud of the artwork, but I'd never considered how he would receive it.

"I love it," Zeke whispered finally, effectively putting me out of my misery. I sighed into him, my back relaxing into his chest. I didn't care about the gym full of people or my friends standing a few feet away, likely watching our interaction.

His chin brushed against my cheek, his stubble scratching my skin lightly, and I felt the sensation from the car take over me once again.

"None of my ancestors turned into giraffes, you know." His chest shook as he laughed quietly. I looked around discreetly, but none of my friends were close enough to hear his breathy comment.

I turned my head and whispered back, "If that's true, how do you even know what a giraffe is? You basically live under a rock."

He laughed out loud at that, and I pegged him with a look that said, *Behave*.

He reached his hand out and touched the giraffe softly. "Just because my community is isolated doesn't mean we're completely stupid. We have a way of sharing knowledge and memories with people who haven't witnessed them, as you well know."

My mind flew back to the Blossoming Ceremony when Zeke's ancestors' memories swirled through my head, connecting me to the rest of the magic wielders. Did they share images like that often? I had assumed the ability was restricted to special rituals like children coming of age, but perhaps they used their abilities during any story time. It was certainly better than watching TV.

Natalie stepped forward at that moment, as if she couldn't stand being left out of our conversation for another second. "Well, what'd you think?"

Zeke detached himself and stood a more respectable distance away from me. "I think you all have a lot of talent."

Natalie grinned and pulled us along to examine the rest of the class's projects.

The rest of the evening was a blur of color on canvases and smiles shared with my friends. With each passing conversation, Zeke relaxed a little more until he was initiating discussions and stories all on his own. We introduced him to a handful of teachers, and the bear story had to be acted out no less than three more times at Jason and Taylor's demands.

By the end of the show, I was filled with a newfound confidence that Zeke and I could make things work. It didn't matter that his family was different and that there would always be secrets I couldn't share with my friends. I could have both of the lives I wanted. This here, whatever this conglomeration was, would be better than anything I could have imagined.

I said goodbye to my friends and motioned to my mother that I would wait for her outside. She was busy talking to my aunt Lacey, although I hadn't seen my uncle all evening.

I pulled Zeke out the door and we slipped into the cool air of the slowly darkening night. Curfew wasn't for another hour, but the sun had set, and the remaining light was quickly being sucked into the dark blue clouds. The night reminded me of Natalie's painting, and I wondered how long it would take for the forest to transition into Jason's.

Knowing we only had a few minutes before my mother came out, I wrapped my arms around Zeke's neck and settled my head against his chest.

"Thank you." I murmured into him.

He squeezed me back tightly. "You're very welcome. But for what exactly?"

I rolled my eyes, knowing he couldn't see them from this angle. "For being brave enough to face a bunch of scary humans for me."

He laughed, the sound vibrating through his chest and buzzing in my ear. He tipped my chin up so that I was looking up at him, then gently kissed my forehead.

"I'd do anything for you, Cami. Anything."

The door opened to our left and my mother and aunt strode outside, giggling about something. They hadn't spotted us in the shadows yet, so I turned to Zeke for a quick goodbye.

"I'll see you tomorrow?" I asked quietly.

He nodded his head and cupped my cheek. "Of course."

Then I was standing in the dark alone. I thought I caught a flicker of movement at the edge of the forest, but it could have been the shadows playing tricks on me. When Zeke wanted to be stealthy, no sound or twitch of a leaf would dare give his location away.

"Cami?" My mother's voice was slightly panicked. I hurried to step away from the wall before she could send the cavalry after me again.

"There you are," she sighed. "Where's Zeke?" She craned her neck around me, as if he would even be capable of hiding behind my much smaller body.

"His sponsor family picked him up," I shrugged. "Let's go home before the crazies come out."

She smiled and looped her arm through my elbow. I was in too much of a good mood to break away from her, so we walked side by side to the car and drove out of the parking lot. Instead of hounding me about Zeke, she let the voice of Carrie Underwood play through the speakers and proceeded to drive all the way home in companionable silence. Maybe Green Peaks was changing my mother after all.

Once home, I ditched my shoes next to the stairs and began the creaky climb up to my room. I stopped abruptly on the third step and turned back to my mom, who was hanging her jacket next to the door.

"Mom?"

She swiveled to face me, surprise flickering across her face that I wasn't already shut up in my room with the door locked.

"Thanks for being awesome." I finished quietly.

Before she could turn my gratitude into a heartfelt conversation full of tears and hugging, I smiled and resumed my trek up the stairs. When I made it to the top, I shot an "I love you!" over my shoulder and escaped into my room before the inevitable tears began to flow one story below.

I collapsed onto my bed and sighed. *What a night*. I didn't think anything could make me feel happier than I felt in that moment.

Determined to prove me wrong, something crinkled beneath my back. I sat up to find a piece of origami, a "Zeke Original" waiting on my pillow. The paper was folded into the shape of a giraffe, its face angled towards me just like the one in my painting. If that wasn't enough to make my heart full to bursting, then the words written across its chest in Zeke's looping handwriting would have finished the job.

Anything.

Chapter Twenty-Five

I awoke to the crisp smell of frying bacon. Sunlight was already peeking through the window, and the clock on my nightstand read eight A.M. sharp. It was way too early to be awake on the weekend, but my body and mind felt exceptionally well rested.

I stretched out my arms and felt something at the edge of the bed. My paper giraffe. I must have fallen asleep holding it.

A wave of emotion washed over me, equal parts excitement that I'd successfully pulled Zeke into my unmagical life, and peace that I could stop worrying about hiding him from my family and friends. I just had to keep up the foreign exchange student charade for the rest of the year and then find a way to keep him in my life for good.

For some odd reason, I didn't feel the need to worry about that. Something told me everything would work itself out if I just sat back and enjoyed the ride.

Slipping into my house shoes, I followed the smell of bacon down the stairs and into the kitchen. My mother's hair was a frizzy mess and there were grease splatters all over the stove and counter tops. A bowl of eggs sat cooling beneath the microwave, and a mountain of pancakes balanced precariously on the plate next to them.

I whistled lowly and hopped into a seat at the bar. "What's the occasion, Rachel Ray?"

My mom spun around, a hand over her heart as if I'd scared her. Flour coated her forehead and bangs, and I couldn't stop myself from laughing.

"You're not supposed to be up yet," she whined. "I was going to bring you breakfast in bed!"

I tilted my head to the side. "Why would you do that?"

She rolled her eyes at me, as if I was the clueless mother and she was the teenager that knew everything. She turned around and quickly threw together a plate, piling it with pancakes, eggs, bacon, and sausage. To add the finishing touch, she stuck an obnoxious looking candle into the pancakes with the number "18" painted in rainbow colors and decked out in glitter.

"Happy birthday, Cami!" She sang, clicking the lighter I hadn't realized she was holding. The candle flickered to life, causing the glitter to sparkle and dance in the orange glow.

Was it already October 5? It felt like I'd arrived in Green Peaks a week ago. Somehow, amidst the craziness of learning that magic was real and accepting the fact that I was falling for a witch, I had turned eighteen.

I was a young adult.

Before any wax could drip onto my pancakes, I blew the candle out and carefully laid it to the side. My mother clapped and cheered like I was eight, rather than eighteen.

"Thanks, Mom." I said before giving her a side armed hug.

"Don't thank me yet!" She squealed. She was bouncing in place, hard enough that I had to worry about the foundation of our very rickety house.

"After you eat your breakfast I have a *real* surprise for you!"

My fork full of eggs paused halfway to my mouth. I narrowed my eyes suspiciously. "What kind of surprise?"

Her smile grew even wider, and she turned to bustle around the kitchen some more. She dished herself a plate and sat down beside me, giving nothing away. "You'll just have to wait and see."

I chewed my food slowly, speculating. I'd held no expectations of receiving a birthday gift this year. We were still hurting financially in the aftermath of my father's death. The funeral expenses and cost of moving had drained us dry, and a teacher's salary was barely enough to keep the electricity running and food on the table.

What did my mom plan on surprising me with? A pie in the face?

My plate finally cleared, I stood up to wash everything in the sink. But before I could take a single step, my mother jumped up to block my path. She was bouncing up and down again, and now I could really feel the floor shifting beneath us.

"Oh no you don't. I'll get that later honey. Right now we need to give you your surprise!"

I rolled my eyes and allowed her to drag me out of the kitchen. I'd always wished my parents would have had another kid so I wouldn't be an only child, but sometimes my mother acted like a little sister all on her own.

"Do I need to be blindfolded?" I laughed. My mom's smile widened even further, and I tried to reign in my sarcasm. It wouldn't kill me to let her be excited about this, whatever *this* was.

I mentally prepared myself for the fake enthusiasm I normally saved for Christmases with my grandparents who always seemed to think I was ten years younger than I actually was. *Another baby doll? Oh boy!*

As my mom led me through the back door and onto the porch, however, I didn't have to hide my surprise. What could she possibly have done for me outside? My curiosity grew even more as she pulled me towards the old shed in the backyard that I'd never bothered to look into. Was she throwing me some kind of weird shed party? At eight in the morning?

The shed had once been painted white to match the house, but now the paint was so chipped and peeled away that the brown wood stood out starkly with a splatter of white polka dots. Two hinged doors were tethered shut with a rusty looking eye latch.

My mom made a point of positioning me perfectly in the center of the two closed doors, exactly three feet away from her surprise. She glanced at me one final time before unlatching the doors and throwing them open in a dramatic sweep of her arms.

The early morning rays shone into the shed, lighting up the millions of dirt and dust particles floating through the air. When the cloud of dust began to settle, I finally got my first look at my mother's surprise and understood why she'd been so excited to give it to me.

It was a car.

A car.

My mom had gotten me a car?

"Mom," I gasped, even as I staggered towards the gift.

It was a Pontiac Grand Am, of that much I was sure, although its model year remained a mystery. It could have been three times my age and I wouldn't have cared. It was a silver beauty, freshly washed and polished by the looks of it. And, more importantly, it was *mine*.

I walked around the car in a daze, trailing my fingers over the slick, cool body. I barely registered the fact that the bottoms of my pajama pants and my fuzzy house slippers were collecting enough dirt to fill a garden. Who cared about clothes when my mother had bought me a car?

"How?" I spluttered, because how indeed had she managed to afford this? She knew the financial crisis we were in. How many house payments had she redirected to pay for this incredible birthday gift?

She shrugged, as if it wasn't a big deal, but her smug smile told me she knew exactly how big of a deal it was.

"One of the teachers at the elementary school was selling it cheap. Lacey and Peter chipped in a little, and I've been saving up to buy it for months. We couldn't have you walking to college next year, could we?"

She walked around the car and gave me a hug that I returned whole heartedly. "Happy birthday, sweetie."

I squeezed her back tightly and tried to reign in my tears. "Thanks, mom."

"I have one more piece to add to your gift." She said as we broke apart.

I gaped at her openly this time. What more could she *possibly* give me than a free car? It was already too much.

"A piece of advice." She continued, winking. I relaxed at the knowledge that she hadn't spent even more money on me.

"I want you to use this car to chase your dreams." Her voice dropped, thickening. But she held the tears at bay.

"I don't want anything to hold you back, and I certainly don't want you to let *me* hold you back. If you want to go to college halfway across the country, I'll help you fill out the applications. If you fall in love with this boy Zeke and follow him back to Canada, I won't stop you.

"I want you to be happy, Cami. Wherever you go and whatever you do, I want you to be happy."

She ended her speech with a firm squeeze of my hands. I opened my mouth to say something, but no words escaped. What could I say that would be good enough to follow that?

My mother had essentially given me permission to skip off into the sunset with Zeke. I wondered if her advice would still apply if she knew what he really was. Would she be excited that I found someone so unique to spend my life with? Or would she be afraid, and forbid me from seeing him?

I looked into her unwavering gray eyes, the eyes she'd given to me, and hoped that I knew the answer.

She nodded as if she understood the thoughts racing through my mind and she agreed. With her encouragement shared in full, she gestured towards the car and told me to continue enjoying the "major" part of my gift. I secretly disagreed, though. Her advice was worth a thousand free cars.

After checking out the interior, however, my mind returned to the present and the impossible freedom this new car would grant me. I couldn't wait to share my excitement with my friends.

The black seats and console matched my simple tastes, but I knew Natalie would take one look at my car and try to transform it into a wad of bubblegum on wheels like her truck. I shuddered at the thought and took a mental note to lay down ground rules before allowing her to make any cosmetic changes.

"Want to go for a ride?" I asked after completing my inspection. My mom had bought me the car, so it was only fair to offer her the first drive.

"That's okay honey," she said as we exited the shed and stepped into the sunlight. "You go and enjoy your car. I have some errands to run, and your first drive with it shouldn't be a trip to the grocery store."

Once back inside, I all but ran up the stairs to grab my phone. It sat on the nightstand next to my paper giraffe, which I'd propped up to lean against the lamp.

I found Natalie's conversation thread and shot her a quick message. *Guess what?!*

Her response was almost immediate, and in my excitement over the new car I didn't stop to wonder why she was awake at eight thirty on a Sunday.

WHAT?! She typed back, in typical Natalie fashion. If she couldn't be loud in person she could always take advantage of those shouting capitals.

I plopped down on the bed, my fingers flying over the keypad. *I GOT A CAR!!!* I might as well join in her shouting.

The bubbles immediately appeared at the bottom of the screen, her message being typed out just as quickly. *OMG, SERIOUSLY?! GET YOUR BUTT OVER HERE AND SHOW IT OFF!*

Jumping off the bed, I wasted no time in getting ready. I was in and out of the shower in five minutes, barely waiting for the water to get hot. After drying my hair haphazardly in a towel, I threw it into a messy bun. One look in the mirror said I was a walking hot mess, but I was too excited to care. My cheeks were flushed without any makeup, my eyes naturally bright. I brushed my teeth and called it good.

Someone had already clipped an air freshener onto one of the vents, so the car smelled like lavender as I settled into the driver's seat for the very first time. The car was old enough to have a real key to turn instead of a fob and button, and I relished the feeling of the metal sliding into the slot, the ignition catching and bringing my car to life as I turned the simple key. I'd need to invest in a keychain if I didn't want to lose it.

There were tears in my mother's eyes as I eased the car out of the shed and rolled onto the driveway. She stood on the back porch, waving, watching me drive away like I was leaving for college or somehow driving out of her life.

I waved back as I drove by, taking advantage of the dark windows to roll my eyes at her usual dramatic behavior. I was only driving to Natalie's, after all. Maybe she was worried I'd make the trek up to Canada without saying goodbye first.

The Pontiac had aged well, driving as smoothly as could be expected up the gravel path. The gas pedal had to be pushed almost to the floor to convince the car I actually wanted it to move. But it *did* move, and that was all I really cared about.

Once I turned off the gravel, dusty roads and onto the main drag, I rolled the windows down and enjoyed the cool October morning. The smell of the Green Peaks Forest flooded the car, replacing the scent of lavender with pine needles and sap.

I wondered what Zeke would think of my new car, and if he'd be willing to go on rides with me. He had handled my mother's SUV well enough.

Zeke had shared the wonders of his magic with me, showing me things I'd never dreamt were possible. Perhaps it was time I returned the favor and shared some of the magic of modern technology with him.

I'd hung out at Natalie's place a few times over the past months, but when I pulled up to her house I saw that her truck wasn't parked in its usual spot. In fact, I didn't see her truck anywhere. Did she forget I was coming over and leave to do something else?

I grabbed my phone out of the cupholder and sent her another quick text. *Are you home?*

My phone buzzed back in response. *Sort of. My dad is using my truck.*

She didn't fully answer my question, but then the bubbles appeared at the bottom, so I waited for her to finish typing.

I'm in the woods. GET YOUR BUTT OUT HERE SO I CAN GIVE YOU YOUR SURPRISE, BIRTHDAY GIRL!!!

What was with everyone and the surprises today? I supposed it should be expected on my birthday, but I'd made a point of not telling any of my friends when my birthday was to avoid this exact treatment. I didn't need or want the attention. Natalie must have asked someone, possibly my uncle or mom when I wasn't around.

Regardless of how she discovered today was my birthday, I figured I might as well get it over with.

I stepped out of the car and took two steps towards the forest bordering her yard before pausing. What was she doing in the Cursed Woods anyway? There weren't any other cars parked at her house, so a surprise party seemed unlikely unless the partygoers had committed to hiking half a mile here.

She knew the woods were banned and had been pretty freaked out about the whole situation, the last I checked. Perhaps Jason's bad influence had finally rubbed off on her and she'd developed a disregard for authority and better judgment. Maybe Jason *had* hidden his car a short drive away and convinced her that a surprise party in the forest was a perfectly rational idea. All my friends could be waiting for me out there, and I was standing around and stalling like a pansy.

Ignoring what was possibly *my* better judgment, I took a deep breath and strode into the Cursed Woods.

As soon as the trees surrounded me, I heard it. Music, coming from deeper in the woods. I walked towards the source, attempting to decipher what the song could be, all while trying not to trip over the vines and underbrush grabbing at my feet. The distance made it soft enough that the drumbeat and low guitar notes could have belonged to any genre. But as I drew closer it became evident that it was an old rock song, not one of the girly pop tunes I'd come to expect from Natalie.

The music grew louder, signaling that I'd almost made it to the source of the sound. I stopped in the middle of the greenery and looked around. Sunlight poured through the half empty canopy, shedding soft light on the leaves and undergrowth I'd been trampling on, but still there were no signs of my friends.

I took a few more steps forward and noticed an overturned tree, its bark half decayed and covered in a thick layer of moss. The sound seemed to be coming out of the tree. I walked the remaining distance until I found the music's source at last.

A cold feeling washed over me as I picked up Natalie's baby pink phone, its speaker blaring the final lyrics of a rock song I'd never heard her listen to.

I'll keep you by my side with my superhuman might. Kryptonite.

Something was very wrong. As the guitar solo faded out and the phone went silent at last, I became aware of just how quiet it was in the forest. No birds chirped, no squirrels scampered along the trees, and my friends didn't pop out to surprise me.

Just when I thought I'd go crazy from the lack of sound, a twig snapped behind me. Leaves rustled. I was frozen in place, a rabbit trapped in the eyes of a wolf. If this was some kind of birthday scare, my friends were going to get an earful, along with several punches to go around.

Before I could take another step, I breathed in the pungent scent of strong cologne. I knew that smell; I'd been hugged by its wearer on several occasions. Confusion swept over me as I whirled around and faced my uncle Peter.

Chapter Twenty-Six

"Hi, Cami."

I stared at my uncle in shock. Had my friends pulled him in on the "surprise" too? I looked behind him to see if they were waiting to jump out and join us, but there was nothing but trees and foliage. Another quick sweep of our surroundings told me we were absolutely alone.

"What are you doing here, Uncle Pete?" He'd made me promise to stay out of the forest, and here he was breaking his own rules. Apparently neither of us cared that there was a killer on the loose.

He smiled at me sadly, his eyes softening in the way a teacher looks at a student who is struggling tremendously with a question that has a very simple answer. He said nothing for a moment, as if he were waiting patiently for me to solve the equation.

I looked down at Natalie's phone, trying desperately to put the pieces together. A part of me whispered that this wasn't a difficult puzzle, and if I only opened my eyes I'd understand everything. I stubbornly told that voice to shut it.

"Why do you have Natalie's phone?" My mouth was dry, my muscles tense. My body was clearly picking up on the situation much faster than my mind.

Uncle Peter's eyes followed mine to the phone, and he snatched it easily out of my hands before I could blink.

"Let's say I borrowed it for a bit. Don't worry, though, I'll be giving it back to her soon." He smirked, as if he'd just made a very clever joke, but nothing about this was funny. His eyes had transformed into a cool stare, that gleam of determination I'd witnessed once before shining through again. But determination at what? What was happening here?

Finally showing a hint of impatience, Uncle Peter sighed and put his hands in his pockets. Natalie's phone disappeared into one of them, and the absence of that pink beacon in the middle of this sea of green and brown jarred me even more than my uncle's next words.

"She was a means to an end, Cami. I needed to bring you out here and pretending to be Natalie was the only way to do that."

Pretending to be... A memory popped into my head, a conversation I'd had with Michael Varner. It seemed like a lifetime ago that I'd joked with my friend about a serial killer using my phone to text him.

A serial killer. The gears in my mind were finally turning, squealing loudly in an agonizing refusal of acceptance. This couldn't be happening. My uncle *couldn't* be a murderer.

"Uncle Pete?" I managed to whisper.

His eyes softened at my tone, his smile delicate.

"Yes, Cami," he nodded, as if he were relieved that I'd finally figured it out. "I'm the Green Peaks serial killer."

There was a buzzing in my head, a current of electricity that started in my ears and radiated all throughout my body. His words bounced around the inside of my head, trying to find the receptor that would accept his statement as fact, but finding nothing but loose wires that crackled and buzzed some more.

I groped for something to say, maybe a demand for him to take it back, to tell me it wasn't true. *Happy birthday surprise, I got ya!* But when my vocal cords finally resumed function only one word escaped.

"Why?"

Peter brushed something off his flannel shirt, his hands unshaking. Calm.

"Why did I kill all those girls?" His voice was even, as if we were talking about the weather rather than murder. "They were distractions from what I really wanted to do. I thought they would be enough, but I was wrong. You can't serve an alcoholic grape juice and try to convince him it's wine. I should have known they wouldn't do."

Again, his words rattled around my head but failed to make any sense. Distractions? Murdering young women was a *distraction?* What kind of black deed could possibly be dark enough that committing murder was an acceptable alternative? If murder was his distraction, what did he really want?

His voice dropped, and he answered my question as if I'd spoken out loud.

"I wanted you."

I stopped breathing, even as the hairs on the back of my neck began to rise. Peter made up for my lack of respirations by increasing his, finally breaking his composure.

"It was always you, Cami. For as long as I can remember, I wanted you. Every family visit brought us closer together, and I knew when you moved here I'd grow closer to you still."

I shook my head. None of this felt real. This was a nightmare, because my uncle couldn't be a serial killer, couldn't be *obsessed* with his niece. This was so wrong on so many levels, and how did one even process this kind of information? It was impossible.

Almost against my will, my mind began showing me clips of memories like a slideshow. My uncle hugging me, always hanging on a little too long. Touching me, never inappropriately, but casually and often. That picture of us at the beach, with me in a *swimsuit* for Christ's sake, living on my uncle's desktop for him to admire anytime he pleased.

The bacon and pancakes rolled in my stomach.

"I thought we were getting along great in the beginning. I got to see you in school and came by the house as frequently as I dared. But you were distant, like something was distracting you from me. Remember that day I brought you soup because you were sick? I thought I'd be able to hang out with you, tell you jokes to make you feel better. But something was off. You couldn't wait to get rid of me."

Peter began to talk faster, his voice growing stronger and louder as if he couldn't hold the words in any longer. He needed to let his story out, and who better to listen to it than me?

"I didn't take your rejection well. I needed an outlet, someone to take your place if only momentarily. As I drove to clear my thoughts, I saw Heather on the side of the road. She had a flat tire and was trying to change it herself. I pulled over to help.

"As I talked to her, I remembered how similar the two of you were when she was in school. She was quiet. Sweet. She didn't call anyone to help her with the tire because she didn't want to bother them, and I knew this was something you would have done as well. She didn't look like you, but something told me she could be my Cami for a while. I hid the evidence as well as I could."

I tasted bile and tried to choke it back down. There *had* been a reason the first murder occurred the day I met Zeke, but it wasn't because Zeke or any of his people were responsible.

In a way, *I* was partially responsible. I hadn't given my uncle the attention he craved, and he'd taken his disappointment out on an innocent girl. I tried to reign in my horror even as Peter plowed on with his story, his confession, whatever this word vomiting was to him.

"I thought I'd gotten things out of my system with Heather. I didn't regret what I did. If her death meant I could avoid hurting you, then she was a worthy sacrifice. I decided to continue to get closer to you. I thought I had things under control. At least, for a few weeks I did.

"Then I overheard Lacey talking to your mother on the phone one evening, gushing over the fact that you'd snuck out and spent time with a boy. *A boy.*"

The last word was almost a snarl, and I saw something in my uncle's eyes I'd never witnessed before, in him or anyone else. He was unhinged, his pupils dilated and wild, like an animal cornered and about to lash out at anything that came too close.

Then his eyes cleared, that dementing fog swept away. He tsked and shook his head, pursing his lips at me like I was a naughty child that had broken the rules. In whatever delusion he lived in, I probably had. I *really* needed to get out of there.

"I was so angry with you, Cami. I knew that this boy was the thing coming between us, the distraction that was stopping you from giving me your full attention. I went on another drive to clear my head and stopped at G.G.'s to buy a drink. And there was Jessie, taking out the trash. Another quiet girl, just like you. I found the release I needed.

"Only I knew I couldn't let things continue the way they were. I needed something to turn you into my arms. A stimulant. So I printed those news clippings of your good-for-nothing father and hung them on your locker. I waited until you found them and swept in to save the day. I was there when you needed me."

I couldn't stop the gasp that escaped my lips. He did *what?*

I knew that committing gruesome murders was infinitely worse than bullying and manipulating me, but somehow the idea of my uncle staging that shameful, embarrassing moment in the hallway stung even more than the revelation that he was a serial killer.

"We had such a good talk in my office after that, I thought we were finally heading in the direction that I wanted. I was someone you could lean on, someone who could put you back together. But then you disappeared into the woods. You were still hurting, and you didn't come to me."

It was ironic, in a way. Peter had taped up those awful news clippings in an effort to draw us closer, but all it had done was send me running straight into Zeke's arms.

As I stood listening to my uncle speak, I felt disconnected from my body, as if I were hearing all of it through a long tunnel. I was able to mull things over in my mind, finally processing them in a way, but knowing with a cold clarity that this wasn't the time to do that. I needed to go, to run, to escape whatever evil was standing before me. But I couldn't move.

"When I found you in the woods, I nearly took you then. But I resisted. I wasn't a monster, Cami, I wanted you to come to me on your own volition. But I needed a release, something to distract me from you until you were ready. I knew Penny was working late, preparing for the art show. So I dropped your aunt off at home and went to the school. She was messier than the others."

Peter's face twisted. His eyes were distant, lost in the memory of my art teacher's last moments. If I was going to get away from him, I'd need to take advantage when he was distracted. I noted that he stood in a way that would block my path if I wanted to run out the way I came in. If I could get past him, maybe I'd have a chance of getting out of this alive.

"After talking to you on the phone following the assembly, I knew things were back on track. You were still distracted, but it was because you were scared. You were talking to me again. I knew in my heart that things were going to be fine with us.

"Then you showed up with that *boy* last night. I watched the two of you from a distance, and I knew I'd lost. It was over. Everything I had worked towards was for nothing. The way you looked at him, like he held the world in the palm of his hand. It was disgusting."

Peter's eyes were cold steel with just a hint of the crazy I had glimpsed in them before. His body shook with his anger, tremors that seemed to roll down his arms in waves.

"Did you think I was just going to let him take you from me? You don't belong with him Cami, you must know that. I knew a distraction wouldn't be enough for me this time. I needed you, before he could take you away completely. Before the night was over I came up with a plan.

"I told Lacey I was going to help clean up and that she should head home without me. Natalie was all too enthusiastic when I asked her for a ride home. She was so *loud*, so obnoxious. I knew I'd find no pleasure from her, this girl that was nothing like you, so I ended her as quickly as I could. Like I said, she was a means to an end..."

I choked on the air that was halfway to my lungs, gasping as the truth of my friend's fate was revealed at last. My fear had been growing as Peter talked, as more of his dirty deeds were exposed. I had still been holding onto the hope that he'd simply stolen my friend's phone, that she was at home and in bed, completely oblivious to this conversation being held less than a mile from her house.

He crushed my hope with an offhand remark, as if the world wouldn't be changed in the slightest with Natalie gone. And she was gone, of that I was certain. Dead. Murdered by my psychotic uncle for no better reason than having the bad luck of being my friend and the ticket he needed to get to me.

I began to hyperventilate, all of my uncle's words pounding through my head. Not only was I the daughter of a drunk, I was now the niece of a serial killer that had murdered young women because they reminded him of me. Even though their deaths weren't my fault, even though I knew I couldn't be to blame for Peter's actions, I still felt the guilt of those atrocities as sharply as if I'd been the one wielding the knife.

A wave of self-loathing filled me once again, its presence familiar and cold as it greeted me like an old friend. I began to bow under the weight of the guilt, wishing I could take back everything that had led to the deaths of all those innocents.

A small voice whispered that it should have been me. *I* should have died, rather than allow my uncle to hurt someone in my place. I knew I wasn't thinking logically, but still I couldn't stop the dark thoughts from permeating my mind. Perhaps I shouldn't run. Perhaps I should face the fate that was meant for me all along before anyone else could be killed on my behalf.

Uncle Peter took a gentle step towards me, his hand outstretched. "It's okay, Cami. We're here now. It's all going to be fine."

His voice was like velvet as he stepped even closer. I closed my eyes, allowing the emotions to overtake my mind. It would be so easy to give into the soul crushing depression and allow whatever was coming for me to simply come.

A picture of Natalie popped into my head, her face as clear and vivid as the day I met her. She was laughing at something I said, being a friend to me just when I believed the luxury of friends was beyond my grasp. She had loved me, not in the twisted way my uncle did, but with a love so true and pure that it filled my very soul.

A hand brushed my cheek. I snapped out of my self-inflicted torment like a current of electricity had shocked me to my core. I staggered backwards, my eyes flying open to take in the look of surprise on my uncle's face.

"No."

I spat the word, horrified that I'd considered allowing this evil man to win so easily. If I died, who would bring justice to those women? To Natalie? I couldn't just let him get away with this. I couldn't roll over and die.

My survival instincts kicked in at last, sending blood to my extremities with a few strong beats of my heart. I had no element of surprise, no moment of distraction to take advantage of, but I didn't care.

I spared the opening behind my uncle half a glance before turning and sprinting headlong into the heart of the Cursed Woods.

Chapter Twenty-Seven

I was not a fast runner.

Back in junior high, Michael convinced me to join the track team with him, probably in an effort to make me socialize more and break me out of my shell. I endured exactly one tortuous week before quitting, and even he couldn't argue with my decision.

I finished last in every sprint, so the coach tried moving me to distance. I couldn't even run half a mile without walking, so they threw me into the field events. There, I made a fool out of myself by tripping down the long jump lane and missing the high jump mat completely, nearly giving myself a concussion in the process. Shot put, you say? I couldn't even lift one of those tiny heavy balls without dropping it on my foot.

Maybe if I'd stuck it out a bit longer I would have been more prepared for the run for my life. This deep in the trees, the vines and brush were so thick that I had to bring my knees up to my chest with every stride or risk falling flat on my face. I should have given the hurdles another shot, and maybe I'd be able to jump over the fallen trees without scraping my knees across the bark and leaving a bloody trail in my wake.

Of course, I needn't have worried about leaving a visual trail for him to follow seeing as he was right on my heels the whole time. It was a miracle he hadn't caught me after my first two steps.

"Please don't run from me Cami," Peter said softly, only a few feet behind me. Somehow he didn't sound winded from the pursuit, while I didn't even have the spare breath to throw a *"Screw you!"* over my shoulder.

As I gulped in the cool October air, its icy tendrils flooded my mind and allowed me to think more clearly than I had since first setting foot in the forest. *Focus*, I commanded myself.

I wasn't dead or caught yet, which meant I still had a chance of getting out of this. But I needed an advantage, some kind of upper hand if I was going to make it out of the woods and then somehow find help before he could catch me and drag me back in.

Even if I had any clue how to fight, Peter was twice my size and would overpower me in an instant. I didn't have my father's gun, or even a knife to defend myself with. My only chance of surviving this was if he tripped and impaled himself on a broken tree branch (something I should try to avoid doing myself) or if someone magically came to my rescue.

Magic... *Zeke!* Why hadn't I thought of him before? If anyone was going to come to my rescue out here in the middle of the Cursed Woods, it would be him. Weren't the witches supposed to be tracking the "evil presence" in the forest? My uncle had been in the forest for at least twenty minutes, probably even longer depending on how long he'd waited for me to show up. Why hadn't they descended on him as soon as he set foot in the trees? Why didn't they stop him from killing Natalie?

Our conversation, spoken through paper birds like a pair of walkie-talkies, came back to me in a wave. *"They could be in the woods right now, but unless they're committing an act against nature we won't even know they're there."*

Apparently talking to me and then chasing me through the trees wasn't an act against nature. No wonder they weren't able to catch him with Natalie. Hadn't Peter admitted that he killed her as quickly as possible? He probably killed and buried her before they could pick up on where he'd done it.

I never thought I would wish for my friend to die slowly, a drawn-out end full of pain and suffering. But if my uncle had taken his time with her, maybe Zeke's coven could have found her before he finished her off. Maybe they could have saved her. This was so twisted, so sick. No one should ever have to think about or wish for the things that were violating my mind.

Consumed by my thoughts, I didn't see the black, gaping hole in the earth until I tripped forward and began to fall straight into it. Before I could plummet into what would surely be a broken neck and death, something grabbed my arm and jerked me up and to the side. My momentum redirected, I hit the ground next to the pit hard, my head bouncing off the earth like it had when I missed that stupid high jump mat.

Zeke? I thought, disoriented. Had he found me after all?

But the voice that spoke over me wasn't Zeke's.

"Not quite yet, Cami." Peter chuckled, his sharp scent assaulting my nostrils once again. "You'll get to go down there later. Right now, we have business to attend to."

My head spun, and I gripped the ground as I tried to make sense of up and down. I definitely had a concussion this time. As the trees ceased their nauseating dance around me and the world finally righted itself, I stared down into the hole and tasted bile as my breakfast started to crawl back up my throat.

It wasn't a hole. It was a grave. An *occupied* grave.

Natalie lay sprawled at the bottom, one arm thrown out to the side and the other resting heavily on her chest. The white dress she'd worn the night before was smudged with dirt, the flowers barely visible amidst all the muck. It was only two days ago that I'd helped her pick it out at the thrift store, and now the dress was used up and ruined, just like her body. I barely registered the blood-stained dirt around her, the line across her neck that created a menacing red smile. Her throat had been cut cleanly, the blade wielded as deftly as a surgeon's scalpel.

Out of the corner of my eye I saw my uncle extract Natalie's phone from his pocket. From another pocket he produced a simple red handkerchief, the bold color catching my attention in this world of dirt and debris. He used it to wipe the phone thoroughly, removing any trace of his fingerprints, before tossing it into the grave to thunk uselessly against Natalie's stomach. *I'll give it back to her soon,* he'd said. I shuddered.

Before I could even try to stand Peter was on top of me, grabbing my wrists on either side as his weight held me down.

I tried to buck him off, tried to wriggle a hand loose in a futile attempt to claw at his face, but he was too strong. I exerted all the energy I had left in my struggle to break free from him, knowing it was no use. We'd just sprinted what felt like a mile into the woods, and I was spent. My uncle, on the other hand, seemed like he'd just been warming up. Seemed like, I realized, he definitely could have caught me sooner.

The truth smacked me in the face, stealing what little breath I had left.

Of course he'd let me run ahead of him, never more than a yard away, always within his reach. He knew I wouldn't try to run past him in the direction of Natalie's house because I would have run straight into his waiting arms. So he allowed me to think I was getting away, all while he was really leading me right where he wanted. Further into the trees, away from any outside help. He had corralled me to this spot like a sheep to its slaughter.

Natalie's grave had been left open because it wasn't full yet. This was a grave meant for two, and its second occupant had just arrived.

A strangled sound escaped my lips before I could swallow it.

"Shh, Cami," Peter purred as he brought my hands together above my head. With his chest directly above my nose, the pungent smell of his cologne was nauseating. Maybe if I threw up on him he'd be too disgusted to go through with this. Or maybe he'd kill me sooner, stealing whatever chance I could give Zeke to find me before it was too late. I needed to give Zeke all the time I could manage, needed to draw this out as long as possible. But how?

Peter adjusted his grip, repositioning my wrists so he could hold them together with his left hand, effectively trapping me against the dirt.

"It's okay Cami, you're safe with me." His words were contradicted by the long knife he pulled out of its sheath behind his back. The silver metal gleamed in the sunlight filtering through the trees, blinding me for a moment.

He shifted his weight over me, locking my body in place. When I could tear my eyes away from the knife, I noticed he was smiling again. It wasn't an evil grin, I decided, but rather the type of smile you share with someone you love. His eyes roved over my face like I was a priceless gem, a relic he'd searched for his whole life and had found at last.

Distantly, I wondered what was going on in his head, if he realized how absolutely insane he was. How could he have acted so normal all these years and hidden the fact that he was a complete psycho? How could he not see that I wasn't safe with him, could *never* be safe with him when this shriveled, twisted part of him was calling for my blood?

Slowly, carefully, Peter held the knife flat against my torso and eased the bottom of my shirt up. Cool air licked my stomach, and I felt my skin break out in goosebumps. My heart thudded wildly in my chest, and I wondered if everything in a two-mile radius could hear it. Were the animals curious as to the source of the incessant, beating drum? Would they notice when it stopped?

"Please, Uncle Peter," I gasped. Tears were streaming down the sides of my face freely now, dripping into my ears. "Please don't hurt me."

Something flickered behind his eyes. Pain? Regret? Whatever it was was meaningless. I could tell he was too far gone.

"You're mine, Cami." He cooed, running a light finger along my gooseflesh. "Everything will be okay because you're mine. I won't let that boy or anyone else hurt you."

He brought his face back down to mine. I tried to flinch away but there was nowhere to go, no slack in his grip. He kissed my forehead softly before returning his attention to the knife and the exposed skin of my stomach.

The first slash was quick and smooth. I didn't process the pain until he was moving on to the second cut, his knife carving a pattern into my flesh as easily as my paintbrush had outlined the Cursed Woods.

A scream was ripped from my throat, a primal sound that I'd never heard myself make. I fought against him even harder, but his body weight held me fast.

I remembered all the times I cut myself shaving in the shower, watching the blood well up and stain the water pink, but the memory of those tiny nicks was like butterfly kisses in comparison to this new understanding of pain.

I was vaguely aware that he was still talking to me, speaking in a calm voice like a mother trying to soothe her child. He was telling me that it was okay to scream, that I should let it all out, that it was okay because no one would hear us this deep in the woods. It was okay for me to feel this pain, because it was *him*, and I was *his*.

Hadn't I been hoping he would drag this out? I was such an idiot. Natalie had gotten off easy with a single slice to her neck, her blood draining out in seconds. But I was going to suffer. He was going to slice me up piece by piece until there was nothing left for Zeke to find except a tic-tac-toed mess, a freshly carved jack-o'-lantern.

I didn't know how long the cutting went on. Seconds, minutes, an hour? It seemed like an eternity. When my uncle finally leaned back to appraise his work, I felt weak and drained. My mind was growing fuzzy around the edges.

The tears were no longer flowing, my body's attempt to conserve as much of its fluids as it could, no doubt. But I could feel the blood trickling down my sides to pool beneath my back. I could still feel the echo of the blade against my flesh.

Peter laid the knife to the side before touching my stomach gently. I fought through the haze and forced myself to look at him, to stare into the eyes of this monster. Perhaps if he could see the hate there, the absolute revulsion, he would realize how truly sick he was.

He touched my face with his palm, leaving a bloody handprint behind that felt sticky against my cool skin. I narrowed my eyes and spit in his face.

"Nice, Cami." Peter rolled his eyes and wiped the saliva away with the back of his hand. He tsked at me again like I was an errant schoolgirl, and then retrieved his knife from the ground. The metal gleamed even more sharply as he brought it near my face.

"Shall we continue?"

I took a deep breath to prepare myself, trying to guess which body part he would target next. That was when I felt them.

Their presence hit me in a warm wave, as though sunshine had somehow been bottled and injected directly into my veins. I couldn't describe the sensation that overtook me, but I latched onto it with all of my being. It was warmth, peace. Hope.

"Stop!" an angel's voice snarled. Could angels snarl? My fuzzy brain didn't think so, but this one had. I ignored the pounding in my head and turned my neck to catch a glimpse of him.

The person that stood before me wasn't human. It *was* an angel, I realized in dismay. A fiery angel completely engulfed in flames. The fire was hot enough to warm my skin even from my place on the ground. The flames licked over the angel's skin in a tickling embrace.

The blaze reminded me of the Blossoming Ceremony, the bonfire that reached towards the sky and moved in a way that suggested it was something more, something alive. Magic. That would explain why the angel wasn't burnt to a crisp.

I squeezed my eyes shut before opening them again, my vision clearing slightly. The flames remained, but now I could make out black hair, electric blue eyes, and a look of fury that was sharp enough to kill. *Zeke*.

Flanking either side of him were two other teens, friends of Zeke's that I had met briefly. I noted that they stood out of the reach of Zeke's flames, their own skin bare and covered only by their usual leathers. They each held a bow in one hand, their other hands occupied by arrows aimed directly at us. Zeke was the only source of brightness in our quickly darkening section of forest, as if he had drawn in all of the surrounding light and warmth and was concentrating it into that inferno.

My uncle's body had frozen in place, his grip tightening on my wrists at the appearance of these strangers. His head began to whip back and forth between them, like he was watching a very exciting tennis match. It would have been funny under normal circumstances, if I hadn't been in excruciating pain. If I wasn't currently bleeding out onto the forest floor.

"What is this?" Peter asked, his voice steadier than I would have expected given the weapons pointed at him.

Despite the pain, despite the fact that I was still pinned to the ground with a psycho looming over me, I smiled.

This was redemption.

"Drop the knife and we won't hurt you," one of the boys said. His voice was deeper than I remembered. Zeke pegged him with a look that suggested someone was getting hurt here whether he cooperated with them or not. Four young women had been murdered, and he was on his way to his fifth. Not to mention, this wasn't just any young woman being carved up in front of them. This was personal.

I couldn't hide my relief any longer.

"Zeke," I croaked. My voice was as soft as a breath, but he heard it. His eyes flitted to mine on the ground. There was anger there, a lot of it, but something else as well. Fear.

Peter gasped. I felt his recognition by the way his body tensed and held me even more possessively before I turned and saw it in his eyes. His head swung back and forth between the two of us, his face changing from surprise, to alarm, and finally settling on disgust.

"He–he's one of–*them*?" He choked on the last word, his eyes coming to rest on mine. I flinched at his inhuman gaze. The madness was back, and it looked as if it were here to stay.

"Camille. Elizabeth. Stone." He breathed, each piece of my name hissed like an insult. "Do *not* tell me you've been fraternizing with these animals. These *monsters."*

I probably shouldn't have pushed him. He was clearly insane, incapable of rational thought, and unpredictable in the least. But the fog in my brain had transformed into a white cloud of hatred. Maybe lack of self-control ran in the family.

"The only monster here is *you,"* I said firmly, finally finding my voice again. He recoiled as if I'd slapped him, but I continued anyway.

"You fed me all those lies about Zeke's community, claiming they murdered innocent women as sacrifices, but it was you all along. They're good people, better than most of the people living in Green Peaks. Why did you tell those lies about them, knowing they weren't responsible? Why did you lie about them to me?"

I could have answered my questions easily enough on my own. *Because he's evil. Because he found an easy scapegoat and was trying to steer the town in the wrong direction. Because he's as crazy as an outhouse rat.*

But I still wasn't prepared for his response.

"Because they're unnatural degenerates that should have stayed dead when my grandfather ran them out of town the first time."

Peter's eyes were wide, his nostrils flaring now. Spittle flew from his lips and crusted on his chin.

"My grandfather worked hard to turn the town against them. He even had to stage some murders to make the people see them for what they truly were. The fact that they survived at all just proves that they aren't human. They don't belong with us, Cami. They don't deserve to live at all."

You could have heard a pin drop in the silence that followed his statement. It was as if the entire forest was holding its breath, waiting to see what would happen next.

The boy to Zeke's right took a step forward. Oliver, I thought his name was. His green eyes practically glowed in the shadows.

"Your grandfather killed those women all those years ago?" His hand holding the arrow twitched slightly, like he had to force himself not to let it fly. "He's the reason our ancestors were killed and exiled?"

I knew my mouth was open wide enough to start collecting bugs, but I couldn't seem to close it. So many revelations today. Too many. If I made it home alive, would my mom add to the fun and declare that she was the Easter Bunny?

"Of course he did." Peter rolled his eyes, as if it should have been obvious. "The sluts deserved it anyway, or so my grandfather said. I found his journals in storage when I was your age, Cami. I'd heard all the stories before, but only my grandfather knew the whole truth. He saved our town when he purged it of those demons."

Peter licked his lips, his eyes narrowing at Zeke. "And here we are, a hundred years later, with the beasts trying to ruin everything again."

He shook his head and looked back at me, the fire surrounding Zeke reflecting in his glassy eyes. "We can still be together, Cami." He whispered, tucking a strand of hair behind my ear with one of the fingers holding the knife. "Just close your eyes, and I'll make everything better."

But I refused to close my eyes, refused to listen to him for another second. So I had a clear view when he raised the blade above my chest and prepared to stab me in the heart.

I watched in slow motion as the knife came arcing down, slicing through the air as it zoned in on its target. It was inches away from my chest when two arrows pierced my uncle simultaneously, one in his shoulder and the other in the forearm holding the knife.

Peter screeched in agony, his left hand releasing my wrists to cup his bloody arm. I was completely soaked in blood now, the river flowing from my uncle's wounds washing over me and mixing with my own dark pool of red.

I could no longer feel my hands and knew I was sure to have bruises from where his grip had restrained me, but I took advantage of his momentary distraction by shoving him off me and jumping to my feet.

It was a terrible idea, of course. My body was weak from blood loss and my head spun anew as my legs tried to hold my weight. The cuts on my stomach screamed as my skin stretched with the movement, but I used the pain to anchor myself to consciousness.

The flames around Zeke vanished in an instant, plunging us into momentary darkness. I felt his warmth behind me as he held me up, smelled his familiar campfire scent as he kissed my hair and squeezed me even more tightly against his chest.

Light returned slowly to our area in the woods, and I watched as Peter staggered backwards, away from us. Oliver and Benson tracked his movements with their bows, waiting for an excuse to impale him with more arrows.

"You're going to regret this!" He spat, backing up another step. "You're going to wish you were never born!"

The pain from my stomach was fading into nothing as the fog over my mind returned in full force. I couldn't help thinking this was very much like an old episode of Scooby Doo, the villain unmasked at last and threatening the heroes. *You kids are going to pay for this! You and your dumb dog!*

That half delirious thought, combined with a blurry vision of my uncle turning and crashing through the trees was the last thing my mind knew before allowing the fog to cover everything with its blissful, silent blanket.

I was sinking in an ocean of black.

I felt the waves toss me around playfully, the water thick and velvety against my skin. Did I have skin though? I couldn't feel my extremities, couldn't feel the tug of my hair as the current swirled around me.

And was I sinking or floating? Was it possible to sink and float at the same time? The water was so dark, it was impossible to know up from down. I had a feeling that up and down were meaningless here anyway.

I didn't know how long I drifted, neither sinking or floating, simply existing in that blackness. Like so many other things, time was meaningless here too. The only thing that mattered was the ocean and the understanding that I was a part of it now. That is, until a light interrupted my peace.

It was a thin golden glow, like when my father would crack my door open and a sliver of light from the hallway would escape into my dark bedroom. I tried to squint my eyes against the sudden illumination, but I had no eyes here either. Who opened the door?

Cami, the beacon of light whispered. The voice was warm, and I didn't realize I was cold until its golden breath washed over my phantom body. The feeling was familiar, and something itched at the back of my mind, demanding to be known.

Cami, you have to wake up!

The voice was louder now, and the glow was growing, as if the door at the end of the light was opening wider. I knew that voice, remembered that warmth, that feeling of hope. It had saved me when I was in a different dark place, one full of pain and hatred and fear. This was a voice I could trust.

So I ignored the fact that I didn't know which way was up. I didn't care that I couldn't feel my body. I focused on the light, on the voice that was calling my name, and swam through the open door.

I opened my eyes to a world of white. It was a slap in the face compared to the darkness I had just swum out of. The walls were white, the ceiling was white, even the soft blanket I was currently tucked into was spotless and white.

You're in a hospital, the part of my mind that seemed to be working insisted. I wracked my brain for why I would need to be in a hospital, and the day's events came flooding back.

The Cursed Woods. Uncle Peter. Natalie.

Zeke!

He must have been the voice that pulled me out of my slumber, although I couldn't hear him now. Something was happening though, something I needed to be a part of. I could feel it.

I jerked myself up in the too white bed and hissed when I felt the painful tearing in my stomach.

"Cami!" My mother exclaimed, hopping out of a chair I hadn't noticed was stationed to my left. She materialized at my side, placing a gentle hand on my back in an effort to soothe me or keep me in place. I wasn't sure which.

"Mom," I gasped reflexively, even as I threw the blanket onto the floor and swung my legs off the bed.

Without the cover of the blanket, most of my body was exposed to the freshly chilled air coming in through the vent above my bed. I shivered, wrinkling my nose at the paper gown I'd been dressed in. The material crunched as I moved and made an odd slithering sound as it scraped against the thick bandage wrapped around my torso.

I ignored the pain radiating out from the bandages and forced myself to my feet.

"No, Cami!" My mother said sternly. I barely felt the pressure of her hands on my shoulders as she tried to push me back onto the bed. She wasn't applying any kind of real force, though, nothing compared to the weight Peter had used to force me to the ground.

"You're going to tear your stitches!"

It wasn't my mother's words that stopped me, but rather the hitch in her voice, the fear she was uselessly trying to hide. I paused and looked at her for the first time since waking up in that hospital room, and noticed she was crying. Had been crying, in fact, for hours by the looks of her splotchy cheeks and bloodshot eyes.

"Mom," I said more gently, sitting back down on the bed. I didn't have time to calm her down. I needed to get out of there, needed to figure out what was happening. Couldn't she feel it too? Electricity seemed to race up and down my body, like I was a live wire capable of catching fire at any moment.

"You need—to rest," my mom choked out. Her breaths were coming in spasmodic sobs now. "The doctor said—so much—*blood!*"

She collapsed onto the bed beside me, her arms wrapping around me in a death grip as her tears overflowed and drenched my hospital gown. I winced at the new pull in my stitches but refrained from pushing her away. She felt the movement and gasped, releasing me anyway. I grabbed her hand before she could move away and clutched it tightly in my own.

"I'm okay, Mom." I whispered.

I wasn't though. Nothing about what had happened to me was okay. But I forced myself to take a breath and squeezed her hand firmly. "I'm going to be fine."

I would have plenty of time to pity myself and be babied by my mother later. Right then, all I cared about was finding out everything that had happened between losing consciousness in the woods and waking up in that room.

Did they catch Peter? How did I get to the hospital? And where was Zeke?

With my free hand, I tipped my mother's chin up and forced her to look at me. It was the same action she'd used on me countless times during my childhood, when I fell and hurt myself or was upset about something and didn't want to meet her eyes as I cried. It felt odd and somewhat cruel for our roles to be reversed now.

"Tell me what happened." I said calmly, just as she had done for me all those times when I was a kid.

Her eyes swam behind the tears, and I willed her to pull herself together. I needed her right now, possibly more than I'd needed her in my entire life. Five minutes of strength was all I asked for so I could find my answers and plan for what would happen next.

My mother nodded as if she understood my urgency. She took a shuddering breath and hiccuped once before beginning.

"Someone found you along the side of the highway." She paused again, as if speaking the words aloud were causing her physical pain. She braced herself and went on. "You must have crawled out of the woods and collapsed there... after they did those horrible things to you."

I allowed my mother another minute to cry as I thought about her words. After my less than pleasant treatment from my uncle, I'd been in no shape to crawl anywhere, let alone however many miles it took to get out of those woods. The last thing I remembered was Zeke's solid form at my back, his arms wrapped around me, and the trail of blood dripping from Peter's wounds as he hightailed it into the trees.

One of the boys must have carried me out of the forest and left me by the road for someone else to find and bring to safety. But why hadn't they brought me themselves? Or, better yet, just healed me? Weren't witches capable of healing humans? There had to be something else going on.

My mother sniffled, interrupting my speculation before continuing.

"No one knew what had happened to you or who was responsible. It wasn't until your Uncle Pete came to the hospital just as banged up as you were and told us what happened."

I froze.

There was a rushing sound in my ears, like running water. I wondered if that black ocean was about to make a reappearance and swallow me whole. Surely I hadn't heard her right, or she was mistaken.

"Uncle Peter... was here?" I croaked.

My mother wrapped her arm around me, carefully this time. Her other hand came up to smooth my hair against my shoulder.

"Yes honey, but don't worry, he's going to be fine. They patched up those nasty arrow holes, and then he discharged himself and left to convene with the other town leaders. He was so upset over what happened to you. We all are. He's going to make sure those *Satan worshipers* pay for what they did."

She squeezed me against her chest in a one-armed hug, but I couldn't return the sentiment. What in the *actual heck* was going on here? Peter had gotten away from Zeke and his friends, obviously, but to come here and spread more lies about Zeke's people after butchering his own niece? This was taking it too far.

I was so wrapped up in my own thoughts I didn't realize my mom was still talking.

"—so thankful for your uncle," she was saying. "He got us our house, gave me a job, and now saved your life. We're so lucky he heard you screaming in the woods and came to your rescue. If he hadn't taken those arrows, I'm sure you wouldn't have been able to get away. Our family owes him so much, and I thank heaven every day for putting him into Lacey's life."

My nostrils flared, and the taste of bile returned to my throat. This could *not* be happening. Peter couldn't just waltz back into town and claim to be the hero after murdering all those women, after almost murdering *me.* I couldn't believe he thought he could get away with this.

"Mom," I interrupted.

She sat back a little at the sharpness of my tone, her eyes soft. I braced myself for the words I was about to say, but they *needed* to be said. This insanity had to end here, now.

"I don't know what all Peter told you, but he's a liar. Actually, he's freaking *crazy*! *He* was the one that attacked me in the woods. *He* killed all those women. He even killed Natalie!"

My voice broke, a sob hitching in my chest. It was the first time I said the words aloud. That Natalie was dead, gone, her life stolen from this world by the hands of my uncle.

It still didn't feel real, but the image of Natalie lying at the bottom of that grave was seared painfully into my mind. The red stained dirt, the ruined dress, that bloody smile of her opened throat.

I tried to blink the images away. This wasn't the time to go into a trauma induced breakdown.

My mother wrapped her arms around me again, her touch tender and warm. I sank into her embrace and allowed her to rock me gently on the bed. If only my problems could be swept away with a hug and a kiss like they were when I was a child.

"It's okay, Camille." She sang gently as we rocked. "You've been through so much. Why don't you lie down and get some more rest, hmm? I'll be here the whole time."

I shook my head and brought our movement to a halt.

"You aren't listening to me," I asserted. "Peter killed those women and he's going to kill again. He's, like, obsessed with me or something. It's *sick*, and we need to stop him!"

My mom smiled at me sadly, like I was the one who was sick here. She brushed my hair behind my ear and began speaking to me slowly, like I was the innocent child I longed to be again.

"You hit your head pretty badly, Cami. The doctor said you have a concussion and could experience some memory loss.

You're just confused right now, okay? You know your uncle would never hurt you. He's the one who *saved* you."

She squeezed my hands with her last sentence, as if she could press the truth into my skin. Only it wasn't the truth, it was just another lie Peter had inflicted on the world.

I opened my mouth to argue some more, to make her understand, but the expression on her face stopped me. I could see it there, written clearly in her eyes and the way she held her mouth. She wasn't going to believe me.

No one will, a voice in my head whispered. And why should they? I was an outsider in this town, someone who hadn't grown up knowing everyone's siblings, parents, and grandparents. Peter was the principal of the only high school around, held a seat on the school board, and was viewed as a city leader in his own right.

He owned this town and everyone in it. He didn't even need to silence the only witness to his crimes, knowing everyone would take his side over hers. No one would listen to a sniveling teenager who had a history of being bullied, one who needed therapy to get over the scandal of her dead drunk father. Throw in a concussion and possible memory loss and he easily held the winning hand.

A noise came from outside the window. It sounded like yelling or chanting, but the voices were muffled by the thick glass. I remembered the feeling that had struck me when I woke up, the chill still buzzing through my veins that something terrible was about to happen. I needed to move, and if my mother wasn't going to help me then she was just another obstacle in my way.

I looked around the small room, thinking quickly. I spotted my sneakers and jeans folded neatly on a table, but the T-shirt I'd dressed in that morning was nowhere to be found. It had probably been cut off of me in the EMT's hurry to clean and patch up my stomach. I looked back at my mom and noticed the plain Old Navy jacket she wore to every occasion. It would have to do.

Schooling my features into the poor, traumatized daughter she expected, I glanced at my mother again and shivered violently. It worked like a charm.

"Oh honey, you must be freezing," she exclaimed, immediately shrugging out of her jacket. "I don't know why they have to keep these hospital rooms so cold."

I nodded demurely, clutching the fabric as she wrapped it around my shoulders. I hoped my shaking hands weren't overdoing it as I slipped my arms through the sleeves.

"I think I will try to rest," I murmured before lying down on my side. I pulled the thin white sheet up to my chin and shuddered again. My lip trembled, and I wondered if it was too late for me to consider a career in acting.

My mom held a hand to my cheek and gasped. "Darling, you *are* freezing!" And I was. The chill spreading through my body had leached into my bones, turning my blood into ice. The next shiver that racked my body was real.

I thought I would need to come up with another excuse to get her out of the room, ask for a drink of water or pain medication perhaps, but my mom continued to make things easy for me.

"I'll go and see if we can get more blankets and let the doctor know you're awake. You just hang tight, hun."

She squeezed my shoulder one last time and swept out of the room, pulling the door closed behind her. As soon as I heard the door click, I threw the blanket off and was out of bed in an instant. I moved too quickly, though, and the ground swayed beneath my feet, the room spinning dizzyingly around me. I clutched the bed frame to steady myself and stared at the walls until the room finally stopped moving. I didn't have much time.

Shimmying into my pants, I silently cursed myself for choosing today to wear skinny jeans. To add to the struggle, my socks were nowhere to be found and I had to slip into my tennis shoes with nothing to cover my bare feet. The comfort of my feet was hardly a priority at this point, but considering I had a lot of running ahead of me it would've been nice to have them.

I left the stupid hospital gown on but tucked the tail into my pants and zipped my mom's jacket up around it. I knew I had to look like a train wreck, and I didn't even want to think about the state of my hair, but it was a step up from running around town barefoot in a flimsy hospital gown. At least no one would be awarded a flash of my butt now.

Fully, if not a little awkwardly clothed, I ran to the window and let out a sigh of relief. For the first time since moving there, I was grateful that Green Peaks was a small town. The tiny hospital probably only held a dozen beds and had no reason to build a second story. If I'd been injured in Plainfield, planning my escape would've been much more difficult from a room on the fifth floor.

I unlatched the window and pushed. For a brief moment I thought it wasn't going to budge, that I was going to be standing there half naked and trying to escape when my mom and the doctor came strolling back into the room. But then it did open, the glass tilting downward into a clear slide and creating a gap just wide enough for me to duck under and climb out onto the other side.

My feet touched the ground and I was immediately hit with a wave of fresh air, washing away the smell of antiseptic. The sky had darkened while I was unconscious, the sun barely visible on the skyline. I estimated I had thirty more minutes before the sun would set completely and I'd be left to run around in the dark.

Not *complete* dark, though. As I jogged away from the hospital, my stitches screaming loudly with every step, I finally learned where all the light was coming from. Where the shouting I'd heard had originated.

The citizens of Green Peaks were preparing to invade the Cursed Woods.

Chapter Twenty-Nine

Suddenly I wasn't outside the hospital anymore. I was thrown back into the horrible memory I'd witnessed at the Blossoming Ceremony when Zeke's ancestors were banished from the town.

In the memory, I watched the people lift their torches and pitchforks into the air, crying for the eradication of the witches. I blinked, and the torches were replaced with modern day flashlights and cellphones, their beams lighting the quickly darkening night and throwing cruel shadows that danced around the mob.

The women here wore jeans and jackets instead of dresses, but the look of pure fury on their faces matched those of their ancestors. The men's old-fashioned firearms transformed into the rifles and shotguns I was accustomed to, and I noticed several people wearing holsters with their pistols and revolvers on display and ready to use.

People were flooding the street, marching down sidewalks and crossing grassy lawns all to gather in the hospital parking lot. I watched a couple of kids try to blend in with the crowd, crouching low so as not to be seen, only for their mother to spot them and send them running back to their house.

It was organized mayhem, and my uncle was leading the charge.

He stood in the bed of his Ford pickup truck, elevated above the horde that was still assembling around him. Someone must have helped him up there, because half of his checkered flannel shirt was obscured by a sling that bound his arm and injured shoulder tightly across his chest. The sleeve of his other arm had been rolled up to display the bandage wrapped around his first arrow wound. The arrow that had saved my life.

I stared at his bandaged arm in disgust. I knew without a doubt he was showing it off, keeping his sleeve rolled up to flaunt his battle wound. *Look what those animals did to me,* the bandage said, *I'm a hero for surviving their attack.*

"Citizens of Green Peaks!" Peter boomed. He didn't need a megaphone or a mic. His voice was already too loud in the darkening evening, his audience waiting silently for him to make his speech.

It was eerie how quiet everyone became, like a heavy blanket had settled over the crowd, muffling even the sounds of their breathing. I hung back, using a rusted orange minivan to shield myself from view.

A part of me was screaming that I needed to run, that a mob of angry people hell-bent on killing my boyfriend was the *last* place I needed to be right now. But I was rooted to the spot, staring at my uncle with my mouth gaping open like the rest of them. While the crowd seemed to be sharing the same look of awe and inspiration, however, I was pretty sure my face held a mixture of shock and indignation.

"I called you all out here tonight so we could finally put our fear to rest and avenge the young women who were stolen from us. The Green Peaks serial killer has been identified!"

A low rumble rolled through the crowd, whispers and murmurs breaking the silence. Based on the number of weapons I could see, I figured everyone had already been clued in on what this assembly was about. But hearing the words spoken aloud by my uncle seemed to light the spark the mob had been waiting for.

"Some of you might be wondering why we aren't handing this over to the police, or even the FBI." Peter continued. "But I think the majority of you know why it has to be us."

There were scattered shouts of *"Yes!"* throughout the mob, encouraging Peter to go on.

"In Green Peaks, we take care of our own. We fight our own battles and we right our own mistakes. We avenge our loved ones!"

Another wave shook the crowd as the people cheered their agreement. The energy in the parking lot was equivalent to that of a state championship pep rally. Only Peter wasn't the football coach, and he wasn't rallying the players up for a great game. He was preparing the mob for the slaughter to come.

"Earlier this morning, another young woman almost lost her life. My niece, Camille Stone." Peter looked back towards the hospital and the crowd followed his gaze, as if they could see through the hospital walls and take in my poor, wounded form. I tried not to gag at the ridiculous gesture and made myself even smaller behind the van.

"Luckily, I was able to save her, and barely made it out of those woods with my own life. The woods are indeed cursed, my friends, but not with the spirits of the past. The monsters are *real*, and the evil breathes and walks through those trees at this very moment, just waiting to strike at us again. Are we going to let them continue their wickedness?"

"No!" The people screamed.

"It's time for justice to be served, once and for all!"

Peter ended his speech by lifting his free arm towards the sky. His fist punched the air as hard as a gavel swinging to strike a lectern, the judgment passed at last. The crowd responded by raising their weapons and flashlights into the air as well, a war cry erupting from their throats as one.

For a moment, I saw myself pushing through the crowd, jumping onto the truck and shoving my uncle aside to tell everyone the truth. That *he* was the monster, and the people in the forest were the true heroes that had saved me.

But as my feet turned to carry me up to the platform, I felt a sharp tug around my navel as if a force was holding me back.

Don't, a voice whispered in my head. The breath was low and warm, just a tickle at the back of my mind, but I immediately recognized who it belonged to.

Come find me, Zeke's voice began again. His words were fainter this time, as if he were speaking down a very long tunnel while walking away from me. *Hurry, Cami!*

I awarded my uncle and his band of executioners one last glance before ducking completely out of sight. They wouldn't have believed me anyway, and probably would have fitted me for a straitjacket if I tried to convince them that witches saved my life. Zeke was right; I needed to find him before it was too late.

Keeping low to the ground, I weaved between cars and trucks as their drivers split into regiments fit for storming the Cursed Woods. I could still hear shouted commands and directions when I reached the edge of the parking lot and slipped stealthily into the forest.

I crossed the line of trees at last and was plunged into a world of darkness. Only two steps into the forest, and it felt like Dumbledore had activated his deluminator, quenching all light within a mile radius. The cellphones and flashlight beams in the parking lot couldn't seem to travel this far, as if the tree line was an impenetrable wall that filtered out the light.

How was I going to find Zeke's coven in a completely black forest? More importantly, how was I even going to navigate two feet without tripping on an unseen root and falling on my face?

As if he were waiting for the question to cross my mind, Zeke's voice gave me the answer. *Close your eyes,* he whispered.

I obeyed.

The moment my eyelids fluttered shut, the forest lit up around me. I could see the trees clearly now, could make out every detail of the leaves littering the forest floor. This world was black and white, a million hues of gray, but my vision was the sharpest it'd been in my entire life.

It was the most bizarre feeling, seeing with my eyes closed. I touched my eyelids tentatively to confirm they were really shut. When I was satisfied this was truly happening, I lowered my hands and gasped at the path that had been illuminated before me.

It was a sparkling blue fog that hovered a few feet above the ground. Starting directly in front of me, the path was about the width of a sidewalk and stretched deep into the forest, twisting between trees and winding out of sight. Because it was the only source of color in this sea of gray, I knew it would be impossible to lose.

I held out my hand and swept it carefully through the mist. I imagined my body would pass through it undisturbed, like trying to touch a ghost. I wasn't expecting it to feel so cool, or for the vapor to disintegrate upon contact, dispersing into even tinier speckles of blue glitter that made a cloud of dust around me.

Magic dust.

I forced myself to focus and pulled my hand back. I'd wasted too much time already standing around and listening to my uncle's ridiculous speech. I took a deep breath and plunged forward into the mist.

I ran through the magical path with my eyes closed. Each time I opened them slightly to peek at my surroundings, I was once again engulfed in darkness. I squeezed them shut and saw the black and white forest again, my body slicing through the blue fog like it was water vapor. Except water vapor didn't sparkle or rise in the air like smoke as soon as a person passed through it.

I observed its weird behavior over my shoulder, the path disintegrating into glittery plumes that disappeared completely once I was a few strides ahead. I had a brief moment of panic when I realized that if the path was gone, I had no way of finding my way out again. Even my weird night vision wouldn't help me navigate these woods if I was lost in the middle of the trees.

I just had to trust that Zeke was at the end of this path, and he'd know what to do when I arrived.

The stitches in my stomach were all but nonexistent as I flew through the mist. I wondered if the magic was healing me, or if a new burst of adrenaline was blocking out the pain. Based on the number of miracles I'd witnessed in the last hour alone, I was guessing it had to do with magic.

I didn't know how long I ran along the path, only that I was gasping for breath by the time I reached the end of it. The blue fog came to an end at the edge of a clearing I thought I recognized. I walked through the last plume of dust before stepping out of the thickness of the trees, allowing my eyes to open at last.

Just as I expected, I stood in the clearing that was Zeke's home. Lanterns were lit up and down the houses, casting flickering shadows across the emotionless faces of Zeke's people. I had to blink a few times as my normal eyesight returned. Apparently the light nullifying blackness was confined to the surrounding forest.

I looked around at the magic wielders gathered there, all motionless and staring at me. They were all there, I realized, every last member of Zeke's coven, from the hunched over form of an ancient looking man to the round cheeked baby in the arms of the woman next to him.

The crowd was half the size of the mob I'd recently escaped from, but somehow their steadfast forms and deathly quiet demeanors made them seem even bigger. The group stood together, breathed together as one, and, I thought, would willingly die together.

"Cami!" A voice shouted to my left.

I turned my head to find Zeke breaking away from his parents and sister, running towards me like I was a fire that needed to be put out. Even though I was exhausted, my legs completely spent, I forced them to move once again and met him halfway across the meadow.

Then I was in his arms, and it was as if the last twelve hours had been nothing but a dream. He squeezed me tightly and ran his hands over my arms, my shoulders, my hair, before stopping to cup my face.

"You came," he breathed. "You're really here."

Despite how romantic the moment was, I couldn't stop myself from rolling my eyes at him. He could be so dramatic sometimes. Although, I considered, so could I. Maybe we really were meant for each other.

"Of course," I said easily, smirking. "You sort of woke me up out of a near coma and screamed at me telepathically to find you. It sounded a little important."

His eyes twinkled at my sarcasm, and he lowered his lips to my forehead.

I flinched at his touch, all joking forgotten. My vision blurred, and I wasn't in the meadow anymore, the clearing replaced with a thick area of forest. Zeke's face disappeared and I was staring into the eyes of my uncle. He had kissed my forehead lovingly before opening my stomach with his knife.

I felt Zeke's hands tighten around my face, and I shuddered before snapping out of the memory. I expected him to be hurt at my reaction to his kiss, but his eyes were hard instead. His nostrils flared.

I had the distinct feeling that he'd shared my vision, had read my mind as I relived the most traumatic moment of my life. Or maybe I'd somehow pushed the images into his head all on my own. He had opened a psychic connection between the two of us on multiple occasions. Perhaps the channel was still open.

Zeke held his murderous expression for another second, his anger undoubtedly focused on Peter, before it crumpled into one of guilt and sympathy. He crushed me against his chest once again, resting his chin on the top of my head.

"Oh Cami," he sighed into my hair.

I allowed him to hold me, to piece me back together as he had done so many times before. I wondered if I would ever reach the point where I was so broken, my mind shattered into too many uneven shards, where no amount of holding or gluing would ever put me back together.

Someone sniffed behind us, and I was suddenly all too aware of our massive audience. I pulled back and gave the spectators closest to us a timid peek. Their faces no longer expressionless, they actually appeared moved at our reunion with soft eyes and warm smiles. I smiled back shyly before returning my gaze to Zeke.

"So," I whispered, my voice stolen away by my embarrassment. "Why am I here?"

Zeke's hands dropped from my arms to clasp both of my own. His lips turned up in what should have been a smile, but there was pain in the lines of his face, regret behind his electrifying eyes.

"Because we're leaving."

Chapter Thirty

"*What?*"

My breaths were deafening in the now silent meadow. I looked around at the faces that had smiled at me moments before, their eyes now downcast, avoiding my own. For the first time I noticed the knapsacks and leather satchels strapped across chests and dangling precariously on fur bound shoulders. Everyone was packed and ready to go. Waiting for me, but why?

Did I come all the way out here just to say goodbye?

Zeke squeezed my hands again, pulling my attention back to him. Recognizing the fear in my eyes, he quickly added, "We want you to come with us, of course."

Of course, as if it should have been obvious. But there was nothing obvious or logical about what was happening here.

Why would Zeke's people want to take me with them? I was an outsider. An outsider who lived in a town that murdered some of their ancestors one hundred years ago and was currently preparing for another round of slaughters. How could they trust me, nearly a complete stranger, when they clearly could trust no one else?

"Why?" I felt the word escape my lips and internally cringed at myself. Apparently, when under stress, I was only capable of speaking interrogatives.

Zeke didn't seem to mind my one-worded replies. His voice turned gentle and slow, as if he were talking to a frightened child.

"The townsfolk are in the forest right now trying to find us," he began calmly. "They shouldn't make it out here with the cloaking spell we dropped, but it's only a matter of time before they find us again and finish what they started. It's time for us to move on."

I shook my head at his reasoning. I knew the mob had surely progressed into the trees by now and were bound and determined to eradicate the witches for good. But I wasn't asking for their motive for leaving. I needed to know why I'd been included in their escape plan.

Swallowing the lump in my throat, I searched the faces of Zeke's people until I found the one I was looking for. While everyone else avoided my gaze, her eyes were trained on mine, as if she had been waiting for me to address her.

"You want me to come with you?" My voice was barely a whisper, but I knew Alexandra heard it. I wondered if she caught my inflection on the word *you*, if she knew I was asking her specifically and not the rest of the coven.

It was true that she'd been kind to me at our last meeting, but only after talking to Zeke. I still remembered the venom in her voice and the fire in her eyes when she realized her son had spilled all their secrets to a human. But if Zeke said they wanted me to come with them, as Leader of the coven, she must have given him permission to bring me along.

Alexandra stepped forward, breaking away from the rest of her family. Her black hair seemed to sway around her even though I couldn't feel a breeze this deep in the forest. She walked up to us before placing a hand on my shoulder. Her other hand came to rest on Zeke's arm, forming a connection between the three of us.

"Camille Stone," she said my name with authority, like it was a title fit for a lord or queen. "You were introduced to our kind by my son, Ezekiel Rivers. You have been taught many things and have even witnessed the Blossoming Ceremony of one of our own. But you still don't know everything about our way of life."

Exactly, I thought. *So why are you inviting me to run away with you?*

As if sensing my thoughts, she smiled. "Zeke was going to tell you everything when he felt you were ready to hear it. As fate would have it, that time has come sooner than we expected."

Her eyes were soft, and she paused for a moment to allow her words to sink in.

I glanced up at Zeke and noted a bead of sweat making its way down his nose. Given the chilly evening, I realized he must be nervous about whatever his mother was preparing to tell me. The fact that he hadn't shared the information with me himself was unnerving enough, but seeing him uncomfortable at whatever it was I was about to hear made my heart pound even faster.

Alexandra squeezed my shoulder, bringing my attention back to her.

"As it is with all important knowledge, we find the best method of telling is through *showing.*"

She winked at me, and her bright blue eyes were the last thing I saw before my vision went black.

It wasn't like the Blossoming Ceremony. Then, I'd had time for the magic to sweep over me slowly, filling me with its pulse and warmth that left me feeling like a bodiless spirit. I had drifted into those visions easily, as though a strong wind had carried me into them. I'd had time to adjust to the weightlessness before my own body was all but forgotten.

This time, Alexandra's magic washed over me in a single wave that threw me into the current of her vision in an instant. I could still feel Zeke's hand in my own and knowing that we would experience the trip together helped me breathe more easily.

I was still unprepared for the scene that materialized before me.

I was standing in front of G.G.'s Oil. The brick building appeared newly constructed, with perfectly clear windows and fresh paint displaying the gas station's name.

Just like in the memory played behind the eyes of Zeke's great-grandfather, my distance to the ground was nauseatingly high. I looked down at my hands that were wiping themselves on an oil spattered rag. Large, calloused, and tanned from the sun, I knew I was in the body of another male.

The emotions of the stranger filled me as though I were experiencing them firsthand. I was tired. Burnt out. My life wasn't going as planned. I used the dirty rag to wipe my brow, not caring if it smudged my face with oil. I could have removed it with magic, of course, but I didn't feel like putting forth the effort. It was taking all of my energy to simply exist.

I was contemplating the meaning of life when a shiny Model T rolled up to the pump.

The first things I noticed were the white gloves gripping the steering wheel as if it would fly off if she loosened her grasp. The woman removed a hand, and with shaking fingers brushed back the blond locks concealing her face.

There was no makeup or any of that gunk women felt the need to paint all over themselves those days. Her face was plain, with a long nose and thin lips that were puckered in a grimace of distaste.

"Stupid hunk of metal," she cursed as she all but fell out of the vehicle.

My feet moved of their own accord. Dropping the rag, I caught the woman in my arms before she could hit the pavement.

Brown eyes stared up into mine, and my crappy existence faded away. The hole in my heart I didn't realize existed was suddenly so full it made my eyes water. This was the reason I was here. This was the part of me I had been missing.

The woman smiled shyly, and then the scene dissipated.

Now I was in a meadow with the same woman and a man standing before me. They faced each other with their hands held between them, and I recognized the man's hands as the ones whose body I had just inhabited.

Their eyes were glued to each other as if they were all that was left of the world.

My own hands stretched forward and tied a simple white ribbon around their joined wrists. I spoke in a high, calm voice, a female's voice, as I conducted a ceremony as old as time itself.

The magic in the air was palpable. The ribbon snaked along their hands, stretching thinner and glowing bright gold in the midday sun. My heart swelled as the couple whispered the words that would seal their lives together.

"Soul to soul, I accept this binding. I welcome nature's gift, my other half in you. Mate to mate, we become one."

The ribbon transformed into a thin, golden thread before sinking beneath their skin.

The scene changed again, and I was standing in a forest. The Cursed Woods, I realized, recognizing the trees I'd walked through so many times with Zeke.

I turned and looked towards the entrance, past the line of trees. A wave of irritation washed over me, or rather whoever's memory this was, at the sight of the red truck parked in front of the house.

My house, I thought distantly. We were in the part of the forest that stretched into my backyard. And there was my aunt and uncle, waiting patiently in the truck's cab.

The person whose mind I currently occupied wasn't as thrilled to see them. I felt his annoyance at my family, a sudden urge to use magic against them. They didn't belong here. I'd have to be creative and find a way to keep them away from the house I had sworn to protect.

Then another car crunched its way up the driveway. A large SUV. The woman behind the wheel threw her door open and sprinted to the truck, crushing the other woman in a bear hug. I stood my ground as a man stepped out of the truck, followed by a dark-haired girl who took the time to walk around her mother's vehicle and close the gaping door.

The girl turned her head towards me, and I saw my own curious eyes appraising the vastness of the trees.

My heart stopped beating. Or maybe it was time that was standing still.

I watched the girl that was and wasn't me greet my family, and every second that passed without me sprinting across the grass to embrace her felt like a physical strike to my chest. The pressure was overwhelming, and the realization at what was happening caused my legs to buckle beneath me.

I perched on my hands and knees, acclimatizing to the fullness in my previously empty chest. I counted my breaths and looked at the ground, at the puddle I'd nearly fallen into. Out of the water's reflection, two electric blue eyes stared up at me.

I gasped as I was thrown back into my body.

Strong hands gripped me before I could collapse onto the ground. I looked up at the same face I had just seen in the memory. At the man whose life had shifted as soon as he laid eyes on me.

Zeke.

My *soulmate.*

I tried to wrap my mind around the craziness of that notion. I had never been a huge believer in soulmates, but then again I'd never given magic much credit either before I'd moved to Green Peaks.

If magic and witches could be real, why couldn't there be soulmates? What was one more piece of supernatural discovery in the wake of everything that had happened to me?

I thought back to our early days spent in the attic, before I knew what Zeke was. Before I even knew his real name.

All those letters he'd written to me, so poetic and full of love. If I'd been paying better attention, maybe I would have realized he was trying to tell me the truth from the beginning.

A few lines from his letters jumped out in my mind.

It wasn't until I laid eyes on you that I realized I had been dead.

There is no life, not without you.

Trust me when I tell you that your presence only makes me stronger.

His words had been deep for a reason. They had been pulled from the heart of a man who was desperate to be with his mate.

Suddenly all those times I felt drawn to the woods made perfect sense. Perhaps I didn't feel the full effects of whatever a bond between mates entails because I wasn't a witch, but I felt something. An itch at the back of my mind, a physical pull towards Zeke.

I knew in my heart it was real.

"Cami?" Zeke squeezed my arms again, and I shook my head to clear it. His eyes were wide, his eyebrows drawn together, as if he were afraid I might run away screaming. I didn't think I would crack so easily, but at least he acknowledged the mental load I carried.

In answer, I smiled at him shyly, much like the girl in the vision had smiled at her mate, before drawing his lips down to mine.

I felt the breath release from the crowd and was horrified when everyone began clapping. As if I wasn't already embarrassed enough at being the center of attention. There were a few whoops and hollers, and the air literally crackled with all the excited magic.

My face was flaming when Zeke finally pulled back and cupped my cheek.

"Does that mean you're coming with us?" He asked, his voice dripping with hope.

I took a deep breath as I considered my options. Now that I knew we were soulmates, I could hardly let him leave without me. I didn't know what would happen if you found your mate and then ignored nature's call to be with them, but I had a feeling it wouldn't be pleasant for either of us.

At the same time, could I really just leave my mother behind? My friends? Natalie might have been gone, but I still loved Carly, Taylor, and Jason and would miss them dearly. They'd have to mourn the loss of two of their friends without the chance of saying goodbye to either of them. Not to mention Michael. I didn't think my cell phone would be welcome on our getaway journey.

It was an impossible decision. Stay with my friends and family or run away with the love of my life?

It's not like your family is normal anyway, a voice in my head remarked. I'd almost forgotten about Uncle Peter, and the fact that staying in Green Peaks would mean facing him again. Not even my mother believed he was capable of the evil acts he performed. I'd probably scream about him being the murderer until they finally decided to lock me in an asylum.

But if I didn't go back, I'd be leaving Peter free to continue his killing spree. I couldn't allow him to take another life, not when so many had already been taken in my name. I had to stop him.

But how?

"You're thinking about your uncle," Zeke murmured, breaking me out of my daze.

Could soulmates read each other's minds? Or did he just know me well enough to discern that I wouldn't be okay with leaving him behind, free to kill again? Whatever it was, I was grateful I didn't have to explain my conflicting thoughts.

"He needs to be stopped." I said simply. My nostrils flared at the idea of him walking around, spreading more lies. "Isn't there anything we can do?"

Zeke's eyes left mine, and I followed his gaze to Alexandra. The small witch looked regretful, but she shook her head.

"We can't interfere any more than we already have," she said quietly. "If we cause him any harm, the person whose magic is used will lose their earthly body. I cannot sentence any of my people to that fate."

The forest was silent as I processed her words. No leaves rustled, and no owl graced us with a hoot out of the darkened trees. Even the rest of the witches were silent and still as they waited to hear my decision. No one moved, except one.

Lucinda Rivers stepped forward. Her white hair glowed in the torches' flames, and her wrinkled hand didn't shake as it gripped the walking stick, pulling her towards us.

Despite how frail she appeared, there was no hint of weakness in the former coven leader's voice when she broke the silence.

"I'll do it."

Mother," Alexandra hissed, her eyes as round as saucers.

I was sure my face was an equal mask of surprise. I'd only spoken to Lucinda once, and the impression I'd gotten was that she was a warm, loving grandmother. One you would expect to sit quietly by the fire while she knit sweaters and fuzzy afghans. She might make tea when you were sick and sing you a song to fall asleep.

She wasn't the type of woman I expected to lay down her life for a complete stranger. That sort of action was always reserved for the young characters in stories that sported a hero complex. Somehow, this frail, white haired old lady didn't fit that stereotype.

The gnarled tree branch she used as a cane thudded softly against the earth. When she joined our party at last, I could barely pick up on her wheezing breaths, as if breathing loudly stole too much energy.

Zeke released me and placed a gentle hand on Lucinda's elbow. I was about to do the same thing, out of instinct for her safety. The woman looked like a strong wind would blow her over.

"Grandmother," Zeke echoed. It was both a greeting and a question.

I glanced back and forth between the magic wielders, the three generations of Rivers gathered before me. Alexandra's expression had taken on a similar look to when Zeke brought me to their coven for the first time. Eyes hard, nostrils in danger of flaring at any moment. She was glaring at her mother like she had just crossed some impassable line.

"Don't act like you don't know it's the right thing to do," Lucinda said gravely to her daughter. Her voice held the air of a teacher reprimanding her student for failing a test.

Both of the women's shoulders were squared tensely, the universal sign of stubbornness.

Alexandra shook her head. "It's not about what's right and wrong. It's about you losing everything. Don't you realize what you'll be giving up?"

Lucinda cackled, a high pealing sound that shook her entire body. Zeke's grip on her tightened, no doubt in fear that she'd knock herself over with the motion.

"You mean this old bag of bones?" She said between chuckles, gesturing to her bent form. "A new body will be a vacation from this wrinkled tomb, even if it has scales or fur."

I watched the altercation between the witches with tightly pressed lips, barely allowing myself to breathe. I didn't want Zeke's grandmother to be stuck in the body of a random animal, but we were running out of options.

And time.

Shouts echoed through the trees. They were still a ways off, but the mob was making more progress than anyone had expected. Even with the cloaking spell and the fact that they were essentially running around blind, they would stumble upon the meadow eventually. The only question was when.

Alexandra turned towards the source of the sound. "We don't have time for this," she groaned. She glanced around at the crowd. At her people. "We need to leave. *Now.*"

Even with the urgency of her voice, no one moved. All eyes were trained on Lucinda, waiting to hear what she'd say next.

I realized then that a lot of the people there, the older witches at least, had spent most of their lives with Lucinda leading the coven. She may have ceded control to her daughter once she reached a certain age, but she still held all the respect and authority a coven leader deserved.

If neither yielded their stance, who would the people follow?

When Lucinda spoke again, her voice was dull and drained of the musical cadences I'd come to expect. She sounded ancient, as if she had lived and endured three lifetimes.

"For one hundred years, this coven has lived in the shadows," she began. "We run. We hide. We isolate ourselves from those who are different, in the fear that they'll never understand us."

Her eyes swept around the company before resting on mine.

"The running stops today."

Alexandra opened her mouth to interrupt but was stopped when Lucinda raised her hand.

"The spell I have in mind is complex, but it will put an end to our solitude and stop the rampage of a murderer all in one swoop. Trust me when I say this, Allie. You don't want to spend your whole life hiding, as I did."

For a moment, I allowed myself to hope that things were actually going to work out. That I could have my cake and eat it too. The universe may have given me a drunken father, a serial killer for an uncle, and a best friend who was taken from this world too soon. But allowing me to keep my soulmate and what little remnants were left of my family would make it all worth it in the end.

I crossed my fingers and turned to Alexandra. It took a lot of restraint not to cover my eyes and peek through my fingers like I was watching a scary movie. My heart fluttered in my chest as I waited for her response.

Her eyebrows drew together, and she reached out a hand. The irrational part of me thought she was finally going to snap, that I'd see sparks fly from her palm as she cursed her mother for speaking against her.

But then her hand closed over Lucinda's shoulder in an approving gesture.

"Do what has to be done." Alexandra whispered.

Lucinda winked at me, as if she'd known she would get her way all along.

Alexandra backed away, rejoining the circle of witches around us. They too were retreating, backing away several yards and giving Lucinda a wide berth.

I took a step to follow them. If they thought this spell needed a lot of space, who was I to argue? I didn't want to be left in the blast zone. But before I could set my foot down, Lucinda tugged me back.

"A spell of this kind requires a link to the target. Hair, nails, blood, or something similar." Lucinda explained. "I understand that you're his niece, so your familial bloodline should do the trick."

I stared at the old witch blankly, feeling my heart plummet to the ground.

She needed a familial link, someone who shared my uncle's bloodline. But I wasn't a blood relative. My aunt Lacey was the one I shared blood with, the sister to my mother. The only thing I shared with my uncle now was a plethora of bad memories.

My eyes widened as I realized what that meant. There was a choking sound at the back of my throat as I struggled to find the words to tell her the elaborate plan she'd concocted couldn't work.

Sensing my despair, Zeke spoke for me. "She isn't related to Peter by blood. Only through marriage."

I felt my distress echoing through the crowd. Normally the face of calm, the witches were showing their discomfort through murmurs and shifts in weight. I noticed more than a few hands shaking, along with nervous sparks of energy that emitted from their fingertips.

We were running out of time. Even if we abandoned our hopes of fixing everything, we might not make it out of the forest alive. The shouts were louder now, the mob closing in on us. Leaving the meadow now would likely result in a blood bath equal to the one I'd watched play out a hundred years ago. And it was all because of me.

I was always the source of misfortune. Always causing problems for others.

I was such a hindrance that Zeke couldn't even look at me. He stared over the top of my head, to avoid eye contact I thought. Tears sprang into my eyes as my insecurities grabbed a new hold.

His eyes narrowed, as if he were inspecting something, and then he did the last thing I expected. He smiled, a huge toothy grin that lit up his entire face.

"Cami," he blurted. "Your hair!"

My *what?*

Was the stress of our situation too much for Zeke, and he finally decided to crack? My mind could find no other explanation as he shook me excitedly and began combing his hands through my hair.

I tried to bat his hands away. My hair was absolutely disgusting. The hospital had apparently thought saving my life was more important than my hygiene, because no one had bothered to wash my hair. It still sported dirt and leaves and probably a decent amount of blood from my skirmish with my uncle.

Wait. *Blood?*

"Oh my god," I gasped, finally understanding.

As it turned out, there was a *lot* of blood caked in my hair, all courtesy of my uncle and the arrow wounds that had sprayed over my entire body.

Lucinda raised her hand, and the blood lifted out of my brown strands and united in the air to form a solid red mass about the size of a baseball. Other beads she allowed to fall carelessly to the ground, and I wondered if those drops of blood were mine. I didn't know how she could distinguish them, but like most of the questions I'd asked about Zeke and his way of life I figured it could be answered in the same way. Magic, of course.

Arm still raised, Lucinda pointed her chin at the circle of witches, gesturing for us to move. I quickly obliged. Pulling Zeke behind me, we evacuated what I could only assume was the soon to be destruction zone.

I'd watched Zeke perform magic on several occasions, simple spells that required nothing more than a flick of his finger, but I had a feeling this one would be different. She'd said it was *complex*. I was equally parts terrified and thrilled to see what that kind of magic would entail.

June waved us over, and I melted into the crowd between her and Alexandra. Zeke's sister was as wild as I remembered. Her black curls were strewn around her face, some tossed lazily behind her back. But her eyes were bright and intelligent, watching the scene play out before her with more interest than I would have expected from a girl her age.

Then again, she'd be the Leader of the coven one day, and this was a monumental moment.

A hush fell over the witches as Lucinda lifted her other hand, allowing her crooked cane to tumble to the ground. I watched in awed silence as the woman walked in a perfect circle around the hovering sphere of blood.

Her steps began heavy and slow, the kind of movement I anticipated from someone who'd lived more than a century. But then she increased her pace, her feet moving lithely across the grass as she mumbled a low incantation. I could feel the magic charging the air, building more with every step she took. It was as if the magic was fueling her, giving her the energy to continue and channel more.

After completing one orbit around the blood, her circling ceased. She began to sway forward and backward, side to side, her body adopting a fluid dance. Her chanting grew louder and the blood glowed brightly, like a miniature sun and Lucinda was its orbiting planet.

She continued to chant and dance, and I became aware of just how loud her voice must seem in the quiet forest.

Too loud.

I heard their shouts then, so much closer than they were before and carrying an excited edge that indicated they knew exactly where we were. Zeke squeezed my hand, and I willed Lucinda to move faster.

I watched in slow motion as she approached the sphere again, her hands raised. She uttered one final incantation before the blood dissolved into thin air. As if a small bomb had gone off, a blast of wind rocked the meadow strong enough to blow June's hair back from her face.

It was done.

Her energy spent, Lucinda fell to the ground just as the first person broke through the trees.

Bodies crashed through the trees, breaking into the meadow like insects disturbing the surface tension of a pond.

Some hit the ground upon entry, their legs no longer remembering how to navigate in the absence of the thick vegetation. Others remained standing, their eyes squinting against the sudden reemergence of light.

I took note of the tattered shirts, the mud stained jeans. I recognized the mother that had shooed her children back to their house. Her hair had been bleached blonde, but now it was so caked in dirt and mud that she could have passed as a brunette. The forest had been unforgiving.

I bit my lip in an attempt to hold back a smile. *Serves them right.*

One by one the townspeople entered the meadow, aggregating into a mass that quickly dwarfed ours in size. Many of them gaped at us in shock, as if they hadn't completely believed in the existence of the witches until that very moment. Others bore a confused countenance that suggested they hadn't considered what they would do once they finally found us.

For several seconds, no one moved. Each group stared at the other in silence, waiting.

Then Peter was pushing his way through the crowd. He paid no mind to his shoulder, allowing it to knock into other bodies as he advanced. It confirmed my theory that his "grave wounds" were all a show to garner more sympathy. He was too focused on the front of the mob to care about maintaining the act, too eager to claim his position of leadership at its head once again.

His eyes were wild. Insane. They held the same look of conviction that had been present as he carved away at my stomach. I instinctively backed up further, melting into our group even more to avoid his gaze.

Relief flashed across faces as their party waited for a command. In that moment, I realized that these people weren't the same as their ancestors. They may have been riled up by Peter's speech in the parking lot, but they lacked the appetite for blood that had resulted in the loss of all those lives a century before. If that thirst to kill had been present, they would have already attacked. Something was holding them back.

These people didn't want to be murderers. They were simply following Peter's lead. Even as they clutched their firearms, some of the men and women appeared to be scared.

Peter reached the expanse of grass between us, the space occupied solely by Zeke's grandmother. Lucinda remained on her hands and knees, and he didn't even acknowledge her presence as he turned back towards his people. His mouth was open to emit what I could only imagine would be a war cry.

This was it. This was the moment we would die or miraculously receive our salvation.

The look of triumph that flashed across his face was only present for a second. Then there was a gust of wind, so subtle I didn't even feel it, that swept lightly over his face and disturbed his thinning hair. I thought I could make out a powder in the air, a small puff of red dust, but it might have been a trick of the light.

Peter gasped as he breathed in the foreign particles, his face falling instantly. He began to cough, choking on the air like it was poison.

Lucinda raised her head, revealing a crooked smirk.

My heart froze at the sight. She'd said her spell would fix everything. That she'd take care of my uncle and the coven's isolation all in the same breath. But what if she'd changed her mind and decided to kill Peter instead? Green Peak's citizens wouldn't simply turn around and go home if their leader had been suffocated before their eyes.

This wasn't the way things were supposed to happen.

Several people looked as if they were debating about running to Peter's aid. He bent over double as he struggled to breathe, his hands gripping his thighs and his face turning pale. I held my own breath as I waited to see if my uncle would recover his.

Before I could lose my mind completely, the coughing ceased. Peter gasped as air entered his lungs and color returned to his face. When he finally released the grip on his jeans and stood up, I saw the change in his eyes.

They were clear. Calm. Almost lifeless.

I had a feeling the madness was hiding just below the surface, but for now it was subdued. For the moment his eyes were perfect mirrors, windows to the task he'd been assigned to execute.

Peter turned back towards the mob. They were all staring at him, breaths held, as they waited for his instructions.

When he finally opened his mouth to speak, his voice held the same authority it had carried in the parking lot and the gym as he conducted the school assembly. He was as much of a captain and principal as he'd ever been, but his words took his charge in another direction.

"Well, folks, I think we can all agree that was quite some hike through the forest."

Several people chuckled at his opening joke, and I rolled my eyes. I wondered how many public speaking classes my uncle had taken in college to perfect his political campaigning.

"Finding our way to the truth has never been easy, though. You followed me out here to exact justice and confront the killer that has devastated our town."

He paused and took a deep breath, ensuring everyone's attention was focused on him.

"I'm here to tell you that you're looking at him."

Peter pointed to himself, and gasps rippled up and down the crowd. My own eyes widened as I realized what he was doing. Lucinda's spell had worked after all. He hadn't been struggling to breathe; he had been choking on his own truth.

We all stood in silence as Peter confessed to every single murder. He even mentioned Natalie and where we could find her body. He admitted to every crime, every black deed, and the people who had considered him their leader simply stood there in shock.

After several minutes of confession, the townsfolk began murmuring among themselves. They looked back and forth between Peter and the witches distrustfully, and I knew his testimony alone wouldn't be enough to convince them of the truth. Their suspicion ran too deep.

My fears were confirmed when someone shouted from the crowd.

"How do we know they aren't making you say all that? They fooled our town before, they can do it again!"

Flashlights bobbed up and down as people nodded their heads and voiced their agreement. They were becoming agitated again, and I didn't know how long this cease-fire would last.

Then I noticed Lucinda, who was sitting back on her heels calmly. Her mouth was quirked up in the same winning smile. If she wasn't panicking yet, then perhaps things were still under control.

"Oh yes, about that." Peter said. My eyes snapped back to him just as he pulled something out of his flannel. "My grandfather lied about that too. I have everything here in his journal."

This time I was the one to gasp. *The journal.*

The journal held all the evidence that Zeke's people had been framed and wrongfully exiled all those years ago. It would prove the innocence of the magic wielders and condemn Peter's grandfather in the process. It was the key to everything.

And it appeared so conveniently.

Suddenly Lucinda's smile made a lot more sense. Whatever spell she'd woven had not only turned Peter into an honest man, but it had also transported the proof we needed right into his waiting arms. I vaguely wondered what else she had up her sleeves.

I refrained from biting my nails as the book was passed around. Men read over women's shoulders and the screens of cellphones shed light on the truth. The younger folk snapped photos of the damning words before handing it off to the next person. Their faces twisted as they scanned the words, realizing just how long they'd been lied to.

The progression went on and on. I stood next to Zeke, keeping silent along with the rest of his coven, and wondering how long this spectacle was going to last. I could just make out the moon through the canopy of the trees, hanging high in the sky and suggesting we'd already been out there for hours.

Were we really going to get away this easily? I watched the people's rising anger, a steaming pot of emotions that seemed inches away from completely boiling over. But they weren't angry at the witches anymore. All of their hate and mistrust was being transferred to the one who had created the hate in the first place. My uncle.

Peter stood in front of the assembly with one hand on his hip, the other arm bound uselessly across his chest. He had remained emotionless through all of the excitement, but now I could see something growing behind his eyes, building in the lines of his face. His body seemed to be shaking, and I recognized the shadows that flitted across his features.

Jekyll was gone, replaced with the unhinged frame of Mr. Hyde. The Peter I'd met in the woods was back.

Of course Lucinda's spell had been temporary. I imagined it would be impossible to permanently change that kind of evil. She bought us time for the truth to be revealed, but now we'd have to deal with the fallout.

The journal had finished making its rounds and was now held in the trembling hands of the vice principal, Mr. Kenny. His own flannel shirt was torn in places and a muddy streak adorned the left side of his face. There was dirt powdered through his bright orange hair and mud speckled over his glasses, but no amount of grime could conceal the fire in his eyes.

"You *knew*," Mr. Kenny spat. "You knew everything we'd been told about these people was a lie, and you used it for your own gain. Why, Peter? What was the point of any of this?" He waved the journal around, gesturing towards the congregation of witches and then the sad state of their own group.

Peter chuckled, as if his followers' fury with him was funny.

"*Why?*" He quipped. "You want to know why I lied?"

He continued to laugh, the sound quickly turning manic.

"I did what had to be done to keep Green Peaks safe, to keep those unnatural brutes off our land." He snarled. "No one loves our town as much as I do. No one would go to the lengths I've gone to keep us safe."

Safe.

The word echoed around my head, hauling me back into the traumatizing moments when I thought I was about to die.

It's okay Cami, you're safe with me. Those were the words he'd used right before holding me down and scarring me for life. No one was safe with this mad man. The only thing he could be counted on was to lie, manipulate, and demolish everything good in his path.

There was a bitter taste in my mouth as I glared at Peter, remembering the nightmare he'd put me through. My heart fluttered in my chest, taking off like a racehorse. I didn't allow myself to think as my feet carried me forward, out of the protection of Zeke's family and into the open meadow. Into the lion's den.

"How dare you?" My voice shook as I neared my uncle, but I didn't allow it to slow me down. "These people trusted you. *I* trusted you. But you turned out to be nothing but a monster."

Mr. Kenny turned to examine me, and I saw the recognition in his eyes. Many people were shifting to get a better look at me, at the girl whose uncle was a serial killer. But instead of the disgust I was used to receiving for my ugly familial connections, all I could see was unbridled sympathy. They actually appeared to feel sorry for me.

Peter's head whipped around at the sound of my voice and then I was locked in his steely gaze, a mouse trapped in the eyes of a lion. But his irritated expression hovered for only a moment before melting into something softer, something more possessive.

I wanted to scream.

He wasn't allowed to look at me like that, like I belonged to him. He wasn't allowed to look at me at all after what he did. I faltered a step backward.

"Cami," Peter breathed. "You're here."

I froze. That lilting voice of his would always haunt my dreams. I stood rooted to the spot as he began stalking towards me, his steps as soft as any predator on the hunt. I couldn't tear my eyes away from him, afraid that if I did he might actually pounce. But through my peripherals I could see the confusion of the townspeople as they became more and more uncomfortable at my uncle's deranged behavior.

"Come back with me, Cami," Peter was saying. "We'll put all of this behind us and start fresh. We'll go somewhere new, and it'll just be you and me."

My nostrils flared at his words and I struggled not to gag.

Mr. Kenny took one look at my expression and it seemed to jar him out of his trance. He handed the journal off to the farmer standing beside him and broke away from the group.

"Hold it right there, Morse."

There was a loud click as a bullet slid into the chamber of his rifle. The barrel was pointed towards the ground, but Mr.

Kenny gripped the gun firmly, prepared to aim it at Peter if the need arose.

Peter paused in his advance, but his eyes never left mine. He turned his head slightly and spoke over his shoulder.

"This doesn't concern you." His voice was sweet as honey, but the warning was implicit.

My focus was so ensnared by his dominating gaze that I almost didn't see his hand reaching for his belt. I almost didn't notice the knife being pulled from its sheath there, or the fact that it was *the* knife. The one I could still feel painting patterns on my flesh.

"Let's end this now, Cami." Peter purred.

The events that followed seemed to happen in slow motion. I watched the knife leave its sheath in a blinding flash, the metal reflecting the firelight from the coven's flickering torches. I saw Mr. Kenny's eyes widen as he realized what my uncle held, and followed the arc of his gun as he swung it up to train on his target.

Finally breaking eye contact, I turned my head and prepared to run before Peter could throw the knife or cross the remaining distance and drive it home at last. As I whirled away, I saw Lucinda's lips curl into one final smile before she awarded me her last wink.

A noise split the silence of the meadow, but it wasn't a gunshot.

It was a scream. Peter had dropped the knife on the ground and was holding his head in his hands, shrieking as if his hair were on fire. He collapsed to his knees, hunched over in agony as he screamed over and over.

"My head! *My head!*"

I glanced over at Mr. Kenny, thinking he'd shot Peter in the head and I'd simply missed it, but he was staring at my uncle with the same look of shock I felt, the gun held loosely in his hands.

Before anyone could move, there was a blinding flash of light, so bright I had to shield my eyes. When I was able to lower my arms, I saw with a trickle of horror that Lucinda no longer knelt on the ground. She had been replaced with the largest bald eagle I'd ever seen, the *only* one I'd ever seen for that matter. Its wings fanned out, revealing the layers of dark, glossy feathers, before it lifted into the air and soared straight for the sky.

Peter lay curled on the ground, his screams receding into gasping sobs. The many versions of my uncle I was misfortune enough to witness were all gone, replaced by a withered, crying man. His eyes were glazed as he rocked himself gently, whispering for someone to please make it stop.

A warm body pressed into my back. It wasn't until I felt his solid form that I realized I'd been shaking uncontrollably.

"It's okay, Cami," Zeke whispered in my ear. "It's all over now."

I didn't know how long we stood there, my mate's arms wrapped around me from behind. Long enough for someone to place handcuffs on Peter and drag him into a sitting position. Three men with guns guarded his every move, but he never so much as twitched. He stared lifelessly at the ground and had to be carried out of the forest. The town leaders conversed with Alexandra and a few other magic wielders, but Zeke hung back with me, humming softly into my hair.

The rest of the night held the distorted ambience of a dream. My ears were muffled to the conversations happening around me, and I didn't bother trying to make out what was said. I was alive, I had Zeke at my back, and the murderer had been detained.

No more blood was shed in the Cursed Woods that night, and I had a feeling it wouldn't be shed again for a very long time. There was peace in the air, a taste of hope.

As dawn's early rays peaked through the leaves and bathed the meadow in gold, I closed my eyes. Somewhere above us, an eagle emitted a single, high-pitched note. It wasn't a cry of loss or a plea for retribution. It was a call of ratification, a song that spoke of a life lived in solitude and chains that were broken at last.

It was free, and so were we.

Six Months Later

I sat before the vanity with my hands folded in my lap. The plush red stool wasn't entirely uncomfortable, but it felt like I'd been sitting there for hours and it was hard not to fidget. Hands flitted around my face, brushing powders across my cheeks and smearing what I could only imagine was a pound of eyeshadow onto my eyelids. I bit my lip and was silent through all of it until I smelled something that resembled smoke.

"Are you burning my hair?"

I turned around to scowl at my mother, but she merely pushed me back onto the stool with a grunt.

"Curling irons are *supposed* to smoke a little. Just relax Camille, you're going to look great!"

I groaned. Agreeing to let my mom handle my hair and makeup had been an easy decision. She'd been gushing about my prom for months, and I knew I couldn't take this moment away from her. I still wondered if I was going to look like a clown walking into my senior prom, though.

There was a knock at the door and we both turned to see Alexandra peeking her head in. Her long black hair hung in the doorway, and I found myself wishing I had my own magical abilities to make my hair shine perfectly.

"Come on in!" My mom called with a smile. I never had to worry about her not getting along with Zeke's parents. She and Alexandra had been inseparable since the day I introduced them. They made an odd pair, my mom an illustration of chaos and Alexandra the calm and composed coven leader who could get any job done. Their relationship reminded me of what I'd shared with Natalie.

The door opened wide and a short, wild haired form darted inside before her mother could offer a warning. June bounced across the room as quick as a cat, her leather moccasins silent against the hardwood. Most of the Green Peaks witches had exchanged their leathers and furs for more modern wear, but June claimed that cotton and denim were too constricting. She was as wild as the day I met her, and I secretly hoped she'd never change.

"Cami, Cami! Look what I brought you!" June squealed as she slid to a stop next to me.

She held out her hands, revealing what appeared to be a bundle of twigs. My lips quirked, and I hastily arranged my face into an expression of pleasant surprise.

"Oh wow, thanks June!" I said enthusiastically as I reached a hand out to take them. I'd have to find somewhere to stash them to avoid getting dirt on my dress.

She pulled the sticks back and giggled. "I haven't changed them yet, silly."

I raised an eyebrow and glanced at her mother.

Alexandra shrugged, a smile playing on her lips. "She wanted to help, so I told her she could do this."

I looked back at June and waited. Joining her hands, she dumped all the twigs together to create a dull brown pile in her palm. Her other hand lifted, and she wiggled her fingers over the sticks until they began to glow. Thinking she was about to start a fire in the middle of our house, I angled my body for a quick escape.

She laughed at my expression and flicked her hand once more over the twigs, extinguishing the glow with a wave. Her work finished, she held them out for me to see. The sticks had been transformed into golden pins, complete with bright pink rhinestones on the ends. I gasped my approval.

"Thanks, June!" I said with more sincerity. Her face lit up as I admired the adornments. There was even more bounce in her steps as she handed the pins to my mother and helped the women finish my hair.

With Alexandra's help, my hair was curled and pinned into a beautiful style over my shoulder in no time. June grabbed my arm and dragged me in front of the full-length mirror so I could see my hair and makeup at last. My lashes were thick enough to make my eyes pop and my lips had been brushed with a light rose stick that matched the rhinestones in my hair perfectly. I had to admit, they'd done a stellar job.

My mom and June went across the hall to grab my dress, and Alexandra helped me shrug out of the robe I'd worn for getting ready. Without the robe, I stood in front of the cheval mirror in my bra and underwear, my skin exposed to the natural light shining through the window.

I stared at myself in the mirror, taking in the scars that still decorated my torso. The letters were no longer red or painful, but reading the possessive word still sent a flush of heat racing to my cheeks.

MINE.

Peter was long gone, of course. What happened in the forest had finally caused him to crack. Mere days after the spectacle in the meadow, he was declared insane and was transferred to a mental facility halfway across the state. I'd never gone and visited, but I heard he spent most of his time in a padded room complaining about a pain in his head of which the doctors could find no cause.

There was a lot of anger over his relocation. Most people thought he deserved to rot in a prison, or that Wyoming's seldomly used death penalty should be taken advantage of. No one had the audacity to ask my opinion on the matter, but I would have held my peace anyway.

It turned out that Lucinda's last act as a human witch was to cause Peter unbearable pain every time he thought about me or any other young woman in an inappropriate manner.

Lucinda may have been confined to the body of a bird for the rest of her life, but the fate she had chosen for Peter was fitting. He would spend the remainder of his days in agony until he could find it within himself to banish his evil thoughts.

A hand squeezed my shoulder gently, and I realized I'd been glaring at my reflection for over a minute.

"I can still remove the scars if you want. All you have to do is ask," Alexandra murmured.

I watched myself shake my head. After Peter had been taken care of and the witches were finally safe, one of the first things Zeke had done was offer to heal my wounds and erase all evidence it had even happened. I had declined.

It wasn't that I liked looking at the scars. They were an ugly reminder of all that I'd been through, and there were days when I wished I could magically forget it had all happened. But the scars in my mind couldn't be wiped away with the wave of a hand. This kind of trauma would heal slowly, and every day took me a step farther away from my past. I didn't want my external wounds to be erased by magic when only time could heal me internally. My scars would heal together, or I wouldn't heal at all.

Alexandra nodded just as June bounded back into the room, followed by my mother carrying my dress. It was floor length with an open back, and was the brightest, most electric blue I'd ever found in a piece of clothing. The gold stitching was lovely, and the sparkles were a nice embellishment, but I chose it because it matched Zeke's eyes.

Alexandra led June out of the room while my mother helped me carefully slide into the gown without disturbing my hair and makeup. She stood next to me in the mirror's reflection and sighed.

"You're absolutely beautiful, Cami. Your father would be proud of the woman you've grown into. I know I am."

I squeezed her hand and smiled, mentally screaming at myself not to cry and ruin all her work. Somehow the tears held their ground, leaving my eyes wet and sparkling but not disturbing my mascara. My mom hugged me tightly before ushering me out of the room and onto the staircase.

Voices were carrying up from the floor below, and I took a deep breath as I started down the stairs. I knew there was no reason to be nervous, but that didn't stop my heart from pounding faster in my chest with every descending step.

A hush fell over the foyer as I came into view. Crowded at the bottom of the stairs was my entire promenade party. Jason was flying solo in an all-white tux, but Taylor stood beside him with a red-haired beauty on his arm who didn't seem to mind that her date was several inches shorter than her. Carly had chosen a dark blue dress that brought out the green in her eyes and was holding Oliver's hand. She smiled up at me shyly and didn't appear to notice the way the magic wielder's eyes devoured her presence as though she was the center of the world.

Then there was Zeke. The breath caught in my throat as it did every time I laid eyes on him. The black tuxedo fit him perfectly, curving around his chiseled chest and arms as if it were tailored for him. I decided the woods could keep its animal skins. I was never letting him out of this tux.

A new thought popped into my head, and it seemed to speak in Natalie's voice. *Trust me, girl, you'll be tearing it off of him later.*

I blushed as I reached the bottom step and accepted Zeke's outstretched hand. He arched a brow at me questioningly, but I just smiled and shook my head. He let it go and took a moment to drink me in, his eyes raving over every inch of my body and further deepening my blush.

"You look..." he stammered. His own face was turning red.

"I know," I laughed lightly. "So do you."

After a minute in which no one moved, Jason cleared his throat. "If we're all done ogling each other, I'd like to get this show on the road!"

We laughed and followed him to the front door where June was pretending to be a porter. She opened the door wide and swept her arm out into the warm evening air, gesturing for us to make our grand exit. She held her serious demeanor for exactly ten seconds before sticking her tongue out at Zeke and slamming the door behind us.

A limo waited in the driveway and the art boys whooped at its appearance. Oliver shrugged his shoulders as he followed the line into the vehicle, muttering something about the questionable necessity of cars that were as long as trees.

I smiled at the conglomeration that was our group. The magic wielders had melded themselves back into our society with the ease of re-growing a lost tooth. There was healing to be done on both sides, past prejudices that needed to be overcome, and scars that ran all too deep. But all of Green Peaks was working together, humans and witches alike, to create a haven where everyone was welcome.

Wards had to be created around the town to protect the magic and secrets that had been exposed for everyone to see. It was agreed that an invisible boundary would be made around the town, and once crossed an individual would forget about the existence of magic and the people who lived freely inside the city limits. Green Peaks had always been a private place, and no one wanted scientists disrupting their way of life or killing innocent people who had already been through enough.

A museum was under construction that would display the town's colorful history, telling the tale of a broken people who spent a century believing lies that kept them apart. A certain journal was thought to be the centerpiece, along with fake animal exhibits to represent all the magical lives lost in a war they never asked to be a part of.

As the limo crunched down the driveway and someone cranked the music to its max, I looked back at the house that had started everything. The familiar tower stood high above the Cursed Woods, catching the final rays of sunlight as it made its descent into the trees. The window glowed orange in its stark reflection, almost giving the impression of a candle flickering in the attic beyond.

I remembered the dust coating the objects within, the treasures that had waited patiently for someone to finally discover them. I remembered the fear of the unknown, and the joy that came with taking a leap of faith and finding a strong pair of arms to catch you. I remembered the original letter that guided me onto this journey and carried me to a place where now, even scarred, I felt whole.

The End

Acknowledgments

I am indebted to so many people for making this dream possible.

First, I'd like to thank my parents for putting up with the many stories I concocted as a kid and all the wasted notebook paper used for the books I never finished. If you search through their basement I'm sure you'll find dozens of half-used spiral notebooks filled with the first chapters of novels I've long since forgotten.

Next, I'd like to thank my husband for believing I could do this despite my lack of degree in creative writing, English literature, or any other college degrees publishers seem to think are necessary in creating a worthy book.

Thank you, Morgan Newell, for being the best sister a girl could ask for and for always being there to talk me off a ledge and restore my sanity. Also, you take some pretty awesome photos (see my author bio for reference).

A big thanks goes out to Jessica Butcher and Myden Fouts for being the first to set eyes on *Letters in the Attic* and for assuring me that my baby was not, as I feared, *ugly.*

Finally, I want to extend a warm thankyou to all of those who have given me inspiration and hope along the way. From my friends and teachers who didn't bat an eye when I said I wanted to be an author, to my coaches who taught me the meaning of hard work, thank you for shaping me into the person I am today.

About the Author

Meredith Lindsey grew up in a patch of woods in Southern Illinois that became inspiration for many stories. She now lives in Vincennes, Indiana with her husband and German Shepherd fur baby. Employed as a Medical Laboratory Scientist, Meredith keeps her fantasies alive by reading and writing about magic, paranormal beings, and anything more interesting than the mundane world. *Letters in the Attic* is her first published novel.

Visit www.MeredithLindsey.com for more!

A Note From the Author

Hello dedicated reader!

I want to thank you for taking the time to read my book. Words cannot describe how amazed and humbled I've been to receive all this love and support after publishing my novel.

If you made it all the way through this book, past the acknowledgments and author bio that no one ever reads and now find yourself here, perhaps you'll be interested in going one step further.

Please tell me what you think! Head on over to Amazon and leave an honest review. I appreciate all feedback, and I can't stress how important reviews and ratings are to gaining future sales.

You all have been so amazing. Thank you again for helping me bring my dream to life!

Amazon Page

Made in the USA
Columbia, SC
16 August 2024

40075030R00183